"I HAVE RECENTLY COME TO THIS WORLD OF YOURS," LAN SAID CAUTIOUSLY. "ALL WE ASK IS SIMPLE PASSAGE."

"We?" said the leader of the armed patrol. "You have companions?"

Lan turned to find Krek tightly compressed into an amorphous lump. It was impossible to tell that a tall spider once lurked so near. "Ah, a figure of speech," he explained lamely. "Besides, I am no peasant to be badgered by your likes. I have every right to walk this world!"

"Kill him," came the sharp command from the grey-clad officer.

Lan whipped his knife forward, ready to die in battle. To his surprise, the horses all reared and bolted. The officer turned pasty white and spurred his horse away, screaming incoherently.

Lan turned to find Krek towering behind him. The spider asked in a mild voice, "Why did they run like that? Did they remember an appointment...?"

CENOTAPH ROAD

ROBERT E. VARDEMAN

ACE SCIENCE FICTION BOOKS
NEW YORK

CENOTAPH ROAD

An Ace Science Fiction Book / published by arrangement with
the author

PRINTING HISTORY
Ace edition / March 1983

Parts of Chapters One and Two originally appeared as ''The Road to
Living Death'' in *Shadows Of. . .* , copyright © 1982 by Robert E. Vardeman.
Chapters Five and Six originally appeared as ''The Mating Web'' in
Swords Against Darkness III, copyright © 1978 by Robert E. Vardeman.

ISBN: 0-441-09845-2

Ace Science Fiction Books are published by Charter Communications, Inc.
200 Madison Avenue, New York, New York 10016.
PRINTED IN THE UNITED STATES OF AMERICA

For Geo. and Lana,
singly and collectively

CHAPTER ONE

Silence fell over the crowd in the Dancing Serpent as the six grey-clad soldiers marched into the room. Their boot heels hit the wooden planking with an ominous rhythm, a rhythm that spoke of doom and destruction and misery. The six arrogantly studied those in the smoky barroom, saying nothing. The tension rose until a man taller than the six strode into the room, his broad shoulders brushing the doorjambs as he entered.

"Drinks for all!" the man called out in a loud, booming voice. The bartender sighed and began putting the heavy glass bottles of potent liquor onto the bar. The others in the room relaxed, and soon nervous laughter echoed through the once-noisy establishment. The grey soldiers were not here to kill. Not this time.

In the corner of the room at a small table, a low conversation went on, neither participant taking much notice of the intrusion by the soldiers. Dar-elLan-Martak gestured in despair, his palms open and imploring.

"Please, Zarella, let's leave this place and talk," the man begged. "With the likes of *them* around, none can relax."

Zarella laughed carelessly. "Oh, Lan, you're such a fool. Do you have my price? I come expensive, you know!"

"Zarella, why do you do this to me? You know I love you. Let me prove it to you." He spoke in such deadly earnest that the woman hesitated to make fun of him. Few crossed Lan Martak, and fewer lived to brag of it. His expertise with the gleaming carbon-steel sword dangling at his side was legendary. And unlike most legends, this had a strong basis in fact. The grips of both sword and short dagger showed wear from long, hard, deadly use by the man's strong hands and thick wrists.

She said gently, "Lan, please, it isn't to be. We both know that. Your world simply isn't mine. I belong *here!*" The woman gestured extravagantly, encompassing the tapestry-hung walls, the gaming tables, the long, stained bar propping up a dozen drunken men. "The Dancing Serpent is my life. Even for you, I won't give it up."

"But there's more to the world than this stinking pleasure palace. I can show you the jeweled towers of Lellvan. Have you ever seen the Sulfur Mountains? No, you haven't. Or the Sinking Lands to the west. To look out over them at sunset and see the very earth shiver at your command outstrips anything this place could offer a fine woman like you." He sneezed once, not used to the cloying dope smoke in the air. The sawdust gritted uneasily under foot. It wasn't clean dirt; it didn't feel right to him. The very atmosphere in the Dancing Serpent was slimy, a thing unclean. The need to be free of the place added urgency to his words.

He glanced at the crowd and heaved a deep sigh. Zarella, lovely Zarella, deserved the freshness of the country and not the prison of this overpriced brothel. To have to put up with men such as those grey soldiers would sicken anyone—psychically as well as physically. Lan's hand drifted unconsciously to his dagger when he saw the self-important KynalLyk-Surepta leaning heavily on the bar. Thoughts of *traitor* flashed through Lan's mind. Lyk Surepta had sold out to the grey soldiers in exchange for a commission, a high one by all accounts. Such was the clientele of the Dancing Serpent.

Zarella deserved much better than this.

The woman pushed the purple-feather-studded comb into the luxurious depths of her auburn mane. The nervous gesture gave her a moment to think. She let her eyes rove over Lan, then sighed deeply.

The rising and falling of her breasts brought forth the wrong response from the man. He did not take it as a sign of hopelessness, of total disagreement with his plans. He saw it as indecision and thought she required only more cajoling.

"Zarella, I love you! Doesn't that matter?"

"Many men love me. That's why I stay."

"That's not the kind of love I mean. We can . . ." He was interrupted by a gruff voice.

"Is this bumpkin bothering you, Zarella?"

Lan turned. Kyn-alLyk-Surepta towered over him, hand resting lightly on the hilt of his sword. Lan realized the officer wanted nothing more than to spill some blood this evening. It mattered little to him whose it was. The grey soldiers boasted of maintaining the peace, of driving the brigands from the nearby forests. They had done much the old sheriff had been unable to do, but their methods were little better than those of the brigands they displaced. Torture was a game for them, suffering a pastime.

Lyk Surepta was the worst of the lot. He was the only local man in the band and, like all recent converts to a new cause, felt the need to prove himself by being more brutal, more daring, more competent than any of the others in his company.

"Leave us, turncoat," snapped Lan. "We are talking." The menace in that quiet voice would have frightened off a less determined man.

"Turncoat, is it, bumpkin? I am Kyn-alLyk-Surepta. *Kyn*, did you hear?"

Lan let his eyes roll upward as if importuning the gods for patience with a small child. But his hand never strayed far from the hilt of his dagger. His emotions seethed inside, turning from Zarella's dismissal of his love to the arrogance of the grey-clad soldier. Still, Lan did not become careless. The man hadn't won his kyn-ranking being a dullard. And a jerky quickness to his movements warned of feral reactions. Lan had seen the type before. A quick kill or a stab in the back—they were one and the same to this man.

"And I am Dar-elLan-Martak, turncoat. *Dar*. When you joined the ranks of those grey-clad butchers, you forfeited kyn-rank. You cannot have it both ways."

Lan felt wrenching surprise when Kyn-alLyk-Surepta laughed at him.

"So you're the buffoon all snigger at behind your back!" He guffawed loudly, throwing his head back and laughing openly toward the ceiling. Lan stood, his movement tightly controlled. He hadn't missed the slight tensing of the wrist, the subtle change in the other's stance. If he'd gone for Kyn-alLyk-Surepta's throat, he would have found a knife in his own gut.

"Only hyenas laugh so loudly."

Sudden silence fell again in the Dancing Serpent. A few timid customers edged for the doors. The six soldiers with Kyn-alLyk-Surepta drew their blades as if a single brain controlled their actions.

"You would have carrion-eaters kill me?" Lan asked. He felt half a hundred eyes watching him, waiting. The tension in the air was electric. And he reveled in it. This was the vent needed for his emotions. Little matter if he had to dispatch this Kyn-alLyk-Surepta to Hell. It had been months since he had killed a man in a fight. And if the other six attacked, he felt insanely confident of besting them, too.

For Zarella, he could perform miracles.

"You call me a hyena?" bellowed Kyn-alLyk-Surepta.

"You name yourself."

A slight snick and flashing arc of silver were all the warning Lan had. His own blade easily parried the death-dealing slash. A quick half-step back gave him fighting room.

"All at once?" he asked. "Or one at a time? Whichever you prefer, turncoat!"

Kyn-alLyk-Surepta motioned violently to his men to stand back.

"This scum is mine. I will bury my blade in his quivering guts!"

"I'd have thought you'd wait for them to kill me. Hyenas are carrion-eaters. Seldom do they kill their own prey."

The thrust came straight for his heart. Lan turned slightly to the left, felt the blade hotly graze his skin. But the sword blade was past his body, beyond the spot where it could do real harm. His own knife point rested lightly against Kyn-alLyk-Surepta's kidney.

"Catching you is too easy. I'll throw you back and go fishing for bigger-finned creatures. What do you think, Zarella?" Lan held the other man's sword arm in a deceptively mild grip. He watched as Kyn-alLyk-Surepta turned red in the face trying to break free and avoid the knife point digging into his back.

"Fighting, all the time fighting. Aren't you two aware this is a pleasure palace? Sarn!" she called to the man behind the bar. "Bring drinks for my *two* friends."

The bartender quickly poured the drinks, his eyes never leaving the frozen tableau that could erupt into bloody death at any instant. He nervously checked the position of the six grey-clad soldiers before venturing out from behind the relative safety of the bar.

"Zarella says we should drink. Do we drink? Or does my dagger drink alone—of your blood?"

The trapped arm ceased struggling and relaxed.

The voice, trembling with impotent rage barely contained, came. "We drink. Such a charming hostess is not to be denied."

"I agree." Lan carefully backed away, wary that the sword still in Kyn-alLyk-Surepta's hand wouldn't find a sheath in his body. His eyes darted to the six soldiers, still holding their swords in white-knuckled grips. They had been ordered to remain where they were. Lan wondered at their discipline. Few from this area were so rigidly trained.

Lyk Surepta put his blade away, then took the small cup of the fierce liquor. He held it up to his lips in silent toast. Lan smiled slightly and reached for his own cup. As he did, Surepta tossed the liquor into his face.

It wasn't entirely unexpected, yet some of the liquor found its way into his eyes. Lan's reflexes worked for him. He was dropping and rolling to his right even as the liquor spattered across his face. The foot intended for his groin scraped his left hip and then harmlessly glanced off, finding only smoky air.

He wiped the liquor from his eyes. The room swam into blurry focus as he saw the grey form moving toward him. Instinct again told him where to roll to avoid the kick aimed at his face.

This time Lan came to his feet, clear-visioned. His hand never moved toward his knife. His voice threatened more than the action would have.

"You will die for that, turncoat. Name your next of kin so they might arrange a proper burial. Or will these soldier-lackeys of yours attend to the remains?"

"It's not my corpse you should worry about, fool. You'll be cooling meat in a few seconds!" In the same breath, he drew his sword again and made a long lunge.

And kept flying through the air. Lan neatly trapped his wrist, started a circular motion, and sent his attacker somersaulting. The sword clattered to the floor. Quick as a cat, Surepta tried to grab the fallen weapon. Even faster, Lan kicked it, spinning, into the far corner of the room. A howl of pain told that the blade's sharp edge had found a human target. Neither Surepta nor Lan bothered with the spectator's minor injury.

"You two, stop it!" cried Zarella, her tone chastising. Yet the carriage of her body, the inflections of her words, told she was delighted to have these two handsome, powerful men fighting for her favors.

"I will have her," snarled Surepta.

"Only in Hell!" Lan's move came with sinuous, flowing speed. A tangle of arms and legs resulted in a stranglehold on Lyk Surepta's neck. A brawny forearm tightened on the other's windpipe. Tendons appeared in bas-relief as the pressure increased.

Try as he might, Kyn-alLyk-Surepta couldn't break the death grip around his throat. He tried to gesture to his men, to call to them, to get help. Every second marked the passing of just a little more of his strength. He couldn't reach the bushy brown hair of his attacker and pull the man over his shoulder. A rock-hard stomach resisted every blow from his elbows. Inexorably, he was pulled back over a knee jammed into his spine.

Lan felt the life slowly ebbing in the man's body. He pressed his advantage—and found himself frozen like a glacier.

He stood as rigid as a statue, his eyes staring straight ahead. Try as he might, he couldn't move his head. His arms were lead-heavy and his legs firmer than any granite. Lan's pulse throbbed wildly in his temples, almost drowning out the faint voices around him.

"But I tried, Honor! Ask the others."

"Zarella tried to stop a fight over her? Now I've heard everything. The sun and both moons can dance a jig tomorrow, and then I'll have *seen* everything, too."

Lan recognized the sheriff's tired voice. The old mage had cast a mild paralysis spell on both him and Kyn-alLyk-Surepta, of that he was now sure. Knowing the nature of his immobility, he began working out of it.

Lips moving the barest amount, he began chanting the counterspell. He was unable to say it loudly, and it took several minutes longer than normal for the debilitating paralysis to leave his limbs, but Lan knew better than to move before the sheriff conjured the counterspell on his own. The old man had pride. It wouldn't do to humiliate him in front of a pleasure palace full of young bucks looking for trouble, nor would it do for the mage's weaknesses to be shown to the damnable grey-clad soldiers.

Any hint that the sheriff was unable to stop them would bring hordes of them down on the city. Lan didn't like all the laws, but he knew what they meant to the sheriff. He also knew what life would be like under the direct controls of the soldiers.

"It's true, Honor. I was talking with Lan when Lyk came over. Lan refused to leave when Lyk made a legitimate nummary offer for my services."

The sheriff looked at Lan, and their eyes met briefly. The sheriff knew his spell had already been nullified but said nothing. He nodded slightly toward Lan, silently thanking him for this small concession to his authority. Lan knew it was the only consideration he was likely to get.

"So Lan is in the wrong? Who drew his blade first? No, don't bother lying. I can see who still has a sheathed sword and who doesn't."

A whining voice from the side of the room came, "He cut me, Honor! Dar-elLan-Martak cut me with the other's sword!"

"Shut up, Lorgan. I'll deal with you later. If I have the time." Turning to his deputy mage, the sheriff asked, "Is Kyn-alLyk-Surepta going to survive his wrestling bout?"

"Yes, Honor. He'd only fainted from lack of air. Nothing more. Not even necessary for any healing spells."

"So . . ." The sheriff's voice firmed with resolve. "Nothing has been done except stir up the clientele of the Dancing Serpent. Zarella, you should be charged for a floor show. But, from what you say, Lan is to blame. He'll be removed from the premises."

"We claim the right to punish him!" spoke up one of the grey-clad soldiers. "He attacked an officer in our corps."

"Your corps?" sneered the sheriff. "I do not recognize your authority. You might have rid us of those annoying brigands, but who are your lords? To whom do you swear fealty? You are strangely silent on those counts. Your pasty grey complexions sicken me. You hardly appear of this world."

A gagging sound interrupted the sheriff. Kyn-alLyk-Surepta sat up, his eyes fiery coals of hatred aimed at the world.

"You ask that?" coughed out Kyn-alLyk-Surepta. "We fight for the law. We desire only to drive out ones such as that." He glared at Lan, who still pretended paralysis.

"Where do they come from? I've not seen their like around here before," asked the mage.

"They come from . . . distant lands. It is of no consequence. *I* command them. We can take care of this upstart. You need not trouble yourself, Honor."

"I so choose. I am the duly appointed lawgiving authority here, and until that changes, your vigilante ways will not be tolerated. Leave. And take them with you."

Lyk Surepta shot a look of pure hatred at Lan,

then retrieved his sword, sheathed it, and jerked his head in silent command to his soldiers. They marched off, boot heels clicking in unison. The sheriff turned back to Lan. A pass of the hand in front of Lan's face caused a jolt to pass through his aching body. The last trace of paralysis was officially removed with this public act.

"Outside, Lan. I desire words with you."

Silently, Lan, the sheriff, and the two deputy mages started for the door. As Lan passed through, he bumped into Surepta. The man sneered but said nothing. The man appeared strangely satisfied at the outcome of the fracas as he turned and went away, his soldiers following like obedient dogs.

"Humph," snorted the sheriff. To his deputies he said, "I won't need you. Go back to the office, and I'll be along shortly. And try studying up on those paralysis spells. You were both sloppy back there!"

As they went off into the blackness along the dusty street, the sheriff said to Lan, "They're good boys. Make damn fine sheriffs one day, if the grey-clads don't overrun us all first."

"Those soldiers cause more trouble than they're worth. Just appear and then scare off some thieves, and they think they own the town," said Lan bitterly. His feelings went deeper, but he couldn't bring himself to say so to the sheriff.

The old man snorted. "You're the one who's trouble, Lan. If there's any more out of you, I'll reduce you where you stand. I'd hate to do it, but I will."

Lan shivered at the threat. Reduced. Turned into a sizzling spot of grease unrecognizable as human. It wasn't a complex spell, Lan knew, but it was a highly secret one known only to the sheriff.

"Zarella is a beautiful woman, I'll grant you that," the old man went on, "but she's wrong for you. You have terrible tastes in women, Lan. You belong in the country, with a woman who can appreciate the things you do best. Go and enjoy the openness while it's still there. Those *things* are taking over all too fast." The sheriff lifted his chin to indicate a pair of the soldiers walking a self-appointed patrol on the other side of the street.

"As you say, Honor, but don't think this is the end of it. I love Zarella, and I'll make her see my way. She's going to marry me one day. Mark it, Honor, she'll be mine!"

The sheriff shook his head in disgust and left without another word. Lan watched the man shuffle along in the dusty street, jumping just enough to avoid being run over by one of the chuffing Maxwell's demon-powered auto cars. The sheriff raised his fist and issued a steady stream of invective at the magical-powered car, then vanished into his office, still angrily muttering about the price of progress.

Lan stood alone in the wide, dusty street, and yet he felt imprisoned. The town collapsed around him, and he felt the need to leave it far behind. Jogging along at an easy lope, he left behind the Dancing Serpent and Zarella and a city bulging with unnatural laws and grey-clad soldiers and motorcars holding demons in their guts. The cool night air gusting through his nostrils poured refreshing power into his body like water into a jug. He felt whole again.

"Oh, kyn-alBin, you're such a lover!" squealed Zarella, sprawled on her huge round bed. She watched with polar eyes as the rotund man dressed. The broad smile playing across his lips told her he would be exceptionally generous this evening.

He'd better be. Having such a pig in bed disgusted her. If he hadn't been so wealthy, she would have let one of the other pleasure girls have him.

Zarella almost laughed thinking of scrawny Luella with this mountain of fat. He would have suffocated the poor child!

"You're a gem, Zarella. None like you. Here's a token of my undying esteem." Zarella's eyes widened with avarice. She was worldly-wise, but never had she seen such a large drell-gem, easily worth a prince's ransom. Its rainbow colors filled the room with a cold radiance. She would have stayed the night with a score of demons to gain such a trinket.

"You're too kind, but then big men have the biggest hearts and . . ." She let her eyes drop slightly and gave him the chance to mentally finish the rest of her little speech. He was pleased; so was she. It was a business deal like any other. What she had for sale, however, wasn't open for barter among the usual commodity brokers.

"Till the morrow!" the man said, pleased with her response.

Zarella fell back on the soft bed, holding the drell-gem lightly in the palm of her hand. The depths of the jewel pulled her gaze deeper and deeper until she became lost in the maze of its reflecting planes. It was the most perfect gem she'd ever seen.

Her attention was dragged away by the sound of her door opening. The soft click of the lock brought her to a sitting position. Standing next to her bureau, arms crossed over his muscular chest, stood Kyn-alLyk-Surepta. A vicious sneer marred his good looks.

"What do you want, low-born?" she snapped. He repelled her in a way she didn't fully understand. That he had joined ranks with the arrogant grey-clad soldiers cast against him, but the distaste ran deeper. He seemed unclean.

"Low-born, is it? Surely you can guess why I've come." He towered over her. A hand faster than thought snared the jewel from her palm and held it up to the dimness of the glow-lamp beside her bed. "A drell-gem? A poor one, I'd say. And small, very small. Did Dar-elLan-Martak give it to you?"

"No. I haven't seen him since he choked you unconscious. I wish he'd finished you then and there!" She felt a surge of viciousness. To degrade this man meant more to her than her own immediate safety. Besides, one scream would bring four guards able to handle any trouble Kyn-alLyk-Surepta might intend for her.

"Another of your many conquests, then. I think it's time for you to be shown a real man's skill." He began stripping off his grey tunic. As he casually tossed it aside, Zarella noticed a tanned leather jerkin next to his skin. The incongruity of the leather with the grey cloth puzzled her. This was something she'd have expected Lan to wear rather than the turncoat soldier.

"Ah, you notice my, hmmm, shall we call it insurance?"

"Insurance? I think you should leave. Already you bore me with your riddles. If you go any further, I might fall asleep from tedium."

He slapped her with the back of his hand. The force of the blow knocked her sprawling across the bed. Zarella tried to escape. A hand gripped a slender white ankle and pulled her back. The man flipped her over and glared at her supine form.

"Don't ever say a thing like that to me again. I should punish you for what you've done this evening. You make a big play for me, then cast me aside. I suspect Dar-elLan-Martak's been enjoying your charms, hasn't he? *Hasn't he?*"

The man slapped her again, this time with the callused palm of his hand.

Zarella clutched at her brutalized face. Hatred boiled from her eyes. If she'd known the proper spells, Kyn-alLyk-Surepta would have been changed into a bug to be crushed under her heel. But she didn't. The only course left her was to scream. The guards down the hall would come to her rescue. She would laugh as they quartered this low-born scum and boiled his pieces in thick oil.

His cold words cut off her cry.

"Your four guards are dead. They smile with two mouths." He pulled out a bloodied knife and showed it to her.

"What do you want?" she demanded. For the first time since she was a virgin, Zarella felt fear gnawing at her insides. She didn't want to die. The fetid odor of death, however, filled her nostrils.

"Isn't that obvious? Martak humiliates me in front of the entire town. I want revenge." He began running his thumb along the edge of the blade as if to assure himself of its razor-sharpness.

"Why come to me?"

"You're his woman. I overheard what he said. He wants to marry you, and you weren't unwilling, just contrary. My revenge on him will be through you."

"So you rape me, is that it? Lan will cut out your liver and eat it raw!"

"No, no, he won't. I will tell you exactly how clever I am. He can't really care if I have my way with you or not. A woman of your profession would hardly consider that much in the way of revenge. No, I'll take my pleasure from you, then kill you."

Zarella went cold from shock. She heard truth ringing in the man's words. Lips trembling but voice steady, she said, "Lan will track you down. No matter where you hide, he'll find you. Even in the middle of all your grey-clad soldiers, he'll kill you."

"Ah, therein lies the beauty of my plan. First, though, satisfaction. And the rest, my dear lovely Zarella, I fear you'll not live to appreciate."

She fought, but against overwhelming strength. He had his will, then left her corpse for the sheriff to find.

*   *   *

"Well, Sarn, tell me again!" barked the sheriff. It had already been a long night. Now the murder of Zarella turned it into an eternity. "I don't care if you repeat it a million times."

The bartender swallowed hard, looking as if he needed a drink to steady his nerves. His eyes darted from the sheriff to the body on the bloodstained sheets, then back to the implacable sheriff.

"I . . . I saw one of the guards on the stairs. I thought he was asleep. When I went to awaken him, I found he'd had his throat slit." Sarn made a descriptive movement with his index finger, showing the exact location of the knife cut. His already sallow face paled even more until he appeared on the brink of fainting.

"I checked, and the other three were dead also. Kyn-alBin had come down earlier, and I'd seen the guard talking to him. Who could believe such a thing of kyn-alBin?"

"Just tell me what you did next. Never mind passing judgment on the customers."

"Y-yes, Honor. I checked a few of the rooms. There were customers in most of them. It was a good night. Then, th-then," he stuttered, "I f-found Zarella. Just like that! It's horrible. I thought you were supposed to protect us from such things."

"Sometimes even a good sheriff requires more manpower," came a deep voice from the stairway. Lyk Surepta stood there, a smug expression on his face. "I hereby offer the services of my men in finding the murderer of one of this town's leading entrepreneurs."

"You and your soldiers aren't required in this, Kyn-alLyk-Surepta," said the sheriff tartly. "I am perfectly capable of handling the investigation."

"Have you performed the investigatory spells yet?"

"You can go," the sheriff told Sarn. "My deputies and I will do some conjuring and see what we can see. You did well in not staying long in the room. It would only blur the picture. Thank you, Sarn." The mousy bartender scuttled off, glad to be away from the scene of the brutal murder. "And your aid is not required, either, Kyn-alLyk. Go!"

"I would stay to watch the conjurations."

The sheriff started to press the issue, then tiredly nodded. The power of the grey-clad soldiers grew daily, and he wasn't sure of the public response if he ordered Surepta away so preemptorily.

"All right. Everything ready?" The sheriff's experienced eye looked over the censers gushing out their fumes at each point of a pentagram around the body. He'd trained his deputies well. In less than a minute, they would see a reenactment of the murder.

The sheriff muttered the appropriate ward spells and settled down to let the chronoregression spell work. Surepta started to speak, but the sheriff motioned him to silence. A ghostlike figure, almost too dim to be seen, entered the room, closed the door, and locked it. The colors mingled and mixed constantly in a translucent haze, flowing from grey to brown to black.

A blur fell across the bed. A large jewel gleamed. Is lambent radiance washed out any picture of the murderer. A frenzy of activity on the bed, then the jewel disappeared. Left was a faint outline of a man dressed in a leather jerkin.

The sheriff began chanting. When he reached the proper resonance, he looked up into the face of the killer. With knife in one hand and body covered with the leather jerkin, Lan's image swam into hazy focus. It lasted for a split second, then vanished in tangled tendrils of brown, garlic-smelling mist.

"Dar-elLan-Martak!" cried Surepta. "He murdered her when she denied him!"

"Silence!" bellowed the sheriff. He sighed, wiped sweat from his wrinkled forehead, and felt years older in an instant. Of all the people, he hadn't expected Lan to be the one to kill Zarella. The sheriff sighed again, his frail shoulders slumped with the weight of evidence. He liked Lan, had thought better of him.

The rest of the sordid scene flickered in and out of existence. The death stroke released a murky aura around Zarella's ghost body. No question remained as to the instant or manner of her death.

Choking on the fumes from the censer, the sheriff ordered, "Clean up this mess, and one of you track down the murder weapon. It'll leave a trail a blind mage could follow. And be quick about it. Another death with the same knife and you'll lose the trail!"

"My men will find him," said Surepta confidently. "The murderer will be brought to swift justice."

"None of that," snapped the sheriff. "You can hang all the brigands you catch out in the woods. That's beyond my jurisdiction. But not this. I want Lan alive to stand trial."

"You've seen his guilt."

"It's not conclusive. Before reduction, I must be certain." The sheriff wished to retire on the spot and let the younger men handle the case. But that would be shirking his duty. A man never let another do a distasteful job. The sheriff looked scornfully at Lyk Surepta and whirled past him. He would find Lan before the soldier. He felt he owed that much to Lan.

Lan looked at his half-sister incredulously.

"It's true, I tell you," said Suzarra. "I was with Tan when the grey-clads were bragging to one another about it."

"You're sure they claimed Lyk Surepta had killed Zarella?" Lan sat in the center of the crude log cabin, stunned. Zarella dead? It hardly seemed possible, yet he didn't doubt for an instant that Surepta was capable of such a deed.

"And they put out evidence to implicate you," the girl said breathlessly. "They mentioned a knife and one of your tunics they'd found in a hut out in the forest."

"I did leave a tunic in my lean-to. But my knife is . . ." He reached and found only empty sheath.

"Surepta! He took it when he brushed into me outside the Dancing Serpent! No wonder he was so smug!"

"Flee, Lan. They have a web of evidence spun all around you. You can't get free of it. Those vicious beasts are everywhere, lying and plotting."

"No soldier will . . ." He stopped in midsentence as he heard the hoofbeats of horses. "Someone comes."

"Hide! Out the window. No, they might be out back already. Down into the cellar, Lan. Hurry!" The girl frantically shoved him down into the storage cellar and slammed the heavy wood trap door above him. Just as the rug pulled across to hide the trap, he heard the cabin door slam hard against the wall.

"You, wench, where's Dar-elLan-Martak?"

"What do you want of him, grey pig?" shot back Suzarra.

Lan heard his sister moan as if in pain. He started to go to her aid, then stopped. He had counted no fewer than ten pairs of boots entering the cabin. Against one he could prevail. Two would be a battle. Against ten—or more—was suicide.

"Speak!"

Suzarra cried out again in pain.

"He's suspected of murdering Zarella."

"He murdered no one," gasped out the girl. "That one, Kyn-alLyk-Surepta, he did it! I heard!"

Lan cursed under his breath, fingering his sword

in the cool dampness of the black cellar. Silly, stupid Suzarra.

He heard nothing but low moans from above. Deciding it might be suicide to go to Suzarra's aid, yet knowing it meant her murder if he didn't, he tried to push up the trap door. The sinews on his arms bulged with the strain. The lock had been turned. The heavy timbers refused to budge. And the sounds from above were all too apparent now. He could never leave his half-sister to the soldiers.

His sword proved useless against the thick door over his head. Frantically looking around the dimly lit cellar, he spied a tiny window. It proved far too small for him to crawl through. Using his fine steel sword as a digging tool, he slowly, painstakingly slowly, widened the window, pulling down handfuls of dirt until his face was caked with sweat and grime.

After what seemed hours of digging, Lan scrambled out, sword swinging wildly. No one was in sight. Cautiously peering into the now-quiet cabin, he sucked in his breath at the sight. Suzarra lay naked on the floor. The soldiers had used her repeatedly, then murdered her.

Just as Kyn-alLyk-Surepta had done to Zarella.

"This shall not go unavenged!" Lan muttered. Silent tears of rage and sorrow cut through the dirt on his face. "I shall feel my blade in your slimy guts, Lyk Surepta! I shall!"

Without another word, he turned and melted into the denseness of the forest.

CHAPTER TWO

Lan sneaked back into town. It was a dangerous thing to do, but he had to know the evidence against him. The sheriff wouldn't needlessly arrest him; the old man was cagey. He'd be certain of the criminal and the guilt before acting.

Lan heard the few citizens gathered along the wooden walkways buzzing with excitement. A crime always brightened their lackluster lives. This was one of the things he found so repugnant about city life. The people no longer thrilled to nature. They had to have more sophisticated entertainment, such as murder and those coughing mechanical cars that seemed all the rage at the moment.

". . . so there's no question about it in our minds," the sheriff was saying to a news-crier.

"How can you be so sure, Honor?" the news-crier asked, his eyes shining brightly like twin black buttons in the sun.

"The usual spells were cast. The three of us saw Dar-elLan-Martak's image in Zarella's room."

A cold chill raced up and down Lan's spine. Zarella! He edged closer to hear the entire story.

"He wore a leather jerkin and forest boots, and we've found the murder weapon. There is no doubt that it's Lan's. I saw him with that same knife earlier in the evening."

"Why do you think he killed Zarella?"

The sheriff shrugged. "I can't begin to guess. He loved the woman. Perhaps she spurned him. I know he wanted her to leave with him. That caused a fight earlier on with Kyn-alLyk-Surepta."

"What was Surepta's comment?"

"Nothing. The man didn't know about Zarella's death. I am certain Lan is the murderer. My deputies are hunting for him. It won't be easy for us to track him down, either. He's wilderness-wise, and if he wants to lead us a long chase, he's capable of it. But assure everyone that Dar-elLan-Martak will not escape justice. He'll be caught, tried, convicted, and reduced."

Lan thought there was a tiny catch in the old man's voice. The sheriff wouldn't like to summarily reduce him—but he would. Duty required it.

He saw no way to convince the sheriff of his innocence. The magical conjurations had shown his clothing present. That it was probably Surepta wearing the leather jerkin and deerskin boots was something he couldn't prove. It might have been anyone. Lan knew he had many enemies, and Zarella might have even more. Denying her favors to the wrong man could have produced this diabolical scheme to even the score before consigning her to Hell.

But it was Lyk Surepta's doing. Lan knew it. And it was Surepta and his grey-clad soldiers who had killed Suzarra, too. Cold hate began to spread like a polar icecap in the man's innards. His hand trembled on the hilt of his sword, but he was powerless to act, a leaf tossed on a high wind and nothing more. That helplessness more than anything else rankled.

Lan noticed the sheriff's office door slightly ajar. Boldly, he pushed his way inside. The tiny room was deserted. He crossed to the rack of weapons. The lock on the case yielded to slight pressure from his sword blade. First he took out a knife to replace the one he'd lost. Then he took out two clockwork mechanism pistols.

He'd seen these fired many times. While they were noisy and produced a choking cloud of smoke, they killed at a distance far greater than any mage could hope to accurately conjure a spell. He wound up the mechanisms and primed them with a firing cap, powder, and a lead slug. Thrusting them into his belt, Lan went out the rear door of the office. It wouldn't do to be seen on the city streets now.

In the alley loomed one of the oil-reeking, demon-powered cars. This wasn't what he'd hoped to find, but it would suffice. A horse suited him better, but a fugitive had to take what he found and not complain about bad luck.

"Demon! Are you in there?" he called to a tiny iron chamber set next to a heat exchange coil.

"Of course I am, you silly human! Where else would I be?" The demon sounded petulant. Lan couldn't blame him. Being locked up inside the iron prison and choosing only hot air molecules and discarding the cold ones seemed like tedious work.

"Begin your selection," Lan ordered. "I wish to leave town."

"You're not the owner of this machine," accused the demon. "I know his voice. Are you stealing me?"

Lan didn't see any reason to deny it.

"Good!" exclaimed the demon, thumping loudly against the iron walls of the cylinder. "I'll take you far from here if you'll promise to release me when you're done."

Lan considered the bargain. If the demon got him far enough away before the sheriff zeroed in on the thefts, he might yet escape the clutches of the law.

"Very well. But you'll have to perform to the best of your ability. I won't accept anything less," he cautioned the spellbound demon.

"You'll get it!"

The boiler began to turn a dull, cherry red. In a few minutes, a full head of steam built up. Hissing and slewing from side to side, he maneuvered the car out of town.

He hadn't been on the road twenty minutes when the demon shouted, "How much longer? My fingers are blistering! And my feet are turning cold from all the discarded molecules!"

"A little farther, that's all." Lan was frantic. He'd hoped the demon would be able to work at top efficiency longer than this.

"Forget it, thief! I don't care if I rot in this metal coffin. I'm not killing myself for any human."

The car began to lose power as the boiler cooled. Lan let the auto coast until it stopped. Looking behind, he saw frost appearing on the engine. The demon worked frantically in reverse now. He selected the slow-moving molecules and discarded the faster ones in way of protest for what he considered Lan's abuse.

Lan shouted, "How do I let you out?" He was willing to keep his bargain in spite of the demon's obstinance.

"Never mind. Just leave me alone."

So Lan did. He knew the sheriff would be after him both for murder and car theft. Lan wasn't sure but thought it might be easier following him now because of the demon. Magic attracted magic in some unknown and unknowable fashion. Lan's expertise was limited, but he was able to sense the use of magic. The sheriff was well trained and better able to follow the broad magical path caused by the demon.

Proceeding on foot now through the forest provided the best way of muddling his trail.

Looking around, Lan realized he was but a few hours' hike from the Old Place. With the distance-devouring pace of a frontiersman, he began striding in the general direction of the shrine. It would provide shelter and protection from magical spells and perhaps even grant him the information he needed to clear his good name.

After less than ten minutes of travel, Lan stumbled. He dropped to his knee, then rubbed his eyes. He felt sleepy. The incongruity of it struck him. He was filled with energy and the need to flee. Falling asleep at a time like this was sheer folly.

Or magic.

He closed his eyes and pivoted, relying on his magic-sensing ability to home in on a tiny brightness in the dark. He opened his eyes to see the sheriff and his two deputies standing in a small clearing behind him. Their hands were extended in his direction. He didn't have to hear their chants to know they were casting a deep-sleep spell on him.

He pulled out one of the clockwork pistols. Lan didn't want to injure any of the three men; he counted them as friends—or had. Now they would reduce him on the spot if he gave them the chance. Intellectually he knew he should slay, if possible. The gun came up and he sighted along the barrel. Something stayed his hand, however. He couldn't murder in cold blood. That would make him the killer they thought him to be, a killer like Surepta.

The pistol kicked backward in his hand as it spat out its leaden message. The bullet careened off a branch and whistled off into the still night. The ear-splitting report broke the concentration of the three men. The lethargy wrapping him like a cotton-wool blanket vanished.

Lan raced the wind into the dense thicket. The sheriff was slow to follow, not from weakness of spirit but from infirmity of body. Still having one pistol left, Lan carefully sighted along the barrel, wondering why some sighting device hadn't been fastened to the top. At what seemed the proper instant, he pulled the trigger, heard the whir of the unwinding spring and a pop as the fulminate cap ignited; then the pistol bucked in his hand. The sharp crack deafened him, and the acrid gunpowder stench robbed his sense of smell of its usual keenness.

But the bullet did its work. One of the deputies—the one Lan hadn't been aiming at—fell, gripping his leg and screaming in pain.

The diversion was enough to allow Lan to run for his life. He knew the sheriff wouldn't pause long. The man's honor was at stake. Without a successful capture—or a dead body—the sheriff would lose respect. Losing that, there would be little left for the old man. In a way, Lan felt sorry for him. But personal survival overrode any such maudlin sentiment.

He wasn't about to surrender himself so the sheriff could keep his job, his self-respect. Being reduced to a blob of animal fat burning with cold magical fire wasn't the way Dar-elLan-Martak wanted to depart this world.

The forest had fallen silent after the pistol discharge. One at a time, the animals began stirring again. The noises soon returned to normal. The soft clucking of a phor-hen was stifled by the sound of a python feeding. The scents came clean and fresh to Lan's nostrils after breathing the vapors of civilization.

A pine-needle carpet crushed moistly under his feet, and a heady odor rose to be savored like the aroma of a fine vintage wine. The beads of salty sweat forming on his forehead were pulled away by the gentle breeze blowing into his face. Sensing the direction of the wind, Lan quickly turned to his right. The sheriff tracked with magic, but spells took time to conjure. Tracking by spoor might prove easier—and Lan didn't want to stay upwind too long.

Lan found a small hollow in a lightning-struck

tree trunk. Breathing heavily, he leaned into the
depression, his hands coming together in front of
him. Tiny sparks jumped from finger to finger as
he quietly chanted spells of his own. This confused predators intent on serving him as their dinner. He hoped it might momentarily confuse the
sheriff's magics as well.

He strained his ears for sounds of pursuit. All he
heard was normal nighttime symphony. No human
scent disturbed the pungency of the forest, and he
saw only dim shapes moving through the night,
predators thwarted from feeding at sunset and now
hunting anything incautious enough to stay away
from the safety of burrow or nest.

Lan felt a surge of power pass through his body.
This was his domain; he belonged here.

To share such glory with Zarella wouldn't have
been possible. He saw this now that it was too late.
She was a creature of the bright lights, of the
teeming city, of the mechanical world. Blown by
the winds of fad and fashion, she never appreciated
such beauty as that surrounding him now.

A fugitive of the law, yes. A criminal? Never.
The forests knew no law save one: survival. Lan
was fit; he survived. Simple to state, difficult to
achieve. That was the way life was meant to be
lived, at the very edge, constantly on the alert. The
weight of a thousand man-made laws pressed down
heavily on him. He didn't understand why people
tolerated such robbery of their freedom.

They did. He didn't. Simple. He would return to
the world he knew best. He heaved himself out of
the charred wooden cradle and continued in a
direction he hoped would further confuse the te-
nacious sheriff's pursuit.

A dark pile of tumbled stone loomed out of the
forest's shadow kingdom. He halted his headlong
run, checked the direction of the wind, making
sure he had successfully turned downwind from his

pursuers, then sat on his heels, breathing heavily. He soon recovered enough to study the rock edifice.

The Old Place was deserted, and few came here. They claimed it was inhabited by evil spirits.

It was.

Lan had spent much time learning the ways of those spirits, finding the nexus of their power, the limits of their ghostly abilities. Here, unique of the power spots he knew, was the Pit of All Knowledge. With a little luck, the Resident would aid him. How, Lan didn't know. There was only one way of discovering that. He boldly walked into the shadow world of the Old Place, barely noticing the humid, clammy air stroking at his skin.

"It's not too bad. You'll live," the sheriff said, examining the bullet wound in his deputy's leg. "You just take a pinch of this powder and recite a level-two painkilling spell. The two of us will get back to you."

"What if you don't, Honor?" the man whined, the pain chewing at his self-control.

"You mean what if we're stupid enough to get ourselves shot to pieces, too? Then, son, you're just going to have to hobble back to town on your own."

"Unless you can talk the demon in that stolen car into working a little for you," chimed in the other deputy.

"Never mind. Let's go get Lan. Damn him to Hell! I hate going after him, of all people," the sheriff complained.

"A friend, isn't he, Honor?"

"Yes. A friend. I just can't imagine him doing five murders like that. Well, four of them I can. Lan was never one to take guff off anyone, and if the guards annoyed him, sure, I can see him cutting their throats. But not Zarella's."

"Women can twist a man around inside, Honor," said the deputy, as if stating a truth of the universe.

The older man didn't answer. He stooped and picked up the discarded wheel lock pistol. Silently he laid it back on the ground and began pulling various phials from his pouch. Assiduously mixing pinches of powder from three of the containers, he produced a violet paste that soaked up water from the atmosphere.

Muttered quietly, the mage's spell caused the paste to turn again into a fine-grained powder. The sheriff tossed this into the air and carefully watched the results.

"See, youngling? The hygroscopic powder shows Lan's profile. If we're careful and the wind doesn't blow too hard, we can get a good trail on him. He's too expert a woodsman to leave any other trail behind."

The deputy headed in the direction indicated by the grainy clouds of powder. Every few feet appeared the outline of their fugitive. Like a fuse ignited, the trail leaped onward into the forest with increasing speed.

The sheriff and his deputy were puffing hard when they came to a small clearing. Only a jumble of violet dust indicated the path.

"May all the gods of Ulfblom take him," cried the sheriff. "He's used some sort of magic to muddy his track. The dust can't figure out how to follow. Damn him!"

"What now? More of the powder?"

"No good. The spell is exhausted for twenty-four hours. Let's get back to our wounded comrade in arms, assure him he won't die a messy death, then go back to town."

"You're giving up?" The deputy was incredulous. The old man had never given up before.

"Certainly not!" snapped the sheriff. "I want a couple sniffer snakes. Lan can confound my magics, but he won't be able to get away from that pair of snakes Lar-ulLen-Beniton trained. Remember how they tracked down that wild howler monkey causing such a ruckus last year?"

The deputy remembered. He also remembered that they'd been too slow in reaching the trapped monkey. The snakes had ripped it apart. No real loss in that case, but to turn those slimy creatures loose on a *man's* trail . . .

He didn't even want to think of the results.

Lan stood in the tumble-down mass of stone for long minutes, waiting, listening. The baleful moan of wind insinuating its way between fallen blocks built up into a harmonic he knew well. The flesh crawled on his back as the sound magnified. Still, he refused to bolt and run.

Every instinct said *flee!* This was an evil place. The spirits would devour his soul and leave him a husk of a man.

Lan began walking with great care through the ruins. There was a safe path, a trail he'd blazed once. He didn't fully understand how the spirits inhabiting the Old Place were kept in check, but there existed spots of safety throughout the ruin. Lan knew about territorial imperatives, had watched animals in the wild exercise their right to hunting space, living space, even dying space. Perhaps the dead ones fluttering up and down the empty hallways of this cold stone mansion wished to preserve their right to a quiet repose.

He couldn't deny them that right.

The winding trail led to a huge room. The vault of the ceiling had been breached in several places. A thin sliver of moon peered down into the center of the room.

Once, this had been a proud, rich estate. Now tatters of tapestry hung rotting on the walls. The stench of decay persisted with the tenacity of death.

The dim light failed to show much more than rough stone and discarded furniture long eaten away by worms. The grit of dirt under his boots told of years—centuries—of desertion.

Still, in the midst of this dissolution was one feature that captured his attention and held it in an iron grip. The casual observer would have thought the pit in the center of the huge chamber to be a well. Closer examination might have evoked one more astute guess at some sort of altar.

Lan knew it was both—and neither.

His prior explorations of the Old Place revealed the secret of this pit. By the light of day, he had examined the ancient cuneiform writing on the rim of the pit. It was painstakingly slow work deciphering those crabbed, curled letters, but he had persisted.

A well, yes. It was a cistern of knowledge. Following the proper ritual brought forth a fountain of information unrivalled in the world. And it was an altar, too. It was the place of worship of a god so old that even its name had been forgotten. Not one of the modern gods of Ulfblom, this one was more elemental, more basic to the fabric of the universe. But, as with all things living, the entropy of existence had inexorably eroded small bits of power. As the millennia piled up, the god became ineffectual, allowing younger, more vital gods to supplant it.

The very name had faded even from the permanence of the well's stone rim. But if power was gone, knowledge remained. All knowledge—past, present, future.

Lan approached the stone ledge with a steady stride, but his heart hammered wildly in his chest. He betrayed no outward sign of fear; inside he seethed with emotion. He alone of all men living knew a fraction of what the Resident of the Pit could do.

He stood, his leg resting against the rough, frigid

stone of the well rim. The room was cold, but the stone was colder. The depths of space were boiling hot in comparison with the existence of this most ancient of gods.

In the blackness, untouched by silver moonbeams, something stirred. A small motion, silent and ominous. This was the Resident of the Pit that Lan must call forth. He swallowed hard, then turned and began searching the chamber for some indication of mortal life. No building, not even one haunted by the ghosts of millennia, escaped the invasion of rats and other small creatures. Lan sought and found such a beast.

The rabbitlike creature was deceptively docile. It sat on its haunches watching Lan advance. With the speed of light, powerful back legs launched the beast at his throat. The sharp fangs of a successful predator gleamed yellow-white in the moonlight.

And blood spurted darkly as Lan impaled the leaping beast on his sword point. As fast as the creature had been, Lan was quicker. The barely perceptible bunching of muscles had signalled its intent. His long sword had already cleared his scabbard by the time the rabbit-thing was airborne.

Lan didn't bother taking the kicking, still-alive creature off his blade. He carried it to the pit, hesitated, knowing the consequences of his act, then snapped the sword toward the depths of the pit. The beast slipped off the end of his blade, teeth clattering mightily against the carbon steel before it fell, kicking, into the pit. Unfortunately, the creature's last snap ripped the sword from Lan's grip. He watched helplessly as the gleaming blade cartwheeled downward.

A pitiful whine echoed briefly through the immense chamber, then silence reigned again. From the bowels of the planet came a deep rumbling. The dark, inchoate mass in the pit began taking substance. A wraithlike creature formed, constantly changing shape as if wind blew through a cloud of dense, inky fog. Even as Lan watched, colors came into the pit. The colors flowed one into another. No rainbow had ever shown more brilliance or innovation of hue.

By the time the deeply resonant voice sounded, Lan had steeled himself to meet the challenge he knew would come. One misstatement now and his soul was forfeit.

"Who beckons the Resident of the Pit?"

"A humble seeker of wisdom."

"I demand payment."

"A life has been given, blood has flowed."

"What is your name?"

Lan began sweating even though the night was cool, the air sluggishly moving inside the chamber. To give his name to a god gave power he wasn't willing to relinquish. Yet the ritual spelled out on the stone rim of the well required him to give voice to his own name.

"I am Dar-elLan-Martak, second son of Aket-elLan-Takus and Marella of Far Court."

A long silence followed, as if the god meditated profoundly on this information. Then: "I will answer your questions, Dar-elLan-Martak. There is one condition."

"What is that condition?" Lan felt fingers closing around his throat. The ritual hadn't mentioned this.

"A question can be answered only once if it pertains to your personal affairs. Questions of science and magic and philosophy may be asked many times by many people, as they have in the past." The Resident sounded wistful about days long dead.

"It is for myself that I ask these questions."

"So be it."

"Will I escape the sheriff? The man who hunts me for murder?"

"Many men hunt you. The one to whom you

refer will capture you in the early morning hours unless a course other than that which you contemplate is followed."

Lan considered this. He'd hoped to slip across the border into Lellvan and offer his services as a forester. The Resident now said this course of action would result in capture by the sheriff.

"What will happen if the sheriff captures me?"

"His evidence is overwhelming. The high sorcerers will uphold the sheriff's verdict. You will be declared guilty and . . . reduced. Let me ponder this term in its entirety."

Lan waited nervously while the Resident thought alien thoughts. He started nervously when the voice again boomed.

"I have studied all aspects of this phenomenon known to you as 'reduction.' It is simple application of disruptive vibrations to your molecules. The answer to your question is therefore: yes, you will no longer be alive if the sheriff captures you."

"If? I can avoid the sheriff?"

"Yes."

Lan waited for a more comprehensive explanation. When none came, he decided to press on. He had no idea how long this spell would hold, how much vitality the animal's blood had given the Resident. It wouldn't do to lose the only source of accurate information of the future he possessed.

"Is . . . who killed Zarella?" His voice choked with emotion.

"The one called Kyn-alLyk-Surepta. It was done with your knife, stolen earlier in the evening from you after a fight. He also stole your tunic and boots to cloud the trail and lend credence to the magics pointing to you as the killer."

Lan realized what the Resident was doing. Giving an answer was one thing, but giving a complete answer totally eliminated any chance of rephrasing the question later. Not that it mattered.

The sheriff wouldn't accept the word of a disembodied spirit as the truth. Ghosts were notoriously deceitful, often intent on gaining vengeance on still-living people who had wronged them.

There seemed no way to convince the sheriff that the Resident of the Pit was an ancient god now physically powerless. Still, the cunning of the eldest god amazed and irritated Lan.

"Why did the murder occur?"

"Two reasons. First, Kyn-alLyk-Surepta desired the woman and she refused him his carnal pleasures. He saw a way of having his will and incriminating you at the same time. The second reason is theft. He stole a most valuable bauble given to Zarella."

"Then this bauble, whatever it is, could prove Kyn-alLyk-Surepta is the one responsible for the murder!"

"No. There are any number of ways he can lie about its possession. At the worst, he would be found guilty of theft. The murder would still rest on your head."

Lan thought how hopeless the situation was. Also, how ludicrous it became. With the sheriff hunting him at this very instant, he sat talking with a million-year-old deposed god, hanging on its every word, believing its pontifications because they matched his own thoughts.

As if reading his mind, the Resident said, "I speak truly. I cannot lie, as you know the term."

"Did Zarella love me? Really love me in a way she didn't the others who came to the Dancing Serpent?" Lan was frightened of the answer. He hoped against hope for a positive answer, feared a negative one.

A pause lengthened into a full minute of silence. Only the wind blowing through the dried, glass-brittle leaves in the chamber came to his ears. Once, Lan thought he heard the chittering of a rat, but he wasn't certain. He didn't dare move. He felt his very sanity hanging in the balance on this answer. Had Zarella been worth all the heartache? Or had she merely been playing him for the fool? Dead, it hardly mattered in a physical sense, but Lan had to know.

"I have thought on this nonthing you call love," answered the Resident. "It is complex and has many manifestations. In the way you mean, she loved you."

Lan felt as if a huge burden had been lifted. He breathed more easily. Yet his love was dead, murdered by a man who escaped justice by sending an innocent victim to legal execution. Lan felt he personally could die happy if only he took Kyn-alLyk-Surepta with him.

That man's viciousness and cruelty had caused the deaths of Zarella, her guards, and Suzarra. Lan swallowed hard and fought back moisture at the corners of his eyes. His half-sister had lost her life and honor trying to aid him. He could never forget that it was Kyn-alLyk-Surepta and his grey-clad soldiers who were responsible.

"Can I get revenge on Kyn-alLyk-Surepta?"

"No."

The answer was short, abrupt. It startled Lan, for he had become used to the Resident's hesitating before answering. His future appeared blighted once again. Zarella was dead. Suzarra was dead. And he couldn't avenge those deaths. A man of honor was stripped of all courses of action.

All except one. The idea came to Lan slowly, painfully. It had always seemed the coward's way out to him. Now he saw it as something else, something more adventuresome. He was a lost soul in this world. The Resident assured him of death if he stayed. If he couldn't survive in this overcrowded, too-many-lawed world, he could flee to another, perhaps better, world.

"Resident, is the . . . the Cenotaph Road open to me?"

"Yes."

"Will I avoid death following the Road this night?"

"No one avoids death. Not even a god. You will, however, not die in this world you currently inhabit. Death will come in another place at another time."

Lan started to ask the time and place of his demise, then bit back the question. If he knew, he would live only for his death. Better to experience all of life and ignore the scrawl of fate slowly inking his name on the Death Rota.

"If I take the Road, will the sheriff pursue?"

"No."

He thought of his friends, his family. Suzarra had been the closest, more a friend than relation. And staying would not aid his friends in the least. To leave behind an entire world frightened him; this was the world of his birth. It held comfort and familiarity. Taking the Cenotaph Road offered only doubt and danger.

"Will I ever return to this world if I follow the Road?"

"No. But you will escape forever the injustice of this world."

"And find injustice in other worlds."

"That was a statement, not a question. Do you wish to rephrase it so that I may properly answer?"

"No. Injustice is everywhere. It's the nature of the universe."

Lan was startled when the Resident chuckled. It was the first show of emotion the nebulous being had displayed.

"That is a paranoid viewpoint. It is also true, in your terms. The only justice is that which you make yourself."

"I only wish I could bring Kyn-alLyk-Surepta to justice."

"You will."

"But you said I will never return to this world, that I'd never get revenge on him. What do you mean? What do you mean?" Lan shouted. But the Resident had begun to fade. The colors dissolved into a jet black indistinguishable from the void of space. Lan knew the being slipped back into the limbo from which it had come.

The Resident of the Pit faded into ebon blackness, patiently awaiting the next questioner. It might be a month or a century or a millennium; to the Resident it didn't matter.

Lan sighed. It was a long hike to the cemetery and the properly consecrated cenotaph. He hoped he could reach the awaiting crypt before midnight—and the persistent sheriff.

CHAPTER THREE

Lan Martak fled from shadows. Since leaving the Resident of the Pit, he had dodged and cut back on his trail and swung through the limbs of the dense trees and done a half-dozen other tricks designed to throw the sheriff off. He hadn't dared use another of his minor magical spells for fear the sheriff could detect it and turn it against him. The old man had taught him a little of his magic, but Lan realized he pitted himself against long years of experience he couldn't hope to match. He held a wide measure of respect for the old man, perhaps too much.

Braced in the crotch of a tree, Lan panted and wiped sweat from his forehead. When his strength flowed back, he dropped lightly to the ground and instantly froze. A sound, so slight a city dweller would miss it, came to his alert ears. He felt his eardrums itching as they strained. Adrenaline flowed through his arteries, sending his heart pounding wildly in his chest. Pursuer or pursued. Those were the only two conditions he knew.

And the rules were different for him now that he had joined the pursued.

He inhaled deeply, sampling the cool night breeze for some spoor to indicate what had alerted him. The sharp, acrid tang of a sniffer-snake made him tremble. The icy hand of fear clutched once at his heart, then relaxed as he stilled his runaway pulse. He hadn't thought the sheriff would loose those vile creatures.

It came again to him how a murder in this

civilized community was the height of crime. The townspeople ignored real crimes, crimes against honor and dignity, while putting too much emphasis on a condition that would occur sooner or later anyway. Better to die with honor, Lan thought, than to be disgraced. Lan only wished he could kill Kyn-alLyk-Surepta and show to all how treacherous the other grey-clad soldiers were. But there seemed no way of even hinting that Surepta had done the dishonorable crimes. Magic failed occasionally, became muddled and obscured. He raged futilely, thinking of Lyk Surepta swaggering, unscathed by justice, untainted by the slightest guilt.

That thought more than any other made his hand tremble and his lips pull back into a thin line.

A slithery sound warned him of the approaching sniffer-snakes. Deaf, almost blind, the snakes tracked only by smell. He could scream and the snakes would take no notice. Let one small hair fall from his head, however, and the snakes sensed it immediately. Even magical potions failed to increase the abilities of lesser animals to equal the sensitivity of sniffer-snakes' sensory pits.

If their tracking ability had been all, Lan would have relished the challenge. Outwitting them and their preternaturally acute sense of smell was a duel worthy of his own abilities. But when the sniffer-snakes tracked, no human dared follow. They hated with an intensity and an elemental intelligence. Anyone would do for their passionate hatred of humanity, including their keepers, but set on the trail of a fugitive, they paralyzed their victim with the bite of poisoned fang, then chewed with teeth. Carnivorous reptiles, they never stopped eating until the victim was totally devoured.

Lan shuddered as the slithering sounds grew louder. He began loping along, his legs covering vast chunks of terrain. The wind whispered through his hair, drew away the cold fear-sweat, soothed him. The stars burning mindlessly in the ebony bowl of the sky all peered down at him, questioning his ability to escape the voracious reptiles. He wondered if the stars held an intelligence and, if so, were wagering on him—or against him—in this death race.

Lan never broke stride as he jumped into a tree and began swinging limb to limb like some oversized monkey. The rough bark cut his hands, forcing him to pull himself up onto a branch and walk along it. The coal-bright eyes of the sniffer-snakes beneath him peered up, malevolent. They coiled, hissing and clacking their teeth together, until one caught his scent on the tree trunk. With a sinuosity that appeared magical, the snake immediately wrapped itself around the trunk and began swirling itself into the tree. Even though his time would be better spent racing the wind to the graveyard, Lan found himself unable to tear his gaze off the hunting sniffer-snake.

It hypnotized him with its boneless movements to and fro. When the snake reached the limb on which he stood, he came to his senses. Never had he heard of such hypnotic power in the reptiles, but he knew it existed. Nothing else explained his failure to run.

He slipped his knife from its sheath as the fiery-eyed snake slithered toward him. Faster than thought, he lunged—and missed. He recovered his balance in time to prevent a fall to the ground. He glanced down to a tight knot of a dozen or more of the sniffer-snakes.

"Keep calm," he told himself. "Calm and you'll still be able to reach the graveyard before midnight. Otherwise, you'll be ready for the graveyard in seconds."

The snake mocked him. It pulled itself up into a coil on the branch and hissed contempt. Lan was loath to throw his dagger at the beast; a miss spelled death. He followed the head as it weaved back and forth, then felt a lethargy spreading to his arms and legs. Realizing it was the hypnotic effect of the snake, he fought successfully against it. As long as he didn't relax his guard, the snakes had to rely on mere physical attacks.

A glance over his shoulder assured him that a jump into the next tree would be futile. Several of the sniffer-snakes already perched on the only limb within reach. As the hissing snake confronting him moved closer, he launched himself straight up.

The snake's strike missed. As it extended along the limb, it opened up its entire length to attack. Lan dropped from the limb above and let his boots crush the snake's back. Hissing fiercely, it fell from the limb to land among its fellows, broken beyond recovery. Lan hastily shot back up into the heights of the tree, transferred in a direction he hoped wouldn't contain more of the slithering beasts, then made his way until he came to a rushing stream.

Walking a limb until the stream gurgled under him, Lan looked around for some sign of human presence. None. He braced himself for the chill water, then splashed down in the center of the flowing river. He immediately dived and swam underwater as far as possible before surfacing. He gulped a lungful of air, then dived once again. With this porpoiselike progress, he hoped to elude the sniffer-snakes.

It worked. He arrived at the cemetery twenty minutes before midnight—alive and uneaten.

Lan scouted the graveyard to make sure it was as deserted as it seemed. While he found no obvious human presence, he did interrupt a pair of mating wolves. They left the cemetery with ferocious snarls to warn him against following them to some nearby place where they would continue their amorous activities.

Lan sat down, his back propping up a tottering tombstone, thinking how his life might have been different. He and Zarella might have been out here this evening with activities in mind similar to those of the wolves. Fate had cast a different role and robbed him of her. And, with cruel jest, fate went further and even held him accountable in human circles for her death.

"It's not fair," he muttered to himself. Yet, he told himself, where was the contract saying life had to be fair? No such agreement existed. Fate could be cruel if it chose; as easily, it could benefit him.

His sharp ears picked up the crunch of booted feet against gravel. He started to bolt for the deeper shadows of the forest, then stilled his impulse. Best to remain stationary, then silently work his way around the cemetery until he found the proper crypt for his journey away from this world.

The sheriff's voice drifted on the light breeze.

"How should I know if he's here, you fool? The sniffer-snakes might have got him already."

"Sure, Honor, whatever you say, but it seems a churlish thing to do, sending those snakes after him and all."

The deputy's voice carried sincere regret, but Lan knew it wasn't born of personal friendship. The man just hated to see anyone trailed by those vicious, carnivorous reptiles.

"Had to be done, boy. No other way of catching one as smart as Lan Martak. Trained him myself, like a son, I did. Damn fine man."

"Then why'd he kill Zarella? It was a bloody crime."

Lan imagined the sheriff shrugging thin shoulders, pulling tiredly at his scraggly white beard, and spitting. The old man's words chilled him more than the cold stone against his spine.

"A man does strange things in the name of love. That whore Zarella twisted him up inside, maybe, and when he found out she never intended anything honorable, he killed her."

"But so bloody," persisted the deputy.

"A man changes." For a moment silence hung like a damp, suffocating fog over the cemetery; then the sheriff continued, "This place always makes me uneasy, jittery. I feel like visitors from beyond are knocking on my door."

"I know what you mean," came the frightened voice of the deputy. Lan smiled to himself. The deputy would be the most easily scared away. He took a quick look at the stars overhead, found the War Dog constellation spinning around the triad of unchanging stars, and knew he had little time left to find the proper crypt and enter it.

He peered out from behind the tombstone and saw the sheriff, his back to Lan, dealing cards to the deputy. The nervous gestures assured Lan of success in the deputy's case. Getting rid of the sheriff without killing him would be more difficult.

Lan found several small pebbles and began flicking them behind the deputy. At first, the man glanced up, suspicious, not sure he'd really heard anything. His hand rested firmly on his sword, but he didn't draw. Seeing nothing, he turned back to the game of magically lit cards, which provided a way of passing time without forcing him to think too much of his unwanted duty in the empty graveyard. Lan dropped another stone just behind the deputy.

This time, the man rose and pulled his sword, shouting, "Someone's here!" He waved his blade and slashed at the darkness, killing only empty air.

"Sit down, you fool. If Lan is anywhere near, he's heard you by now."

"A ghost brushed me. I felt it!"

Lan let the man's imagination prey on itself for a few minutes, then rubbed his hands through some dew-laden grass. Dripping with moisture, he snapped his fingers in the deputy's direction. The sparkling droplets arced through the air and landed on the man's face. The deputy blanched death-pale, wiped the water away, rose on shaky legs, and let out a frightened howl.

"I felt them! I tell you, I felt them! A ghost. Hundreds of ghosts!"

The sheriff reached out and pulled hard on the man's sleeve. Lan cursed his luck. Another few seconds and the deputy would have run into the night, leaving only the sheriff. The old man's basic good sense prevailed over ignorant fear.

"Sit and be quiet. There are no ghosts, not around us. I cast a spell to ward them off," he lied for the man's benefit.

"Y-you did? Wh-why didn't you tell me?"

The old man shrugged it off.

"It's nothing. One of these days, I'll teach you the spell. Quite simple when dealing with ecto-plasmic beings. Much easier than lighting the cards." He glanced down at the spread of softly glowing cards on the stone between them. "I see why you wanted to run, Miska. I have you beaten easily this hand."

"Your spell wards off ghosts? All types of ghosts?" persisted the deputy.

The sheriff nodded. "Let me tell you of some of the residents of this graveyard. My conjurings told me that Lan would head here, possibly to follow the Cenotaph Road."

"No!" gasped the deputy. "No man would be so foolish. To go into . . . into nothingness."

"Is that so silly?" mused the sheriff. "I think not. Listen good, Miska, and learn how a man might think. In Lan's case, it's salvation. Another world, another chance. In a way, I hope he makes it."

"H-how is the Road taken? I've heard of the dire results but never of the actual path."

"See yonder monument? At the center of the cemetery?"

"Lee-Y-ett's tomb? A brave man, from all accounts."

"Truly a brave man. He was among the first to explore the el-Liot Mountains. He braved those heights, mapped the passes to allow commerce with the Boc-traders near Burning Sea, and even did some mining. That cost him his life. While mining drell-gems, a rockslide buried his body so deep it'd take the gods themselves a million years of digging to uncover the remains."

"But, Honor, yonder is his crypt. I see it. You mean he's not in it?"

"No. The full ceremony of death was performed, but without his corpse. Respect was due him for his accomplishments, and thus it was granted. A fine monument to a man who enriched our lives. But only an empty grave yawns."

Lan circled the pair and situated himself closer to the cenotaph. He tossed another small stone so that it bounced off the deputy's booted foot. This was all it took to send the nervous man lurching into the night.

"Stop, damn your eyes, Miska, stop! Don't run off!" the sheriff yelled, knowing even as he said it that his deputy was beyond hearing. He squinted a bit and called out in a softer voice, "Lan? Lan Martak? I know you're out there, boy. I don't want to make a night of this, so why don't you give yourself over?"

Lan had to bite his lower lip to keep from laughing. All that awaited him at the old man's hand was death. He'd rather find that along the Cenotaph Road. Be it ugly, messy death in the jaws of some vicious beast or a peaceful death in bed with a loving family at hand, he didn't care. Either was preferable to being rendered down into a pool of molten animal fat by the sheriff's diabolical spell.

The Road beckoned. He knew not where it led, nor did anyone else. Adventure, yes. Possibly treasure and fame. He wondered why he had never considered this before. Zarella had held him back, certainly. His love for the woman had blinded him to the world—worlds—stretching in all directions around him. If he couldn't avenge her death, why not seek glory in other worlds?

He knew there'd be no returning once he laid down in the cenotaph of Lee-Y-ett, but what matter? The restless power of that brave, lost, roving spirit would whisk him away to another world, perhaps to a better world, but certainly away from this one, away from the sheriff's order of reduction, away, even, from memory.

But he knew that wasn't possible. Zarella would remain firmly embedded in his mind until he died. And Suzarra. Even the old sheriff, who *had* been like a father to him.

On his belly, Lan wiggled closer and closer to the empty tomb. He knew the sheriff awaited him. Only this one gravesite provided the path he must take. But the sheriff nervously paced around the perimeter of the small stone edifice. Lan hesitated; he couldn't kill the man. The sheriff deserved his respect. To rob an old man of the final few years of life would be a sin greater than the one with which Lan was charged.

Glancing at the wheeling stars overhead warned him that midnight approached, less than five minutes remaining before the cenotaph's magic worked on any living being inside the crypt. Lan gathered his feet under him, then jumped out like an attacking panther. A hard fist drove for the sheriff's head and connected with a greying temple. The man uttered not a sound as he sank to the ground, unconcious.

Lan hastily checked for a pulse. It still beat strongly.

"I'm glad, Honor, really I am," Lan breathed. "I'd hate to harm one such as you. The town needs your strength, especially now." He pulled the sheriff into a more comfortable sitting position against the cold stone tomb, then confronted the task of removing the heavy marble slab over the cenotaph.

Grunting mightily, Lan worked open a tiny space through which he barely squeezed. The inside of the grave smelled musty, yet not so oppressive as the youth thought it might be. No cobwebs adorned the insides, and he discovered no creatures of any sort lurking within. Only a pedestal of hard pink granite stretched in the center of the tiny room. With trepidation, Lan went to the bier and placed a shaking hand on the stone. To his surprise, an inner warmth radiated outward. He jumped onto the bier and reclined. Staring overhead, he saw the small opening through which he'd entered and the stars in the night sky beyond. The small angle of vision prevented him from working out the time from the few visible stars. He only hoped he'd arrived in time. He might be off a few minutes in his reading; the stars rarely provided a casual observer the accuracy that a good chronometer did.

"Lan," came a weak voice. "Lan Martak! I know you're in there, Lan. Don't do it. Come out."

The sheriff's voice filled Lan with fear. He didn't dare leave the cenotaph, not now. Midnight was too close. Yet his magic-sense stirred, telling of potent spells being conjured by the sheriff to lure him forth. The old man knew an infinite number of spells to bind him to this world and his fate.

"Very well, Lan. By logic and reason," the sheriff began the mnemonics of his spell, "in every season, stumble, faint and fall, at my beck and call."

Lan's toes tingled as the spell slowly possessed him. He'd never attempted to thwart such a potent spell as this before. He allowed the coldness to spread, still hoping he'd arrived in time for the cenotaph to take him.

Then he dropped through empty space, screaming at the gut-wrenching pain.

Lan Martak fell through nothingness for an eternity. The pain twisted him inside until he was sure that he had died and gone to the Lower Places. Then he splashed down into waist-deep water, nearly drowning himself in the muddy lake as he floundered about, gasping and blowing spumes of froth.

Spluttering, he fought to get his feet under him. When he began to sink in the soft mire of the lake bottom, he leveled his body and tried to float on the surface of the blood-warm water. A gentle pressure freed his boots from the sucking mud, and soon he kicked his way into the center of the shallow lake. As far as he could see in all directions stretched the silent, decaying lake. The surface of the water reflected a turbulent sky hung with thick rain clouds. The humidity and the heat were truly oppressive, but the usual flights of insects failed to take wing and buzz annoyingly around his face.

Lan continued kicking until the mild paralysis left his legs. He had been lucky to escape along the Cenotaph Road when he had. Another few seconds would have immobilized him. But the sheriff and the other world were behind him now. His home world. Lan fought down a sudden surge of irrational panic at the thought of abandoning all he had known for a lifetime.

All that mattered now was his continued survival in this strangely quiet lake.

"Come on, arms and legs, take me to shore," he

said, and waited to hear the returning echo of his words. The reassuring echo failed to come.

Sighing, he resigned himself to being totally alone in this world. As he stroked slowly for land, he wondered if he had gone backward in time or if this might be a world layered next to his own like the skin of an onion.

Lacking five minutes of shore, he became vaguely uneasy. In the forests, the source of his tension would have been instantly obvious. In the watery world of this filth-ridden lake, it took several seconds for him to realize that tiny ripples were overtaking and passing him. The lake had been unnaturally still when he unceremoniously tumbled into it. Now the ripples indicated some large body in the water swimming away from him.

He turned and tread water, peering into the mist now veiling most of the lake. The bow waves from whatever beast also occupied the water were plain, but no creature surfaced to confront him. Lan debated heading for shore at the fastest pace possible, then decided that that would only waste strength and gain him nothing. The swimming creature paddled away from him, after all, not toward him. What danger did it really present?

Still, he felt growing panic. The fog hanging like liquid lead over the lake thickened, swirling and billowing over his head. The muddy water became increasingly oppressive, its warmth insinuating itself into his body and robbing him of strength in odious ways, the thick waters clogging his flaring nostrils, the very nearness of the mud bottom sucking up his courage.

He swam faster. The presence he felt grew stronger. Lan wished fervently he had solid dry land under his feet again. He was a fierce fighter— on the good earth. Here, virtually helpless in the water, he could fall easy prey to any watery Hell-creature. The ripples passing him stopped, and only his own turbulence winged back from his frantic strokes.

His left hand slammed hard into a bumpy surface rising from the murky water. Lan opened his mouth to scream and was rewarded with a lungful of the boggy, tired water. Sputtering, he thrashed about trying to get his feet under him. He rapidly discovered the mucky bottom was too distant; he had to tread water while he spat out the mud clogging his throat.

Then he saw the solid object he'd struck. Baleful yellow eyes peered at him, totally lacking in mercy. He knew that look. It was the way a predator studied a prospective dinner. Lan refused to be food for any creature living in such squalid surroundings.

"Away!" he yelled, hoping the sound of his voice would momentarily startle the aquatic beast. It didn't. The silence quickly returned and became even more frightening as the beast swam in ever-narrowing circles, spiralling slowly in to look him over. "Away, I say! I don't want to kill you!"

He fumbled out his knife and clumsily brandished it. The beast's eyes never blinked. It came closer.

When the ripples vanished, Lan moved instinctively. He gulped in all the fetid air his tortured lungs were capable of holding, then he dived. The creature attacked underwater, and Lan had to meet it on its own terms or have his slowly kicking legs neatly sheared off by powerful jaws.

The murky water prevented his seeing farther than an arm's length. He didn't need sight, though, to sense the alligator surging in for a quick kill. A shock wave preceeded it. One second it poised at the limits of sight, then jaws swung open so far that Lan realized the creature might swallow him whole and not even chew. He dived deeper and came up under the maneuvering alligator. His knife ripped into the soft belly and pulled out a long, thin line of red blood. Then the creature went berserk. The froth from its struggles made vision impossible. Lan continued stabbing blindly, hoping to inflict mortal wounds on the beast. When his lungs burned and approached the bursting point, he relaxed and let his buoyancy take him to the surface. As his head popped into the still air above the invisible battlefield, he gasped. Hurried breaths refilled his aching, straining lungs in time to dive under again when he felt teeth chewing into his leg.

He had seriously wounded the alligator during the first encounter, and only this saved him from the loss of a leg and his life. The weakened creature snapped down with its usual bone-shattering bite, only to find the necessary muscles severed by knife slashes. But it remained a formidable opponent underwater, using its bulk to good advantage.

While it couldn't cleanly bite entirely through Lan's leg, it gripped with ferocious strength. It rolled over and over under him. He knifed it repeatedly, feeling his strength waning as he did so. The pressure in his lungs mounted with frightening speed. He allowed a few bubbles to slip past his lips. His knife moved with agonizing slowness in the viscous water. The wounds he inflicted seemed increasingly minor. The alligator bled, yes, but the man faded from lack of oxygen faster than it did.

When he was certain only breathing water remained, Lan's head cleared the surface again. Gasping painfully, he found himself pulled under too soon. He went back down, the alligator still worrying his leg with its once-powerful jaws.

Lan succeeded in driving the point of his dagger into one of the unblinking yellow eyes. The alligator's thrashing had been frantic before, but now it turned into a tempest sucking all into its vortex.

Whirling in a tight circle, it dived for the bottom of the lake, taking Lan with it. The rush of water past his ears exerted extreme pressure and made him feel as if someone had invaded his head to kick the inside with heavy boots. As a powerful tail lashed past, he stabbed out in panic, his knife sinking repeatedly into soft, unprotected flesh.

The alligator instantly freed his leg. Lan shot to the surface, more dead than alive. He swam along slowly on his back, gasping in the humid air and relishing its now-sweet taste in mouth and nose. His leg trailed behind him, useless from the mauling, but he lived. And, unlike the alligator, he was still able to father another generation.

CHAPTER FOUR

Lan Martak struggled out onto solid land for the first time since blundering onto this world. His leg throbbed abominably, and he bit his lower lip to keep from crying out in pain. Only when he had a tree to guard his back did he rest, however. This was a strange, dimly lit land, and all manner of beasts might be prowling for dinner at this very instant. The huge and hungry alligator-creature had been one small hint at what lurked behind the seemingly placid exterior of an unfamiliar country-side.

He pulled away his pants leg and allowed the wound to bleed freely. He doubted the alligator carried poison on its fangs, but the filth floating in the still water might be laden with any number of noxious germs. When his leg began to run chill from lack of blood, he wiped away the caking accumulation of mud and blood and began to dress his wound. When he satisfied himself he had done the best job possible under the circumstances, he put away his small medical kit and began massaging the limb.

As he did so, he chanted a minor healing spell. He felt itching begin deep within the bound wound and he knew the healing had begun satisfactorily. Before long, needles of returning circulation danced along the entire length of his leg.

Having assured himself that he wasn't going to bleed to death, he surveyed the land around him. This world differed so much from his native one that he sucked in his breath in surprise. The

grey, leaden overcast seemed perpetual. No hint of
a bright, blue-white sun shone on this dismal
swampy place. The trees were mostly blue cypress
and willows, tired limbs dragging the muck of the
land, only occasionally stirring to the caress of a
vagrant breeze. The air itself was fetid, cloying,
possibly even carrying the sick sweetness of death
in it. Somewhere near, something decayed and no
one cared. Lan used the tree for support and pulled
himself erect. From his added height, he discovered little better view of the scenery. There stretched
an endless array of the willows, and the glasslike
smoothness of the treacherous lake multiplied the
effect like a hall lined with mirrors.

Still, he lived. He could boast about that—if he
found anyone to brag to. He massaged and tugged
at his leg and found virtually unimpaired mobility.
The minor magical spells he used had closed his
wounds. Now only time and his own body's pro-
cesses were required to finish the healing. A more
powerful mage might have conjured a deep-healing
spell, but such potent chants were beyond his capabilities and knowledge. Content with the healing
already occurring, he jumped up and down a few
times to test the strength in his leg, then stopped,
deciding not to push himself to the limits of en-
durance unless it seemed vital to his continued
survival.

"Which way?" he wondered out loud. The words
were swallowed by the deserted countryside. For
the first time he realized that, outside of the breeze
rustling the willows, not a sound could be heard.
Although straining his acute hearing to the ut-
most, he failed to detect a single animal moving.
"Is this such a desolate land, then? Hola! Is anyone within hearing?" he shouted.

Stillness mocked him.

"Best to find a stream and follow it," he said to
himself, anxious for the reassuring sound of his

own voice. "But first, where is north?" Pulling a compass from his pouch, he studied the freely swinging needle. After almost a minute of the random movement, he put it away, confused at the lack of reading. This world apparently had no magnetic pole. Lan knew of no other way of determining position as long as the clouds obscured the evening stars and the daytime sun.

Lan decided one direction was as good as another, since he knew nothing of the terrain. He spat on the back of his left hand, then snapped his right index finger down smartly into the wetness. The direction in which the tiny bullet of spittle sailed marked the direction of his march. To ensure as straight a course as possible, he marked every fifth tree with a blaze. The utter sameness of the bog country would betray him eventually if he didn't do something to warn himself of unconscious circling. A lifetime spent wandering aimlessly in this morass of muck and bog wasn't as attractive a prospect as a nice cozy fire, a full belly, and all the beer he could drink.

He trudged for eternity before his wound began shooting painful lances of fire into his leg. The wound opened once on him, then threatened again less than an hour later. He bowed to his own weakness, chanting the healing spell over and over. Gathering dry wood for a fire proved difficult, but he had all the time in the world. A tiny pyramid of dried wood in front of him, he closed his eyes, remembered the fire spell, and felt sparks jumping from fingertip to fingertip. He reached out and applied the ends of his hands to the wood. When the fire began to leap cheerfully and dance in the tiny pit he'd dug, he settled down and warmed himself. The insidious wetness of the swamp had completely soaked through his boots. Drying them out and cleansing them of the fungus he'd accu-

mulated on the thick soles and sides ranked high
on his list of priorities.

A few mouthfuls of his dried rations and one
swallow of water from a small flask was all he
allowed himself. Tomorrow, he had to hunt for
game and try to find a source of clear water, pref-
erably lacking in large, carnivorous alligators bent
on eating him. But now, sleep was more important
to Lan. In the span of a few heartbeats, he slept,
snoring peacefully, the only other noise disturbing
the night being the fire crackling down into embers.

The shrill keening brought him instantly awake,
knife in hand. For a moment, he couldn't locate
the source of the awful noise. His ears finally fought
off the last remnants of sleep and zeroed in on a
dense brush thicket a short run from where he'd
slept. The keening was drowned out by a loud
thrashing noise, then the unforgettable lament of a
dying wolf.

Lan struggled into his still-wet boots. If the wolves
of this world were as vicious as those in his, he
wanted to be able to fight and run at a moment's
notice. He packed together his meager belongings,
slung them securely around his waist, then faced
the thicket again. He wished for the first time that
he still had his sword. A tiny dagger hardly seemed
adequate to go into battle against powerful predators.

He also worried over the first sounds he'd heard.
An animal in distress didn't make such a noise;
this had an oddly intelligent tone to it. But he put
no name to the kind of beast screaming out in
terror with such a high-pitched, wordless cry.

Instinct told him to flee. He wasn't at full fighting
capacity yet. The wound on his leg was no longer
serious, but it might slow him at a fatal instant.
Yet all his training, all his ethical upbringing, demanded that he aid another caught by wolves. The
wilderness was a dangerous place alone; those sol-

itary souls stalking the most distant reaches of it
had to band together against the perpetual tide of
death.

A human owed it to another to rescue anyone in
trouble.

Balanced on the edge of dilemma, he heard the
shrill sound of anguish come again. This time it
was followed by fluent cursing. He picked up only
the trailing words of the imprecation.

". . . damn you beasts to Ajo! I will devour your
livers! If you do not devour me first. Damn you all!"

That pushed Lan Martak back onto the track of
honorable behavior. He felt a passing resentment
that he had even considered failing to aid the other.
He had to rescue the person in the grove. He
couldn't abandon anyone to the savage hunger of
the wolves. He vividly remembered finding the
remnants of an exploration team in the foothills of
the el-Liot Mountains. Three men and a woman
had been partially eaten by the filthy predators. He
had the stomach of one who had seen much death
in his travels, but those gnawed corpses sickened
him more than he had ever admitted to a soul. It
would be impossible for him to now let another fall
in that identical way if he could aid him.

That renewed desire to succor didn't cause Lan
to rush in foolishly, however. He picked up a pair
of the driest limbs, wrapped cobwebs of desiccated
moss around each, then thrust them into his dying
fire. In a few seconds, he carried two flaming
torches to frighten away even the boldest of wolves.

He made his way to the thicket, glad for the
added light cast by the flambeaux. The depths
were veiled in impenetrable shadow; he made out
only the dim outlines of the skulking wolves.

"Away, I say! Aieeeeee! My leg! You repulsive
four-legged menace!" came the cries of rage and
pain from the denseness. A large wolf flew through
the air to smash into a tree bole several feet beyond

Lan. Surprised, he turned and saw the creature's crushed body sprawled bonelessly at the base of the tree. Whoever fought inside the thicket did a noble job of it. To bodily throw so heavy a wolf required strength far beyond Lan's.

But he knew that a wolf pack, if hungry enough, would tackle even a ferocious jann-pard and chevy it to death. First one snarling wolf would attack, only to be driven back. While it retreated, another wolf would attack. And then another. As they backed away, still others would leap and bite until the prey fell exhausted.

Lan cautiously entered the dense thicket, holding his torches high above his head. His eyes adjusted to the flickering light. He counted on the wolves' eyes taking even longer to adapt. In that short time, he had to attack and, with luck, so would the pack's prey.

"I'm going to rescue you," he shouted. "Don't worry. I'll help you get free of the wolves." He crashed through low tangle of heavily thorned brush until he came to a small clearing. Voicing a wordless scream, he momentarily distracted the circling wolves. A savage lunge with his knife disemboweled one careless enough to turn and attack without first studying its intended victim. His torches were knocked from his hand by the leap of another; then he heard the soul-chilling howl of pain and anguish. The wolf had set itself on fire. As it ran from the clearing, it emitted sparks like some child's unsupervised fireworks.

The other wolves milled about, the thrust of their attack now parried. Lan charged another wolf, one easily waist high. Because he held a retrieved torch in front of his body, he forced the animal to circle directly into his blade. Others seemed disinclined to press the attack now that their prey had an ally.

"Are you all right?" Lan bellowed to his still hidden companion in arms against the wolf pack.

"Damn, it is such a sorry state I am in! And you, you fool! Watch how you use that torch. You are sure to set me afire!"

"Don't worry about that, worry about the wolves."

"Pah! These animals are nothing. But what if you set fire to my legs? How should I fight something as terrible as that?"

"Just roll around on the ground, dunce!" Lan had little time to argue. These wolves proved themselves more determined than any he had encountered on his own world. Either they were starved or, as their harsh yellow eyes hinted, they possessed more than a rudimentary intelligence. It was nothing less than a miracle that anyone fended these creatures off, and here his companion had nothing better to do than complain about the careless use of his torch.

"Easy for you to say, you stupid human."

Lan Martak stopped dead. A quick toss of the torch ignited still another wolf and sent it screeching into the night, a living funeral pyre. The last statement from the rescued party struck him as being so peculiar that Lan felt he must investigate immediately. He turned, facing the voice. As the torch flickered out its dull light, he saw revealed a huge hairy-legged spider, cowering away from the flames.

"Get away from me with that torch, I say! You will do me grievous harm if you get too careless." The spider seemed to be the source of the voice. Lan wondered if he had somehow become embroiled in a nightmare and no longer seperated reality from dream.

He mentally checked all the clues assailing his senses. The torch crackled and popped brightly in his hand, and warmed him. Hot resins from the wood seeped forth and dripped painfully onto his flesh. The smell of the burning wood and charred wolf-flesh told him he received the very spoor expected. His mouth felt as dry as a boll of cotton from fear and adrenaline. His boots squished from dampness—if this were a dream, why didn't he simply wish them dry?

"Are you all right?" he asked lamely.

"Of course I am," declared the spider indignantly. "I am quite able to take care of myself. Not that it matters," came the voice, self-pitying now. "I am nothing. Nothing!"

Lan imagined salty tears welling at the corners of huge, unseen eyes. Deciding his back was too vulnerable, he circled to his right, holding the torch in front of his body for protection. A large-trunked tree soon pressed, rough and reassuring, into his spine. To his immediate right loomed a tangle of iron-grey berries, the thorns on the bush dripping poisonous ichor. His left flank remained open as was the area directly before him. Only when his defense seemed adequate did Lan allow suspicious eyes to scan the monstrous spider squatting in front of him.

Had he been at home, he would have thought someone played a joke on him by constructing this overlarge spider with the matted fur legs and lumpy body. He wasn't at home; this wasn't a joke.

"Who are you?" he asked, barely able to trust his voice.

"I am Krek-k'with-kritlike," came the voice again. "You may call me Krek. Humans never get the second syllable out properly." An odd chitinous clicking noise echoed from the dancing shadows surrounding the spider.

"What manner of beast are you? I've never seen a spider so huge before."

"Indeed." The spider sniffed. "You must be one of the provincials from this world. Little wonder you have never seen a mountain arachnid from the upper fastness of the Egrii Mountains."

The spider jumped forward with startling speed. The hairy ropes on each side of the central mass that Lan ascribed to tree roots stiffened to lift the creature upward. He took a deep breath as he studied the towering beast. It was easily half again as tall as he, and Lan measured as a giant among the lowlanders. The hairy legs spanned a full five paces, and the body suspended at the juncture of those copper-wire-studded appendages weighed at least as much as Lan.

To fight such a beast would be foolhardy. Besides, he had rescued it from the wolves. It should be grateful.

"Either set fire to my legs"—a visible shudder rippled through the creature at the mention—"or hold the torch away. There. Thank you. I see now that you are indeed human." Again the odd sigh. "Long have I fled your kind on this world. No longer. I am so weary. Come. Kill me."

"I mean you no harm. Didn't I risk my life to save you from the wolves?"

"You humans seldom do things with logic. Why not save me from them for your own perverse killing pleasures? Straying so far from my web has worn down my will to survive."

Lan planted the butt end of the torch in the ground and moved away from the sputtering fire. Sparks flew everywhere now, and he began to share Krek's fear of being set on fire. He sank to the ground, cross-legged, and gave the spider his closest scrutiny. It was even more repulsive than Lan had anticipated. The huge mandibles snapped noisily, in a menacing manner. The man had a momentary vision of being neatly clipped in half by those powerful death scythes. The only feature of the spider's "face" that softened the fierceness proved to be the eyes. They were an odd dun color, as limpid as the eyes of a maiden in love and as far-focused.

"Why did you leave your web in the first place? I can't see you being native to this world. There isn't a lump of muck large enough to call a mountain, much less the lofty spires that must be your domain."

"Ah, you are another traveller along the Cenotaph Road." For a moment, the self-pity evaporated and Krek talked with some animation. "I left my lovely web seeking adventure. Nothing ever seemed to happen. Just hang around all day, dangling at the end of a sticky strand, waiting for some ugly humans to caravan by. They would either pay the tribute due me or . . ."

A resounding clack of huge mandibles graphically showed the alternative to tribute. Lan's hand moved to his sheathed knife with an instinctive jerk.

"But I frightened you! I am sorry. You humans are so fragile. Why, the last one I encountered on this miserable, wet, soggy ball of mud hardly struggled at all in my hunting web before he was entangled so badly he hanged himself. A pity. And it was such a *tiny* web. I was casting forth for a wild boar or a roe, perhaps, nothing more. But along he gallops on that silly four-legged beast you humans are wont to sit astraddle and that was it. Whish! All caught up and quite dead before I could rescue him."

Lan blinked rapidly at the idea that this spider's web actually caught and held not only a human but his horse. He felt the developing silence to be ominous. He wanted to babble to fill the quiet. Instead, he stilled his impulses, swallowed, and considered what he would tell this bizarre arachnid.

"I'm an unwilling traveller," Lan confessed. "There was a slight misunderstanding, a lady dead— not by my hand!—and I fled to avoid the unpleasantness of being reduced."

Krek wasn't listening. A thin sigh wheezed from

him as he settled down to the ground. With his legs pulled in, the spider appeared no more than a shadowy boulder in the clearing.

"No, this is not the terrain of my personal choosing. So true," the spider mused, "so true. How I wish I had not been struck with the obscene desire to explore other worlds. Not a one of my ancient and noble race has left the web of our ancestors. None, save me." Its entire body shivered as if infected with the shaking palsy. "I, Krek of the Pinnacles, the one who yearns for other worlds, ventured out. Look at my sorry straits now. I, who once bragged of warrior prowess, rescued by the likes of you. A mere human!"

Lan let out a short, harsh laugh, more from nervous release than any other reason.

He said, "You don't look like a warrior at all."

Again came the crashing of powerful mandibles. Lan felt the blood rush from his face. His hand gripped the handle of his knife with feverish intensity, ready for a fight, even though he knew he could never overpower such a large creature.

"If I've offended you, many pardons," Lan said hastily. "I only meant . . ."

"I know what you meant, and it is regretfully true. My vitality has been sapped. The farther afield I travel from my superb, mountain-spanning web, the weaker I become. Once, I was a noble among nobles. I traversed the highest reaches, and none matched my fighting abilities. When the accursed yearning to explore erased my good sense, my powers slipped away like water through the fingers of that ridiculous hand of yours. It has been too long since I returned to the web of my hatching, for too long. I am torn by my inner need to return to mate and my physical weakness from being too long gone from my clan's territory."

Lan nodded, understanding. It was never good to be away from a personal place of power. Krek's problem was compounded by being a traveller on the Cenotaph Road. Lan knew of no way to return to the world of one's origin, though. The Resident of the Pit had warned him that he could never return home. Krek carried the same burden.

"I would give my entire web treasure if only I could return to Klawn-rik'wiktorn-kyt."

"What?"

"Not what, who. My betrothed. Such a fine mating web she spins. Such delicacy and intricacy of pattern. It is a joy to race along the strands, feeling the vibrancy of the web under your legs. Ah, it makes the very fur on my legs tingle thinking of her. All lost to me, all lost!"

Lan watched the spider shrink to rock size. If he hadn't known the large dark lump in the center of the clearing was Krek, he might have blundered along and mistaken it for an inanimate resting spot off the mucky ground.

"I wish I could help you, Krek, but that first step along the Road is a permanent one. There's no going back. You and I are cut off forever from our home worlds."

Krek uttered a sound that seemed a cross between a snort and a cough. Lan wondered if the spider had fallen ill. When Krek spoke, he knew differently.

"Foolish human! Of course you can walk backwards on the Road. Whatever gave you the idea you could not?"

"But I was told . . ."

"Told wrong. All one has to do to find the appropriate spot is to close your eyes and drift. The cenotaphs glow inside the mind, and if you concentrate on any individual one, images dance about it. So simple. I know precisely the way back to my web."

Lan thought over the spider's words. To go home! He could persuade Krek to show him the way!

Then the desire faded like a night-blooming flower facing the dawn. Nothing pulled him home. Zarella was dead. Her murderer would come to grief, so said the Resident. But the Resident had been wrong once. Could it have erred on this? Somehow, Lan thought not. Discounting this, what did his home world have that couldn't be found elsewhere?

The negative points outweighed the positive ones. Why not let Krek guide him along the Road?

"Krek," he said with more spirit then he'd felt in days. "What exactly comprises this web treasure of yours? You said you'd give it all simply to return to Klawn-whatever-you-said." The spider didn't seem a bad sort, and if a little gold could be made escorting him back into those Egrii Mountains he mentioned, so much the better. But Lan didn't want to end up with a few cocooned bugs. Treasure to a spider might differ vastly from the treasure of a foot-loose adventurer.

"Web treasure?" Krek asked dully. "I seldom think of it anymore. It was once a noble stash. Rubies as large as roc-eggs. Silver chains a mile long. There is even the Eye of the Rainbow."

"What's that?"

"According to human tales, all rainbows leap from the center of of this gem. While it does possess a certain brilliance, I have seen other stones with better clarity and color. And this is so small, too. Hardly as large as your fist."

"How did you get this Eye of the Rainbow?" Lan doubted this jewel would prove too valuable, but the silver chains and the rubies sounded enticing.

"A careless human caravan. Refusing the tribute due me called for their deaths. The Eye was in a large box filled with the softest silks I have ever seen spun by mere-spiders. It will be an inspiration to my hatchlings."

"The Eye of the Rainbow?"

"No, no, no! The silk. Such a fine draw. The

expertise shown in spinning those uniform threads, the unique composition, those are the things our young'ngs can learn."

"Would you give me the pick of your web treasures if I escorted you safely back to your web and, uh, your mate?"

For the first time, Krek rose and bounced as if his legs were made of spring steel.

"Yes! Oh, yes, *yes*! To return to lovely Klawn-rik'wiktorn-kyt! For that, anything!"

Lan Martak wondered what sort of task he'd just volunteered to perform. Still, he had nothing to lose and everything to gain. And if by some chance he learned Krek's trick of locating the cenotaphs—and was able to glimpse the world beyond—that would be worth more than any jewel or trinket.

"Good," he said. "We'll leave in the morning."

Krek stirred slightly, then said, "It *is* morning. Cannot you tell the difference between day and night?"

Lan looked above to the heavy, black rain clouds drifting just above the treetops. The glare seemed less intense in the woods, but he definitely had much to learn.

"We'll leave after I've rested. Does that suit you, Krek?" he said testily.

"Why not?" blandly replied the spider.

Lan found no answer for that. Curling into a tight ball, he slept.

CHAPTER FIVE

A bug burrowed its way into his nose, making him snort and sneeze in protest. This was the rude awakening Lan Martak had the next "morning." As soon as he pulled the offending insect from his nostril, he looked up to the leaden rain clouds swirling above the trees. There seemed no difference at all in the light intensity, yet Lan felt this should be morning. He had slept long enough to take the edge off his nervous exhaustion from fighting the wolf pack and meeting his strange companion in arms, Krek—if a spider might be considered a companion in arms.

Lan looked to the dark shape, still crouched in the middle of the tiny clearing. Krek hadn't moved a hair since their encounter. The man tried to figure out the spider, then shook his head. It would take much work to do something as complex as picking apart the inner workings of that intelligent arachnid's brain.

"Ready to do some hiking, Krek?" he called out, unsure of the spider's reaction. When the spider only let out a very human groan, Lan feared some injury had gone unnoticed in the excitement of the "night" before. He went to the hulking beast and laid his hand lightly on the ridge above Krek's eyes.

The spider was crying.

"Krek, are you hurt? Did the wolves nip one of your legs?" He looked in confusion at the tangled array of furry legs curled around the spider. If one had been injured, he wasn't sure how he would attempt fixing it. A bite, even a deep one, required only a bit of bandaging and a simple healing spell, but an outright break posed grave problems. He didn't know how to splint a spider's leg, and his mind reeled at the thought of Krek using a crutch.

"Oh," sobbed Krek, "it is all so useless! I shall never see the lovely Klawn-rik'wiktorn-kyt, light of my life, again. She is gone, gone forever!"

"Krek? Have you had a vision? Can you foresee the future?" Lan shook the spider hard now, trying to get information. Precognition was rare on his world; few claimed it and fewer actually possessed the talent. Once, he had gone to a spring fair years before meeting Zarella and watched the acrobats and jugglers perform. Tiring of them, he found his attention drawn to a tiny booth. The crone propped in the chair inside had spoken to him, telling of things in his future. At the time, he had laughed them off as ravings of an old woman wanting to impress him into giving her a few coins. He had, but when the very things she foretold came to pass, he experienced déjà vu feelings for months. When the Resident of the Pit had foreseen his future, it had *felt* different. The Resident was not human by any definition and had lived for eons, the study of time but a hobby. It seemed fitting that such a being could peer into the clouded depths of the future for a few pertinent facts.

If Krek could foresee the future, what a boon!

"A vision? Whatever are you talking about, you silly human? I bemoan my fate, my pitiable fate, being marooned on this wet world, so far from my Klawn."

"You're not hurt? Nothing's happened to your mate? Then why in all the seventeen hells of the Lower Places are you weeping like a spinster at a wedding?"

"My fate seems so cruel at times," the spider explained. As the tears stained the fur under his eyes, he reached out and brushed the moisture away with a quick front claw. "Are you ready to travel?" he asked abruptly.

"Yes."

"Then why didn't you say so? You humans waste so much time with your petty intrigues, it's a wonder you accomplish anything at all."

The spider rose and began loping off in what appeared to be a totally random direction. Lan watched, open-mouthed, then trotted after Krek, hard-pressed to maintain the speed of the multi-legged creature through the boggy lands.

Lan used the time travelling to think, to sort out all he had learned in the past several hours. This storm-wracked watery world seemed a hollow shell, devoid of surface life. Yet something vicious occasionally sprang out to devour the unwary. The pack of wolves had to live off food more substantial than the damned, all-pervading fingers of fog drifting through the interminable swamps. Lan wondered if the cenotaph providing a gateway between worlds had to be one of a human to open the Cenotaph Road. While Krek was decidedly unhuman, he had mentioned accidentally killing a human in his travels on this world.

"Krek?" Lan panted, speeding up enough to pull alongside the spider. "Was that human caught up in your hunting web from this world?"

"I had not thought on the matter. The unfortunate occurrence happened not fifty days' travel from here, but I doubt he was of this world, now that you bring the question to light. I was so wrapped up in my own concerns at the time, you understand, I never thought on it."

"Surely, Krek, but if he wasn't of this world, did he come through the cenotaph you took to get here?"

"Doubtful. The one in the Egrii Mountains is at such an altitude that you humans begin to wheeze and faint from lack of air. It does not bother me, of course."

"Of course," Lan agreed, to keep the spider talking. "So there are many paths leading to this world?"

"Certainly, and many off it. Why, I can see no fewer than four of them. The ones shielded by the bulk of the planet are beyond my sight, so many others might exist elsewhere. I am not perfect, friend Lan Martak."

Lan bit back a retort.

"How many of those four cenotaphs lead directly to your world? Only the one you came through?"

Krek's head wobbled about until Lan thought it might fall off. Then he decided this was the spider's equivalent of an assenting nod. One cenotaph, one world linked through it. This assumed that only one death had occurred to create the universe-strain required to traverse the myriad worlds. But he had heard of others with many worlds attached, and he had fallen some distance through thin air before hitting the surface of the lake when he'd walked the Road.

He asked and Krek answered, "That can mean only one thing. The empty grave on your world's side was improperly consecrated. A one-way gate formed instead of a door leading in both directions. Not uncommon, especially in lesser-developed human cultures."

Lan bristled at the implied insult, then held his barbed reply in check. The spider was larger than he, and it did possess knowledge he needed if he wanted to walk the Road successfully after parting company. At this moment, Lan wished the appropriate cenotaph gaped in front of them. He didn't trust his temper much longer with this self-important creature.

"Let's stop for a few minutes' rest, Krek. My leg was injured yesterday."

"Last night," the spider corrected.

"I don't care when it was, it still hurts." Lan stumbled to a halt, then fell to the ground. He rubbed his leg until the stiffness faded, then chanted his healing spell. He wished he'd learned more of the healing magics, but life had always seemed so filled with other, more important items. Looking up, he saw Krek passively standing, waiting for him to finish his odd human rituals.

"I want to rest awhile, Krek. My leg will give out under me if I don't."

"Very well. I tire of running like this in the middle of the night."

"There's no difference," Lan flared, irritated in spite of himself.

"If you say so."

Lan massaged his muscles and changed the bandage on the alligator-bitten leg. The terrain where he rested differed not one iota from where he had so ignominiously splashed down on this world. He wondered if Krek actually knew where he was going or if the giant spider simply wanted to play him for the fool. He was tired of sloughing around in knee-deep scum.

"How do you keep oriented on this world?" he finally asked. "My compass needle felt neglected with no magnetic field. And the sky and all those damned clouds prevent a sighting on stars."

"I know nothing of such things," the spider said. "I simply sight in on the cenotaph I desire, then go directly toward it. I am surprised you humans lack this talent. You boast of all manner of other, less useful talents."

"Such as?"

"The oddest one you call taste. It has something to do with the interaction of food on your eating orifice. I never understood that, though many lower animals apparently have it. They choose certain foods over others, simply due to this strange trait. Take the carrion-eaters, for example. They prefer their food dead several days, just as you do. What difference does it make? Dead a day, dead a month? Is it not all the same?"

"You don't taste your food? How dreadful. I don't know what I'd do without being able to savor a juicy steak, cooked only until it's red encased in a light brown skin. The salty tang of it as it works against my tongue is indescribable."

"That is what I said." The spider continued, unperturbed. "No, this sighting talent of mine is akin to vision, but differing."

"That makes as much sense as my description of taste," admitted Lan.

"The empty graves yawn wide and glow a variety of colors. They are so necessary to keep sanity on this dreary world. All seems bland here. Very depressing." For a long moment, the spider said nothing. Then: "It forces me to remember my plight, how I am adrift in a world of woe." Krek sank to the ground and pulled his eight legs under him. A gusty sigh vented like a fumarole before he said, "All this saps my strength. How can I go on?"

Lan stood, twisting to make sure his own legs were up to the task of pacing the spider's loping gait. Sure that he was ready for a few more hours, he softly said, "Remember Klawn. Remember your mating web. And I'll help you back to it."

"Ah, yes, I had forgotten precious Klawn-rik'-wiktorn-kyt in the midst of my sorrow." The spider's eyes came unfocused and it stared, dewy-eyed, at nothing Lan could discern. He began to worry about the creature. Its flights of fancy took longer and longer. This might be a form of sleep or relaxation for the beast, but Lan was leery of taking such a chance. His experience included a creature—almost human—that could dissociate its spirit from its body and roam the world at will. Not quite a ghost, the *therra* usually managed to return to its body before it died of starvation. If it failed and the body perished, the *therra* had to be hunted down and exorcised by an experienced mage. But all that lay behind him on his home world.

This world was . . . different.

"Krek. Krek! I hear voices. Men. Wake up, dammit!"

"Hmmm? Oh, yes, of course. I heard the men and all those silly four-legged horses some time ago. I assumed you had, also. Shall we go meet them?"

Lan's exasperation at the spider knew no bounds. Krek had actually heard them before he had and said nothing. He stamped his foot, then regretted it as tiny stabs of pain jabbed into his wound. Controlling his voice with great effort, he told Krek, "I don't know if they are peaceful or not. If there are too many of them, we can't fight them all if they're after our necks."

"Once," mused Krek, "I could have fought them all. But that was ever so long ago. My powers fade. Oh, why did I ever choose to roam? Fool that I am, it still seems a dream."

"Too late for recriminations," muttered Lan. "Our well-armed friends have seen us. Let's hope, at least, they *are* our friends."

It took several minutes for the horsemen to trot into full view. Lan felt his stomach tighten into a knot. He thought he'd left such men as these behind him. The leader of the grey-clad soldiers reined in and peered down at Lan. His tunic and trousers were slightly different in tailoring from those Lan was familiar with back on his own world, but the arrogance and demeanor were identical. These grey-clads were of the same band as those led by Kyn-alLyk-Surepta.

Lan did a quick head count. Fifteen of them, all mounted, all armed with sabers, some of the soldiers wearing body armor. He failed to detect any longer-range weapons such as bow and arrow or even the bulky wheel lock pistols of his own world.

"Good evening, sir," he said, assuming Krek to be right about the time of day.

The officer in charge said nothing. He stood in his stirrups and stretched, as if he'd been long asaddle. Finally, he deigned to notice Lan.

"What manner of man are you?"

Lan wondered how to answer such an odd question.

"The same as you," he said cautiously.

"You dare say you are of my clan!" roared the soldier, glowering down at Lan from his superior height. His hand rested on the hilt of his saber. From the whiteness of his knuckles, he would draw and slash at any instant.

"No offense intended," Lan hastily said, but his own hand slipped his knife free, hiding it behind his forearm. If the grey-clad soldier intended drawing the sword, a tiny wrist motion would send cold steel into his throat.

The soldier relaxed a little.

"We are the Saviour Waldron of Ravensroost's outpatrol. We guard the far borders for our lord and master. I ask again, what manner of man are you?"

"I am Dar-elLan-Martak, recently come to this world of yours. All we ask is simple passage."

"We?" repeated the soldier. "You have companions?"

Lan turned to find Krek tightly compressed into an amorphous lump near a cypress. In the dim light it was impossible to tell that a tall spider lurked so near. Lan decided this was part of the duty he had shouldered. Krek either feared these men or had retreated into his own personal spidery world for reasons of his own.

"A figure of speech."

"No," demanded the soldier. "You said 'we.' Where are your travelling companions? Tell me!"

"I'm no peasant to be badgered by your likes. I have every right to walk this world unmolested by you."

"Kill him," came the sharp command from the officer.

Lan whipped his knife forward, wondering if he could hamstring a couple of the horses and escape in the ensuing confusion. He doubted it. These men carried their sabers as if they knew how to use them. All the accursed soldiers seemed superbly trained and ready to die in battle. He'd find his head severed from his torso the instant he dived for the horses.

To his surprise, the horses all reared, one even throwing his rider. The others bolted and ran, no matter how their riders tried to slow them. Lan saw that most of the grey-clad soldiers weren't trying very hard to control their steeds, either. Even the officer turned pasty white and spurred his horse away, screaming incoherently.

Lan turned to find Krek towering behind him. The spider asked in a mild voice, "Why did they run like that? Did they remember an appointment? It was one like them who died in my hunting web. I feared they would inquire about that misfortune, as the others have done in the past. Perhaps they are willing to live and let live."

"Something like that, Krek. Let's get moving to that cemetery. I think this world is getting too hot for us."

"Too hot? It seems the right temperature to me. A bit moist, perhaps. I hate water, you understand. But . . ."

Lan shut out the rest of Krek's likes and dislikes. As long as the spider continued frightening patrol officers, all was fine.

* * *

"I feel stronger, friend Lan Martak, much stronger now that we head for the sorry mountains this world offers. Having you along to fend off some of the minor annoyances has done much to restore my courage and good humor, too."

Lan snorted. Minor annoyances, indeed. He didn't consider the grey-clad soldiers to be minor. The fact that they were on both this world and his own caused him to wonder. The time to ponder this was granted him by the utter sameness of the cloudy countryside as they wearily trudged onward. Each step seemed a hundred and each hundred multiplied into millions. The single day's journey had lengthened to the point that Lan worried about Krek's cosmic sense of time.

Still, minor variances in the terrain became apparent after another long day's walk, and by the end of the third tiring day, small, rocky hills sprang up in front of them, hardly mountains but promising relief from the slop caking Lan's boots and making each foot weigh half again what it should.

"Krek? How well do you know these hills? I feel the need of a spot to stop."

"In midafternoon?" Krek's ungainly bulk swayed from side to side as he lumbered alongside Lan. "I know little of this area. It seems no different from any other span of lumpy hills. Do you feel danger?"

"Nothing positive, but I'm uneasy. We haven't seen any of those grey-clads for some time now, and they didn't appear the type to forget even a passing insult, much less a rout like we staged. And there's still the matter of the soldier who was hanged in your web. Does that crevice yonder appeal to you for a resting spot?" He had come to find that Krek had odd instincts concerning his resting places. If any hint of running water was nearby, Krek became nervous and snappish. The last thing Lan wanted was for that powerful set of mandibles to inadvertently close on him while he slumbered.

The spider accomplished the reconnaissance in a few minutes of jumping about. Lan took this to mean approval.

"Let me explore the depths of the cave. Best to stand back," he cautioned. Lan had also learned that fire wasn't merely something the spider disliked—his fear was a mighty phobia. For a self-proclaimed fearless warrior, Krek exhibited strange weaknesses.

Lan soon found a small opening outlined by the flare of his torch. The valley opening on the other side of the hill stretched deep, peaceful and deserted. Satisfied he wouldn't be boxed in, he returned to his spider companion with the good news.

"Looks secure," he said. "Now all we need is some food. Maybe a nice squarrat, basted in its own juices and—Krek! What's wrong?"

The giant spider hadn't moved a hair since Lan's return. All eight legs stretched wide, claws digging into solid rock in a manner Lan had never before witnessed.

"Lan Martak! They come! I can feel the vibrations of many men. They come to kill me for that accident with the commander's hatchling!"

"What do you mean?"

"The one caught in my hunting web was the hatchling of the grey-clad's commander. Oh, woe! I am to die this day!"

Lan's mind raced. To be trapped in this small chamber was out of the question. No doubt existed in his mind that these were from the company of grey-clad soldiers Krek had so ably frightened off earlier. If a more bold officer rode with them this time, a second such scare tactic would fail. They had evinced such a proprietary interest in this dismal country that Lan feared they would kill any traveller, not merely him and Krek. If Krek were right about the youth he'd accidentally killed, no escape at all was possible. The commander would track them to the ends of this world.

"Pull in your legs and get that hairy carcass of yours moving. We can be through this passage and down the valley on the other side before they discover us. Hurry, curse you, hurry!"

"It is no use, friend Lan Martak. I am too weak. Once I could have fought them all and laughed while doing it. Now I am nothing. Riven from my web, an outcast, unable to mate, what is left for me? Go. Save yourself from my sorry fate."

Lan surprised himself by going to the prostrate spider and kicking him hard in the spot where a human's ribs would be.

"On your feet. All eight of them. I've nursemaided you this far, and I'll be dragged naked through all the Lower Places if I'm going to give up on you now. No fatalistic spider is going to keep me from my reward."

"Go to my web," said Krek, "and tell them I grant you your prize. Now, leave me be. My death is imminent. I feel it."

A shuddering sigh wracked the spider's body. Lan was torn by indecision. He could run and save himself. That was the only sensible thing to do. His life had to be worth more than any stack of gold coins, no matter how high. But something rooted him to the spot. He couldn't leave Krek to the fate decreed by the soldiers.

More than simple oath backed his resolve. The arrogance of the soldiers and what others of their kind had done back on his home world goaded him.

Grabbing a convenient hairy leg, he began tugging. The spider's bulkiness surprised him. He'd thought it mostly illusion caused by the eight long legs. For the first time, he realized how massive the creature was.

"Move, you lovelorn pile of legs. Come along or I'll have to try to hold them off here. That's a damned messy way of dying, too, since I'll be outnumbered dozens to one."

"You would do such a thing for me? Oh, well, maybe I should prolong my dreary life a while longer if it means so much to you."

They stumbled along the dark passageway until they burst into the secluded valley, the harsh glare of the overcast causing Lan to squint. Krek hesitated, spreading his legs wide and digging into the soft dirt. Though he lacked a sense of taste or smell, his tactile senses were vastly more refined than those of a human. They had to be, in order to feel the lightest of twitches in a monstrous web.

"They come," was all Krek said.

"So be it. Let's move before they can close in on us. The only chance I see is that they'll have to leave their mounts outside the cave. On foot, an armored soldier will be slower than we are."

The words cheered Lan more than Krek. The spider plunged into a fit of depression, and nothing Lan said brought back the bright sunlight of cheerfulness. They hurried along in stoic silence, legs straining to cover as much land as possible with each stride.

When they came to the cul-de-sac, Lan felt his own cheeriness drain. The sheer walls of the canyon rose to a height that would require a half-day's climb. The only escape was back down the valley in the direction of the pursuing soldiers.

Lan looked at Krek. The spider collapsed into a heap of hairy legs.

"I knew such a thing would happen," he lamented. "My life is fated. Never will I know the loving caresses of my Klawn-rik'wiktorn-kyt. Her mating web will fall to sticky strands and never will our joys be as one. Never!"

Lan had to admit things looked as bleak as his

friend predicted. His hand strayed to the dagger at his side. A pitiful weapon against a trained soldier. If only they were in a forest, that dagger would be more effective than a dozen great swords. What he lacked in armament, he made up for in stealth and cunning.

Whether that cunning would aid him now, so far away from a forest, was a question begging for a quick answer.

"Stay well clear, Krek. I'll try to divert them away from you. If I succeed, we'll both be on our way soon." He hoped he sounded confident. The way his stomach churned and knotted as hard as a hangman's noose put the lie to any real feeling of impending success.

"As you say, Lan Martak. It is all hopeless. If only I could move my limbs. The weakness assaults me in waves. I drown in it." A shudder shook his body and made the hair on his long legs bristle. "Such a worthless death mine will be."

"All deaths, when they come too soon, are worthless," Lan told Krek. Then he slithered, snakelike, atop a massive boulder overlooking the path they'd just traversed. Glinting in the distance were soldiers swinging swords. They had shed their heavy armor, but this was only a slight additional factor in Lan's favor. Their swords had the reach his dagger lacked.

Lan's nervousness evaporated when the soldiers neared. The hunt always affected him this way. Adrenaline pumped fiercely into his arteries. He came alive, flowing with the invisible force that guided him in the kill.

He was not invincible; he still bled if cut. But he became something more than before. Now he called on all his wit and ability and abandoned himself to the inevitable.

As the first soldier drew abreast of his perch, Lan leaped. His hurtling weight smashed the man to the ground. A quick slash sent a fountain of crimson life spurting from the neck. Lan stood, the fallen soldier's sword pressing heavily into his hand.

"There! Attack! Fifty crowns to the man slaying him!" echoed the voice of a hidden commander.

Lan savagely slashed the legs out from under the next man presenting himself at the notch in the rock. But swarming over the still-struggling body came another and another and still another.

Lan faced three experienced swordsmen. No novice with the sword, he knew he could never match these grisled veterans if the fight wore on too long.

"Die, lover of animals," snarled the one closest to him.

Lan was almost duped into turning to face the man mouthing the curse. The soldier at the opposite end of the line lunged, barely missing his target in Lan's gut. Lan's dagger drew a red line of agony along the man's ribs, not fatal but enough to remove him temporarily from the fracas. Lan barely leaped back in time as the two remaining swordsmen weaved a net of steel death around him. His mind settled to the deadly fighting. He couldn't penetrate their singing blades, but he could still run and dodge.

Rolling to his right, Lan put one of the men between himself and the other. He lunged. His blade was deflected by a sharp parry but still found a meaty shoulder.

As he cursed in pain, the soldier continued fighting. Lan felt the sharp sting of his own skin being scored by a razor-sharp edge. Ducking, he barely kept a second thrust from lopping off an ear.

"Krek!" he called. "Help me. I need you!"

The expression on the soldier's face told Lan that Krek had come. The spider need do nothing save loom large and menacing. The flush of abject fear turned to agony as Lan buried his sword into the man's sternum.

Unable to pull the blade free as the corpse sank to the ground, Lan attacked the other man with his dagger. One swift toss and the steel spike found an exposed throat. The bubbling noise and the sight of pink froth gushing from the pierced windpipe were not pleasant. Still, better the soldier dying than Lan.

"You will die, scum! More men come. You will bow to the power of our Saviour, Waldron of Ravensroost!"

Lan saw the guard commander standing, legs widespread, atop a boulder, cape fluttering in the blood-warm wind. The black rage masking the man's face would vanish only when he witnessed death—the death of Lan and Krek.

"We made it past the first wave," Lan panted. "But I can't keep fighting them off forever. They'll wear me down soon." He hoped Krek didn't notice how his hands shook. His mouth had turned dry, and his breath came in ragged gusts. Fighting for the sake of fighting as sport invigorated him; killing sapped him of strength.

"I will never see my mating web or the lovely Klawn again. Never! And all because of those humans. A chance encounter and they hunt me like a rabbit! Me! Webmaster of the Egrii!"

Lan stood back, amazed, by the spider's sudden vicious frontal attack on the soldiers. The charging arachnid killed a full score before the battered survivors fled in confusion. Dripping gore from his hairy legs, Krek ambled back to the stunned Lan.

"That taught them respect. Imagine their impudence!" The spider seemed unaware of the monumental transformation in his attitude. One moment, he cowered docile and willing to die. The next, he was a fighting terror even highly trained men with steel weapons couldn't contain.

"What brought all that on?" Lan inclined his head toward the bloody carnage.

"I have no idea. It simply seemed the thing to do." Krek considered the problem for a moment, then said, "You humans come apart easily."

"I agree, I agree!" Lan babbled. "But we've still got to get out of this trap. He's got more men than the two of us will ever be able to kill."

"Speak for yourself," declared Krek. "I, mere human, am a Webmaster!"

"Krek," pleaded Lan, worrying about the sudden surge of overconfidence. "Listen to me. They'll bring in crossbows and shoot us at their leisure. They can call up hundreds of men. They . . . they might even set fire to us." He watched as the horror of flames assailed the spider. As much as he hated doing it, he had to play on each and every weakness to prevent the spider from pursuing a course that was as suicidal as simple surrender.

"We can't attack. We've got to escape. Do you understand? Our lives will be forfeit if we continue fighting them on their terms."

The spider strutted about, flexing mighty sinews in his legs. He leaped from one side of their sandy arena to the other, almost faster than Lan could follow.

"I must bow to your superior knowledge of humans. After all, you are one."

"It's going to be difficult, but we must creep by their sentries and get out of this valley."

"They will catch us. I am too large to creep."

"Until we can climb those canyon walls, that's our only hope."

Krek looked up as if for the first time. "That is all we have to do, climb these puny stone walls? Every day in the depths of the Egrii Mountains, I swing from pinnacles higher than this."

Lan watched in amazement as a sticky strand of web material jetted from a nozzle just under Krek's beak. In the span of a frenzied heartbeat, the spider had a long cable stretching into the hazy distance, fastened firmly for climbing.

"Why didn't you tell me, Krek? We could have avoided the soldiers altogether!"

The spider gave his equivalent of a shrug. His entire body quaked as he said, "I never thought of it. I assumed you knew of this insignificant talent of mine. After all, spiders do possess the ability to spin webs." It was a matter closed.

"Hurry, then. I hear the commander goading his troops into action again." Lan watched the spider deftly scale the wall of stone, legs seldom touching the smooth rock for more than an instant. The man envied his friend's agility, but as Krek had commented, he was a spider and to the web born.

"Kill! Kill them! They escape! A hundred crowns to the man who slays them."

Lan turned, his back pressed against the cold stone, and saw a full dozen armored men advancing. Bravely, he confronted them with his sword held en garde and his dagger ready for a quick, eviscerating stroke.

He knew, however, it would be he who died.

Closing with the foremost, he executed a deft stop thrust. The recoil of his sword off the man's armor wrenched the blade from his grasp. He managed to drive the point of his dagger into the soldier's armpit as the man foolishly watched Lan's sword go spinning through the air. With blood seeping over his hand, Lan gathered his strength and heaved the dead soldier back at his comrades. Lan had to laugh at the incongruous sight. Men fell like skittle pins. In the confusion, he grabbed a fallen sword.

Even the best couldn't have stood for long under the onslaught of armed and armored might. First Lan's sword, then his dagger flew like a silver bird. He stood weaponless in the face of stark hatred.

As a dozen sharp sword points pricked his body,

a cold voice commanded, "Stay! He is mine. The spider-thing has escaped, but this scum is mine!"

The commander strode into Lan's field of vision. Clad in a grey cape held in front by a crimson frog, he presented an imposing figure, but it was the great sword, clutched as if it were a matchstick, that held Lan's undivided attention. The man swung the massive blade with reckless ease. Each hypnotic pass through the air came a fraction closer to Lan's head. Involuntarily, Lan ducked as he felt hot air and hotter steel rush by his ear.

"Coward!" roared the commander, his men supporting his case with angry curses.

Lan looked into the man's eyes and saw only madness. Nothing but death would appease him. What manner of man was this soldier's sworn liege lord that he allowed maniacs to represent him?

"I know nothing of your plans or your ruler or . . ." Lan flinched from the nearness of the swinging great sword. The arc blurred silver and edged toward his eyes with every stroke. Just as the huge blade rose for a last, killing stroke, Lan shrieked— and found himself dangling upside down far above the heads of the surprised soldiers.

Twisting, Lan saw the infuriated commander below him. The ponderous great sword smashed into the cliff face, sending electric blue sparks shooting high.

"Kill them! Kill, *kill*, KILL!" the man screamed in an inhumanly shrill voice.

Lan's stomach turned over as he bounced repeatedly off the cliff face. But inexorably he jerked higher and higher. At the top of the precipice, he dared open his eyes again. Standing there as unconcerned as only a spider can be was Krek, a coil of web-stuff at his feet.

"Krek! But how?"

"I cast my snaring web. I have not lost a bit of

my skill," the giant spider said smugly. "Again I prove my worthiness to be Webmaster."

"Why didn't you get me out of there sooner? That madman damned near split my head with that demon sword of his."

"I thought you intended scaling the cliff on my climbing strand. After all, I could. When I realized you were incapable of a simple feat that any feeble-minded hatchling could perform, I aided you with a bit of stick-web."

Lan wanted to argue and rail against the spider's logic. He found himself too weak. His insides tumbled, and his morning meal threatened to choke him. Soon, his nerves calmed enough, he asked, "How far is it to the cenotaph off this thrice-damned world?"

"Another day's travel. And I shall be reunited with my mate!" chortled Krek. "Ah, how we shall rejoice. Such a web she will spin for me, her betrothed."

Lan shut out the rest of the spider's fulsome praise for his mate. He simply rejoiced in his own continued life.

CHAPTER SIX

"How much longer, Krek? My legs are killing me."
Lan valiantly worked his way up the steep incline
amid sharp rocks that contrived to slip under his
boots. His hands were scraped raw, and his knees
carried the marks of too many painful encounters
with the mountainside. The only cheery prospect
lay in the fact that the soldiers pursuing them
wouldn't have been able to scale the walls of the
canyon, now almost two days in the past. Lan
doubted if their commander's anger could whip
them to do the impossible.

"Not far. I twitch with the nearness of the Road.
The cemetery rests atop this mound of dirt."

Lan cast a furtive glance over his shoulder. If he
did take a tumble, he would be airborne for long
minutes before striking the ground far below. Luck-
ily, the clouds covering this world hid the worst of
a fall from his eyes.

"Let's hurry. I'm tiring again, and my leg hurts."

"You always complain of your leg. Humans are
so weak," the spider observed as he agilely leaped
from boulder to boulder. "Spiders are obviously
superior creatures. We have a sufficient number of
legs to support us."

Lan had learned not to argue with Krek over
trivialities. The spider's world view differed so much
from his at times that he wondered at the fate
casting them together. The man had to work harder
to keep up with the spider as the pair climbed
higher up on the lone mountain. Whatever the
spider's philosophies, he proved extraordinarily adept

at scaling rock. Lan's brief excursions into the
el-Liot Mountains on his home world had been
minor jaunts compared with the climbing he'd done
this past day. Yet, as he'd grown more and more
weary, Krek's strength had burgeoned. Gone was
all trace of the pliant, woeful beast he'd met in the
midst of the boggy lands. Krek had found his ele-
ment in the craggy reaches of rock. Lan envied
him his climbing ability; with every aching, sore
muscle he envied him.

Finally, the mountain leveled and a mesa sprawled
with small rock spires shooting up across it. Lan
stood for a moment, panting. An ineffable feeling
took control of him, and he knew this to be the
cemetery they sought. Under each stony monument rested a corpse. Under all, save one, the one
they needed to escape this festering, slimy world.

"Come, friend Lan Martak, we must hurry. The
time is at hand for the Road to open to us."

"So soon? On my world, it is only at midnight."

Krek made an odd up and down motion, his
eight legs never leaving the rock.

"It is the same here. Midnight approaches, you
silly human. Why do you think I am so nervous?"

Lan blinked. He hadn't realized the spider was
in the least nervous. His actions hadn't seemed out
of line with those the man had come to expect.
Still, the spider's innate sense of time on this oddly
clocked world had proven accurate in the past.
There existed little to dispute it now.

"Which tomb is it we want?"

"That one," said Krek, one leg quivering in the
direction of a solitary grave marker. "The cenotaph
of . . ." and only a clacking noise mixed with a
sound similar to frying bacon came from his mouth.
Lan knew better than to ask the spider to repeat
the name. It didn't matter; all that counted was
their hasty departure from this world and their
arrival on Krek's web world.

"Oh, Lan Martak, with the goal so near, I find myself quivering and weak once again. I fail to lift such a puny stone." The spider's claws scooped out stony ground on either side of a huge slab of limestone, but no matter how the creature struggled, the slab refused to yield up the cenotaph below. Lan immediately added his strength to that of his companion and went tumbling into a heap as the stone sheet grated to one side.

"So weak am I. Who can blame me? The promise of adorable Klawn-rik'wiktorn-kyt makes me woozy." Krek sat down in a hairy pile and simply shook. Again Lan felt an electric tension in the air, similar to that he'd felt in the tomb of Lee-Y-ett back on his home world. Powerful magics danced in the air around him. The time for transport to another world neared, too near to argue with Krek over trivial matters. Lan kicked the spider into the yawning pit and, as a thunderclap sounded, dived after him.

Lan landed atop Krek, but gone was the surrounding rocky mountaintop. Replacing it stretched a storm-wracked landscape more to Lan's liking. The cemetery stood out in bold relief every time a jagged blast of naked lightning slashed the night. But nowhere could be seen greyness. Colors ran wild in the inky darkness: lush green trees with brown trunks, oddly shaped purple shrubs barely knee-high, intense yellow stalks of some wheatlike grain; even the very tombstones were boldly etched in vivid pink granite.

As the tiny fists of rain jabbed at Lan's face, he felt tears of joy mingling with the natural moisture. Unabashed, he dropped to his knees and cried out his relief at being free of a world where he didn't belong. Here, no matter what lurked in the forest, was more like home to him. This was terrain he understood, loved.

"Rain! The putrid water!" shrieked Krek. "I drown in this filthy downpour."

Lan clambered to his feet and pulled the spider half-erect. Bending over him, Lan formed a temporary shield from the pelting rain. Then Krek darted for the overhanging limbs of the nearby forest. The distaste for water added speed to his loping gait, and Lan found himself hard-pressed to keep up. He had to laugh aloud at the sight of the wet, furry spider shaking himself like a mongrel dumped into a lake.

And he was safe from the sheriff and the grey-clad soldiers and persecution. Free, free, free!

The heavy rain vanished as if it had never existed, leaving a world scrubbed clean and fresh. Lan inhaled deeply, savoring the crisp scent of the countryside. Myriad odors crowded in on his nose, vying for attention. Flowers in full bloom, all colors of the rainbow, scattered across verdant green fields like droplets from the palette of a drunken painter. Lan stooped and plucked one small golden flower and studied it. Feathery petals as fine as spun glass formed an intricate geometric pattern that gathered the sun's rays and bent them into new and wonderful hues. The heady aroma reminded Lan of the most expensive perfumes, the texture of warm honey.

Krek stood by, watching his friend in the odd pursuit of sniffing each and every flower. Finally, the spider spoke.

"What is this insane delight you receive from those bits of food?"

"Food? I don't eat flowers. Rather, I drink in their beauty, I savor their redolence. I . . ." Lan stopped and smiled. The spider lacked a sense of smell. Perhaps he was also unable to detect the subtle differences in shading among the flowers that so appealed to the man. On impulse, Lan laced the long green stem of a flower through the coppery strands of hair on one of Krek's front legs.

"Why did you do that? The pollen makes my leg

itch." A convulsive shiver dislodged the flower. As it fluttered down, Lan grabbed it with practiced ease.

Holding it aloft, he said, "Beauty, Krek, comes in all forms. You have no appreciation for the finer things the universe has to offer."

"What more would I want than plenty of insects to eat, my mountain web, and, of course, Klawn? You humans complicate your lives to the extent that I fail to see how you can possibly survive."

"Never mind, friend Krek. Let us make haste for your mountain fastness and your mate. I must explore this world further. It appeals greatly to me."

"It does have a certain attractiveness," conceded Krek, "though not in these lower reaches. Wait until we spy the Egrii Mountains. Those are noble peaks."

Lan abruptly stopped in the middle of the road, feeling unreasoned dread. Tense, alert as if a challenge to a duel had been issued him and he was unsure where the first blow would come from, he dropped to one knee and pressed his ear to the hard earth. A distant rumbling sounded loud and clear. From the rhythmic pattern, the man recognized the hoofbeats of many horses galloping toward them.

"Do you feel it, Krek? The vibrations?" He waited until the spider dug hard claws into the dirt. A violent shaking indicated Krek's assent. "Think it's likely to be anyone we don't want to meet?"

"I have no enemies on this world, but it has been many years since my departure. The humans here were always kindly, if a bit distant to the web-born."

Lan felt a growing unease. The paranoia of fleeing the grey-clad soldiers had etched itself firmly into his consciousness. And the flight from his lifelong friend, the sheriff, back on his home world heightened his need to be absolutely certain of the horsemen's intent before revealing himself to them.

"Down. We hide until they've passed by," he commanded. Krek obediently sank into the field of flowers and twitched several times as if sneezing. Then he became indistinguishable from any of the other rocks jutting up amid the flowers. Lan approved of the camouflage, then saw to his own in a narrow ravine. He had barely dropped into it when the leading horseman galloped into view.

Lan sucked in his breath and held it. The rider could have been the twin of the commander left angry and frustrated on the swamp world. Dressed in grey with crimson piping at the collar and cuffs, the horseman spurred his mount down the road with a fury that was an echo from the other world. Lan waited. Soon, trotting at a more leisurely pace came the main body of soldiers.

All were similarly dressed.

Their leader's voice carried with surprising clarity. "Lord Waldron wishes all the roads patrolled, Sergeant. You and five men patrol the Highlands Pike. I will . . ." The remainder of the words was swept up in a clatter of hooves and the widening distance. Only when the dust had settled back to the roadbed did Lan poke his head up and study the terrain, as if all the soldiers lay in wait to pounce on him.

Seeing no one, he went to Krek's side and told the spider, "Your world is overrun by those greys, too. What is this Highlands Pike the sergeant is supposed to guard?"

"Oh, I will *never* see my dainty bride, never, never, never! Why does such woe befall me? Why did I ever leave my web in the first place?" Again the spider wept large, gelid drops from the corners of his eyes. Lan sank to the ground cross-legged and allowed his churning mind to settle. Becoming as disheartened as Krek accomplished nothing.

"Krek," he said in a voice both measured and calm, "how do we get you back to your web—and Klawn? I don't even know in which direction the Egrii Mountains are to be found. Please tell me so I can help you." Running in the back of his mind, too, was the promise of treasure. If he had to be fleeter than the grey-clad soldiers, a horse of his own would prove beneficial, as would a few more weapons than the pitiful dagger carried at his belt.

A shaky leg pointed across the field. Lan squinted and fancied he saw a snowcapped mountain peak. If so, at this distance, that mountain literally gutted the azure sky. Quite a climb lay ahead. Undaunted, he got to his feet and urged the spider on. By the end of the day, he had to fight down the urge to strangle the self-pitying creature with its own hairy legs.

Gasping in the thin mountain air, Lan pointed and said, "There it is, Krek. Your web." He knew with innate certainty that he was correct. The monstrous web spanned an entire mountain valley. The silvery strands of the web swung thicker than his thighs, and the complex pattern confused his mind as he tried tracing it. Just what the web was supposed to catch and hold—if anything—he didn't want to ask.

"My web, and my mating web! There, high up! Klawn awaits me! Dear little Klawn!"

Lan shuddered involuntarily when he saw "dear little Klawn." Krek's mate easily massed half again as much as the gigantic spider. Lan vaguely remembered hearing that the female of most arachnid species tended to be larger than the male. He hadn't believed it possible; now he was forced to reconsider.

"Krek, old friend, it's been some adventure. I'm almost sorry to be parting company with you." And he was. The spider's ability in the mountains far exceeded his own rock-climbing skill, and more than once Krek had saved him from tumbling untold thousands of feet to his death. Even the spider's attitude had changed for the better. Looking at Krek confirmed this. The once bedraggled fur on his legs now bristled and gleamed like copper wire in the sun. The limpid eyes of melted chocolate had firmed and became windows on a warrior's soul. Powerful snaps of the mandibles would have instantly severed an armored man's torso. This was a formidable opponent, this Krek.

"I, too, shall miss your quaint views, friend Lan Martak. But so spins the web, so goes life itself. One moment."

The spider leaped and caught a strand of the web with deceptive ease. Faster than any hunting wolf, Krek raced along the great aerial highway. Lan sat on his haunches, back against the stony wall, and vainly tried to force enough oxygen into his protesting lungs. Far above, Krek met Klawn. For a brief instant the pair remained motionless in the web; then the entire valley whistled as the web whipped to and fro with their frenetic movements.

The two spiders, still high in the air at the center of the web, separated. The smaller one vanished, only to reappear in a short while with a blazing gem clutched in his beak. Lan's attention instantly fixed on the jewel. He had actually forgotten the promise to receive part of Krek's web treasure for his aid in bringing the two arachnid lovers together once again.

The blazing jewel turned out to be a large chest, its sides encrusted with indescribable gems. As it weaved a crazy pattern in the spider's clutches, it touched every color imaginable. His eyes ached from the strain of trying to focus on light not meant for the human eye. Most of all, as the jeweled chest came closer, he felt himself pulled deeper and deeper into its crystalline perfection. Never had he seen such flawless gems—and the best was locked within.

"This is yours, Lan Martak. May you do well with it."

Krek dropped the heavy chest into Lan's be-numbed grip. He lowered the treasure trove to the ground and opened the silent-hinged lid. Inside glowed gems of all kinds, many types of which Lan had never before seen. His heart beat rapidly as he allowed the cool gemstones to run through his fingers like expensive water. He was rich beyond his wildest imaginings!

If only Zarella had lived to see this. He sighed, then forced his thoughts away from his dead love.

"Krek, I couldn't. This is too much."

"For the service you have performed, it barely suffices. I am content. For the moment. Take this small portion of my web treasure and buy the flowers you seem so fond of nuzzling."

Lan laughed. With wealth such as this, he could buy more than flowers to nuzzle. And he would, as soon as he reached a city!

"Another drink for my good friend, barkeeper," cried Lan, drunkenly weaving through the smoky room. His head buzzed as if inhabited by a hive of fire hornets, yet he didn't want this elusive friend-ship he'd so carefully fostered with drinks to fade and vanish from his side. She was too lovely to disappear forever.

Like Zarella.

Lan shook his head to clear it slightly, then put his arm around her slender shoulders and pulled her closer. Lan didn't even notice the slight tense-ness as she endured his wine-sotted embrace. The fiery redhead laughed too loudly and gently stroked along the line of his jaw, then pulled his mouth to

hers for a kiss. Lan failed also to see her shudder
when she'd finished with her onerous duty.

"Linnde, my lovely seductress, you are lovely,"
he said, his compliments drunkenly redundant.
The room refused to stop pumping up and down,
but Lan didn't care. Being drunk was something
new for him. Back home—worlds away—he had
never allowed strong spirits to dull his senses. He
had needed them for survival, for appreciation of
the forests, the oceans, the mountains. But that
was a long way off, a long way back. A twinge of
homesickness assailed him. He could never return.
His friends all thought him dead, and worse, his
memory lived on as Zarella's murderer. A tear
formed in self-pity.

Cut off. He was cut off from the world he knew so
well. But the spider's treasure cask had opened up a
new world to him. Before, in his previous life, every
coin had to be watched closely. Now he discovered
the world of the easy spender and how simple it
was to find new friends to share his good fortune.

Like Linnde. She pushed back a strand of fiery
hair that contrasted so beautifully with her milky
white, translucent skin. Never in his life had
Lan hoped to find a companion so lovely. Even
Zarella, dead, lovely Zarella who had spurned his
love on the far-off world, lacked the lissome grace
of Linnde.

"Another drink, milord?" she asked, motioning to
the man behind the long wooden bar. Lan started to
decline, then found the drink being held to his lips
for him. This was the life! Service such as he'd never
experienced before, and all because of his good
fortune in helping a lovelorn spider back to his mate.

Lan tasted the potent brew, felt it blaze down
his gullet; then the room spun so fast he tumbled
to the floor. Sprawled gracelessly, he laughed.

"Linnde, come join me!" he called before passing out.

When he regained some semblance of consciousness, he discovered he was in bed, neatly covered with a quilt. Still a little drunk, he sat up and watched the room spin crazily around him. A quick search told him that Linnde had relieved him of the burden of carrying several jewels. He didn't care. The few poor stones he'd had on him were small payment for the service of getting him up here. And he had to admit ruefully that he might have had all manner of fun with Linnde before passing out. He simply didn't remember.

"Auction!" came the loud cry from the street. "Our Saviour, King Waldron of Ravensroost, declares an auction of slaves taken in the recent Amisha campaign. Auction!"

The strident bellowing cut through his head like a hot knife through a snow bank. Lan held his head for a moment, then tottered to his feet. He propped himself against the window sill and peered into the street. For a few seconds he blinked; then his eyes adjusted to the brilliant light of day. It comforted him knowing he was on a world that experienced discernible day and night.

Still, the grey-clad soldiers irked him. While in this tiny hamlet, they had ignored him completely, and for that he was glad. His cask of jewels was a prize any of those surly bastards would slice his throat to steal. But he had not been treated well by Surepta. Back home.

Again came the pang of self-pity he had tried to drink away the night before. Surepta had killed Zarella, and there was no justice. Somehow, Lan generalized his hatred of Surepta into hatred for all the grey soldiers. They had inched their way into his world, like worms gnawing away at the innards of an apple. They infested an otherwise placid country in such a way that all appeared normal on the surface. Underneath crawled murderers and liars and thieves robbing him of his lover, his family, his friends, his world.

The drunken buzz continued inside his head, but over it he shouted, "I'll stop you!" Lan regretted the vow instantly. His head felt as if it were going to split. More quietly he added, "I have money now. I'll use *that* to stop all of you! If I can't have Surepta's life, all of yours will have to do."

He thought of the jewel-studded case and rushed to the panel in the wall behind which he kept his treasure. Lan let out a gusty sigh when he saw the box residing exactly as he'd left it. Linnde might have stripped him of his portable fortune, but the greater treasure had eluded her.

Lan wrapped the jeweled cask in a spare cloak he'd purchased, belted on a rapier of the finest steel and deadliest edge, then swung a luxurious cape around his broad shoulders. For a moment, he allowed it to flow and billow richly. As he turned, it spun from his body to settle properly, the fur-rimmed bottom scant inches above the ground. He looked to be a young nobleman in his fine garb.

He paused to admire his finery in a dusty mirror, then hefted the cask and went down into the street to see what type of auction had interrupted his drunken stupor.

Lan Martak couldn't believe he'd heard the soldier properly, but he had. A slave auction. On the block were half a dozen men and women in various stages of undress and dishevelment. Two of the men appeared to be emaciated and fighting a losing battle with death. One woman's face was too badly scarred for him to determine even her age, much less any features. But the remaining man and two women held his attention.

The man was a sturdy enough sort and not ill-treated, not yet. The two women were gems beyond compare, even matched against any of the baubles he carried so snugly under his arm. The tall, dark-haired one stood with head held high and an arrogance that showed, no matter the chains rattling at her wrists, that she possessed an indomitable spirit. While no beauty, she had a comeliness that pleased Lan. The other woman, a petite blonde, simply stunned him with her beauty.

"This one," called out the auctioneer, pointing to the blond woman, "will keep even the most discerning happy. Smile for the gentlemen," he ordered. The blonde pouted, a tiny tear tracking down her cheek. "See, gentlemen? She is without peer."

"She is without more than that. She is without courage to spit on you!" The dark-haired woman started to carry out her threat, but one of the nearby guards tugged strongly on the chain around her neck and forced her to kneel, head bowed.

"And that one has spirit. Only the strongest should bid for her." The auctioneer glanced at the kneeling woman and saw her arms shaking in reaction. Nervously, he gestured to the guard to hold her down until afterward.

Lan heard a voice cry out, "Fifteen crowns for the three remaining," and then realized he'd spoken. His upbringing had been such that the idea of slavery sickened him. Bidding so openly, so drunkenly, shocked him into sobriety. His mind remained a bit fogged, but he slowly worked out the problem to his own satisfaction. He did not bid for the desire to own a slave—even one as beautiful as the blonde—but to free them.

He would buy them and manumit them immediately. He didn't bother examining his altruistic urges further. Deep down he realized this was the first opportunity he'd had to fight against the grey soldiers and the slavery they brought with them. He need no longer fight with sword; he had wealth to do battle now. The bidding became more intense and required his full attention.

"Twenty crowns," came a cold voice from the front of the crowd.

"Twenty-five," countered Lan.

A fat merchant rubbed his hands together, then plunged into a thick pouch before shouting, "Thirty and not one silver piece more!"

Lan laughed at the merchant. The bidding sparked some instinct in him that had remained dormant for most of his life. This thrilled him in some way he didn't understand. Stalking elusive game gave a similar rush of excitement, but the knowledge that he controlled the destinies of three human beings surged even more powerfully in his veins.

And he thwarted the grey-clads' scheme for domination. By purchasing these three and then freeing them, he formed a cadre of resistance. Given time and his riches, this world would be rid of the soldiers. If he could not return to his own world and fight them there, he'd make his stand on this world and form a bastion of freedom to rally all those who hated the greys.

"Fifty!"

"Fifty-five," said the man in the front. Lan pushed through to find the man sitting in a folding chair, a huge box filled with gold pieces in front of him. Markers from five other slaves dangled on a necklace around the man's neck. Lan knew he bid against a veteran slaver, one who might go to any lengths for one as lovely as the blonde.

"Sixty," Lan said without hesitation. His wealth was vast. Holding back this churlish slaver's financial attack amused him.

"I wish to inspect the merchandise before bidding further," the slaver said. The soldier conducting the auction started to motion the man to the platform when Lan interrupted.

"No! Either bid or drop out." He smiled as he saw the flash of consternation cross the slaver's otherwise impassive face.

Turning to the three on the auction block, Lan saw a complete array of emotion displayed. The man tried to keep his rampaging emotions in check and failed. Sheer terror was mirrored in his bloodshot eyes. The blonde trembled like a thoroughbred before a race, but the dark-haired woman stood with back as straight as a ramrod and glared defiantly at him. For some reason, he had expected some show of gratitude and encouragement from the trio.

Wasn't he going to free them?

"I bow out," said the slaver, waving his hand as if it no longer mattered.

"Sold," rapped the soldier. A few of the jewels changed hands, and Lan found himself the possessor of three markers indicating ownership of the slaves. He repositioned the jeweled cask under his arm and imperiously waved the trio down from the platform.

"Master," begged the man, "be kind to me. I . . . I'll try to please you however I can."

Lan's gorge rose at the servile attitude. He expected a man to be a man, not a grovelling dog. But the blonde clung seductively to his arm. This made him swell with pride. She, at least, recognized his true intentions.

The black-haired amazon said only, "You are careless with your riches. The soldiers have both eyes and greed."

"Never mind that," Lan said uneasily, recognizing the truth in her words. "Let's go to the edge of town. I want to tell you what I plan."

"At once, master," came the instant reply from the man. Lan restrained his initial impulse of kicking the man senseless. Instead, he pointed down the road and let the man follow, three paces behind as slaves did. The blonde, however, stayed on his arm.

"I am called Velika, master, and am so grateful to you!" The adoration in her grey-green eyes warmed him and drove away the last tendrils of drunkenness entangling his brain. For a brief moment, he had worried that he hadn't done the proper thing in buying these three. Now he knew that his wealth had been put to good use keeping them from the clutches of a real slaver.

Just to meet Velika, it had been put to the best use possible.

"And your name?" he asked the other woman.

Her eyes danced with a bright blue ferocity that told him she cared not at all for him. The words dripped ice water.

"I am Inyx, a traveller of the Road and warrior of the Klendalu. I bow to none."

Lan felt obligated to hurry through his explanation of how he intended freeing them all, how he hated the very concept of human ownership of other humans.

"So you see, I wanted nothing more than to free you from those grey-clad tyrants."

"But, master," pleaded Velika, "what am I to do? I cannot defend myself in this world! Not with King Waldron's soldiers pouring out of thin air. My parents are dead and I am alone. Even my dog has run away. Protect me, I beg you, protect me!" She gripped his arm with a steely need that touched him.

Gently, Lan told her, "Very well, Velika. I'll be more than happy to protect you."

Inyx cleared her throat and stared across the field at the edge of town.

"Here," Lan said, tossing the keys to their chains to the man. "Free yourself and go home. I have no need of a slave." As Velika tightened her grasp on his upper arm, he hastily added, "But a companion is always a welcome addition to one like myself who walks the Road."

"You," sneered Inyx, "have also followed the Cenotaph Road? Amazing." She stopped and cocked her head to one side, listening. "That roar. What is it?"

Above the treetops some distance away rose a parti-colored globe, a hot-air observation balloon. Lan watched it for some minutes, marvelling at its use on this world. On his, they were little more than toys for the wealthy. The soldiers contrasting greyly against the brilliant colors of the fabric and the multihued banner dangling from the gondola told him that this was a weapon of war on this world.

The roar and hiss of the burners carried across the field as the balloon rose in search of the proper air current. A hundred yards above the ground, the balloon sailed at right angles to its original drift. It glided silently toward the foursome.

"No," cried the man, "not again! They rained fire from the skies on me once, but not again!" He bolted and ran for the cover of trees. Lan called after him, but it was to no avail. He shrugged it off. Let the coward flee from this pretty aerial globe. As long as Lan felt the heft of his fine sword at his side, he could defeat anything this interloper warlord Waldron threw against him.

A jingle of chains indicated Inyx had freed her wrists. She cast her bonds aside and declared, "I agree with him. Standing in the middle of an unprotected area is folly. Let's find shelter away from their prying eyes." She glanced up at the balloon, now almost overhead. While the man had displayed nothing but fear, Inyx showed only concern.

"Don't worry. We're all free citizens now," Lan told her. "They won't attack simply out of spite." Lan felt Velika move beside him and a flutter of worry tugged at his mind. How much of what he said was bravado intended to impress the blond woman and how much was common sense? Inyx spoke from experience—experience he, too, shared. The grey-clad soldiers displayed nothing but a viciousness that was inexplicable. He knew from

his brief but bloody encounters with them—damn
Kyn-alLyk-Surepta!—they were treacherous.

"At least let me have the dagger so uselessly
dangling from your belt," demanded Inyx. "With
that, they'll never be able to take me alive again."

"Again? How did they happen to catch you before?" he asked the young woman. He saw her
stiffen and her features harden.

"They ambushed a merchant's caravan, killing
all save that craven who just fled and me. An
arrow grazed my skull and knocked me unconscious; otherwise I'd have fought to the death.
When I regained my senses, I had already been
chained like some zoo beast. Never have I been so
humiliated!"

Lan shook his head in wonder. He believed this
proud woman fought with the best. Still, he vastly
preferred the blonde so desperately needing his
guidance and protection. Inyx obviously desired
nothing but to be left alone. But how could he
shirk his duties and cast Velika out into such a
cruel world?

He couldn't. Not after he had taken it upon
himself to free her from slavery. That line of thinking made him wonder exactly what real good he'd
done any of them. The man, now fled, had a slave's
mentality. He would cower and refuse to fight no
matter what honor dictated. Sooner or later, he
would again feel the chains of slavery that matched
his behavior. And Inyx would never suffer such a
fate. Too proud, too stubborn, she might wear a
slave's chains only until she escaped or died. Lan
couldn't see her accepting any other option. Lan
had to admire her more than either of the others,
but still he felt flattered at Velika's need for him.

"Oh, master," cried Velika. "You are too kind!"
The tears rolled down her full cheeks, leaving salty
tracks behind. He reached out and touched the
tear on her left cheek. For an instant, he recoiled,

as if bitten by an insect. The fluid stung his finger and caused a sensation similar to needles being thrust into his flesh to race up his arm.

"You're so lovely," he said, in a voice that sounded as if someone else spoke. He touched the other tear and experienced the same sensations, though less intense. Lan felt momentary confusion and reeled. Velika supported him.

"Master, are you well?"

"He'll be better under cover of those trees," said Inyx, pointing.

"He's in no condition." More tears welled in Velika's eyes before starting their liquid tumble over her cheeks. Lan felt an overpowering urge to hold her. He bent and kissed her. Tears lightly caressed his parted lips, sent animal surges throughout his loins. Again the vertigo assailed him.

"How do they power those balloons?" he asked, craning his neck to peer upward at the globe. This brief question allowed him to hide the unexplained confusion inside him. The three grey soldiers in the gondola waved their arms frantically as if signalling. "Do they use a demon spell to manufacture the hot air?"

"Of course not. Too wasteful," came Inyx's tart reply. "The burning gas is manufactured on the bleak world. But enough of that. Let's go before they drop their flame nets on us."

Lan twisted to get a better view of the colorful balloon. He might have heard the crunch of boot heels in the dirt. He heard nothing else, unconsciousness claiming him before he struck the ground.

CHAPTER SEVEN

Lan Martak might have had a worse hangover at some time in the past. The pain intensified to the point, however, where any mental feat, such as remembering when this might have been, drowned out the purpose. He groaned and found that even this hurt. Everything hurt. Terribly. He rolled onto his back and stared into the patches of blue sky. For long minutes, he wondered if his eyes were focusing properly. The billowing clouds formed mind-confusing patterns in their mad haste to co-alesce into a raging storm.

The first heavy droplets spattered coldly into his face. He groaned again, this time feeling better for the movement. Lan managed to sit up and waited for the whirling world to calm. When he had re-gained some semblance of control, he saw he was naked. Whoever had robbed him had been extraor-dinarily thorough in not leaving him even one thread. Gone were his jewels and fine sword and cape and even his newly liberated slaves.

"Velika!" he cried out, immediately regretting it. Pain shot through his ribs and around the purple and green bruise blossoming there in the general shape of a boot sole. "All the gods take them!" he raged impotently, knowing the grey-clad soldiers had again entered his life. He banged his fist against the ground, as much railing against his own stu-pidity as anything else.

After a time, his anger at the soldiers changed into something colder, something more controlled. He felt himself returning to his old self, the man who knew intimately the ways of the forest, who prided himself on the things he did well and never pretended to be something he wasn't. Lan sat down in the mud and ruefully shook his head. He knew quite well now what a complete fool he'd been. The money had given him a false sense of security; the only real security lay in what he was, not what he fantasized being. His dreams of riches had come true, and they had almost ruined him.

If he wanted to fight the greys, he'd have to do it with the weapons he was most accustomed to using. And most of all, he'd have to rely on his wits, something he'd failed to do since delivering Krek to his web and mate.

The rain became bolder as the clouds formed into the proper configurations. The lead-heavy drops pelted him unmercifully now, stinging coldly, savagely, against his bare hide. He made a vain attempt to reconstruct the site of his defeat, but the rain rapidly turned it into muddy soup. Lan hardly needed the evidence of the ground to relive the events. Inyx had warned him, and he had ignored her sage advice. While he had stared at the pretty hot-air balloon, those soldiers inside had signalled to others on the ground. He had felt so confused after kissing Velika that he had failed to hear others sneak up on him. The rest was obvious.

Lan sheepishly smiled to himself. It could have been worse. Only some quirk of fate had allowed him to survive the attack. The lesson had been a hard one, but one that was burned indelibly into his brain. The liquor and women and sudden wealth had changed him, and not for the better.

Turning his bare feet toward the beckoning green overhang of the trees, he slipped and stumbled in the glass-slick mud. Soon covered with brown slime, he succeeded in reaching the shelter promised by the forest. For a few minutes, he stood naked to wash off the mud. He soon found himself singing loudly and off-key. He lived. What more did he need? He walked the Road like Inyx and, like her, he took care of himself. After a fashion.

Sitting under the protection of the thickly woven leaves, he started making a simple loincloth. It didn't provide the warmth needed, but it was a start. As his nimble fingers traced familiar patterns, he heard a piteous whining noise. He stopped work on his project and concentrated. Not quite human, the keening noise raced up and down the scale, passing the upper limits of his hearing, only to return again, almost a child's cry.

Curious, Lan investigated. This time history aided him. A dark lump appearing to be a rock with ropy tendrils extending to either side pulsated near a tree bole.

"Krek?" he called. "Is that you? Really you?"

"Oh, silly human, who else in all the world is as miserable as I? This rain! My fur is wet, and I wish to die. Never has one so noble born been subjected to such base treatment."

Lan went and hunkered down beside Krek. The giant spider was completely drenched, sitting under a natural rainspout formed by leaves. The man dragged the arachnid a few yards deeper into the forest, where the boughs formed a more perfect rain shelter.

"Now, you sodden spider, what are you doing here? I thought you'd be swinging high up in your web, mating with Klawn."

"Oh, you saw the mating!" cried the spider, showing signs of excitement for the first time. "Was it not the most glorious mating of two noble spiders you have ever witnessed? Such bliss! We lived for that wonderous ecstasy."

Lan moved closer. The spider might have been damp, but he also radiated warmth necessary to keep Lan from shivering. The coarse fur on the legs had softened in the rain and now caressed his naked flesh like a velvet comforter. He burrowed deeper and was rewarded by Krek's shifting position. He found a berth between two of the large legs and settled down to listen.

"I don't understand. I didn't stay for the nuptials. All I saw was the web swinging back and forth when you greeted Klawn."

"Ah," sighed Krek in remembrance, "the sweet epithalamion of our bliss! Such poignancy, such dexterity of spinning!"

"You mean you've already mated? You did it while I was there, watching?"

"Certainly," Krek said snappishly. "You silly humans prolong the moment of bliss to ridiculous lengths. We spiders concentrate our joy into one intense movement. I shall remember it forever," he sighed, sounding more like a maiden in love than ever before.

"If you're so damned happy, what are you doing out here in the forest getting soaked through and through?"

Krek rose up and peered at Lan. The limpid eyes were as expressionless as ever.

"I simply will never understand you humans and your peculiar ways. Klawn must try to devour me as the ultimate act of our coupling." He didn't have to add, "You stupid human." It carried in his tone.

"So you decided to explore again?"

"Of course. The Cenotaph Road provides a modicum of excitement for me. If I must leave my lovely bride, at least I can experience all the many worlds have to offer, in way of small recompense."

"Seems fair," muttered Lan. He again began weaving together more strands for a covering, then stopped. The universe's finest silk was at his beck and call. All he had to do was ask. So he did.

"A cape?" murmured Krek. "I assume you mean one of those square things you toss around your frail bodies. Hmmm, yes, quite easily done, for one of my skill." In less than an hour, Lan securely wrapped a strong, warm silk cape around his chilled body.

Lan contemplated starting a fire with one of his simple spells, but he decided against it because of Krek's aversion to flame.

Instead, Lan asked, "Have you been near the city recently?"

"I skirted it. My kind has little intercourse with those from that village. They most unkindly scream and flee from us as if we were some sort of monsters. On occasion, they have been known to use fire." The giant spider's body shuddered until Lan thought it would fall apart under the vibration. Krek finally controlled himself and continued, "I have seen the patrols of the grey-clad soldiers, however, and decided that it was pointless to antagonize them further."

"Did you happen to see a small patrol with a woman prisoner?" Lan rapidly described Velika, hoping that the spider's oddly different sensory apparatus had picked up a clue as to her whereabouts.

Lan felt his pulse rate increasing as he described the woman. His forehead dotted with sweat and an uncomfortable feeling mounted in his loins. He turned to keep the spider from seeing his arousal. Worse than the embarrassment was the confusion that accompanied the physical response. Just thinking about Velika excited him, yet he had seen her only briefly. She was lovely, yes, definitely! But a single kiss shouldn't create such mental turmoil.

He remembered vividly the tears rolling down her face, and the acid burn as he touched them. The kiss. The tears on his lips. The surge of stark animal *desire* throughout his body. The confusion. He shook away the rest of the memory. Reliving his stupidity over and over accomplished nothing.

"I saw a mounted guard with two females. One as you describe and the other with black fur on her cranium. She fought well, but the chains binding her wrists prevented much damage. A shame she did not possess proper snippers." Krek grated his mandibles together in an awful sound that made Lan cringe. "*That* would have been a fight truly worth witnessing."

"Where were they taking her—them?"

Krek shivered in way of a shrug. "It is difficult to say since I have the feeling that the soliders are not native to my world."

"Then they're from still another world," mused Lan.

"I mean what I mean," snapped Krek. "They do not belong on this web world. All these grey ones come from some other world lying along the Road."

Lan thought this over, slowly nodding. It explained the encounters on the boggy world. The grey-clad soldiers expanded across world after world in an attempt to establish a real empire. He sighed. This was conquest on a cosmic scale. On his own world, many had established vast empires ranging over entire continents. N-Yalch of the Timbers had welded together a confederation spanning four continents less than a generation before, only to fall victim to an assassin's poison. None had risen to take his place; few of his commanding, charismatic power appeared in any given century.

But the idea of conquering entire worlds, treading along the Cenotaph Road, took Lan by storm. The audacity of it! No simple barbarian warlord could attempt such a feat. The logistics, the movement of men and supplies alone, boggled the mind. Lan considered other aspects, then realized why Surepta had been recruited. Scouting ahead onto new worlds slated for conquest required knowledge. Locals enticed to accept high commissions as Surepta had done would prove invaluable when the main body of troops moved in to conquer.

Lan raged again against the turncoat and his back-stabbing ways. Yet he recognized a still greater danger. The old sheriff had considered the grey-clads a local phenomenon, nothing more. He and all the deputies in the world couldn't resist the onslaught of a well-trained, disciplined army march-ing along the Cenotaph Road. With whole worlds to supply and support, no individual world could stand for long.

Yet the very act of invasion posed a major problem.

"Who can move so many men through one tiny cenotaph?" he asked Krek. "It seems a life's work trying to get enough soldiers into just one world, much less several. Remember the numbers of soldiers we found? They seemed endless."

"I remember, oh, how this woe-filled one remem-bers!" Krek returned to pitying himself. "My fur has never been matted from more foul mud and water. And they humiliated me mercilessly. Me, Webmaster of the Egrii Mountains. Never again will I bear up under such scorn. My bravery then amazes me."

"You can be brave like that again, Krek. Now tell me, how is this being done, this invasion? Surely, a single man armed with a crossbow would be able to kill the soldiers one by one as they emerged from the cenotaph." And, he mentally added, the crossbowman wouldn't even have to stand a long duty watch—merely a short span around midnight when the cenotaph activated.

"The obvious solution is that Waldron Ravensroost has discovered a way of generating his own Road." Krek sounded disgusted with Lan for missing such an obvious idea.

"Waldron?"

"Of course, Waldron. The grey king. The man they all call Saviour. But what matters all this to a dried-up husk of his former self? I am useless. My mate seeks to devour me, and I flee. So craven of me! How can I bear the shame when my hatchlings discover I have not been properly cocooned to feed them? Poor Klawn must capture millions of tiny insects for them instead of giving them my plump, cocooned body. I am a failed spider, failed utterly and beyond redemption."

Lan allowed Krek to pity himself without human intervention. He had much to consider. This Waldron would be the logical one to order the release of Velika and Inyx. All he had to do was find the base of operations and talk with him. Even ruthless conquerors listened with a knife at their throats.

To regain Velika, Lan Martak was willing to barter with forty demons from the Lower Places.

"The rain's over, Krek. Let's get out of here." Lan pulled the silken cape tightly around his flanks. Although the rain had stopped sometime earlier, a razor-sharp wind from the north had been seeking out his naked flesh for hours. Exercise would help keep him warm, and what better way than walking toward his goal of freeing Velika from the grey-clad soldiers?

"You go, Lan Martak. I wish nothing more than to die here. Oh, why did they not leave you with a sword?"

"I wish they had, too, but for different reasons," said Lan grimly.

"You could have dispatched me and put me out of my horrid existence."

Lan decided the spider meant what he said about not budging from this spot. He wondered if threats would work. Deciding against such overt violence, he tried a different tack.

"Krek? Why don't you help me get some clothing and a weapon? That'd help us both, according to your logic."

The spider raised his head, brown eyes softly unfocused. "How could such a bungler as I aid the likes of you?"

"You're always pointing out how clumsy we humans are. Show me how good a spider really is."

"Hmmmm, yes, you are right this time. You are clumsier than the most spastic of spiders. My newest hatchlings show more coordination in their movements along the web. Even old Klork, the seven-legged spider living over in the Estaman Gorge, is better able to get around than you, it seems. Very well, I will help you in exchange for your aid later in dispatching me from this sorrow-filled world."

Lan marched off beside the spider, figuring on arguing later with Krek—after he was decently clothed and had a sword and dagger weighing heavily in each hand. The way Krek's moods oscillated, the spider might talk himself out of suicide soon. The cheerful countryside, dotted with delicate flowers and flowing green ground vines, certainly perked up Lan's flagging spirits. The rain cleansed the air and left it sweet and heady. The porous ground sucked up the fallen water and left only dust, so that their path wasn't through the mud of the bog world. Most of all, Lan enjoyed being able to survey the sprawling country dotted with stands of forest and know that none pursued him.

Rather, he had become the hunter. The grey-clads had left him for dead; they wasted no time hunting corpses. He was free to work as he saw fit until the proper moment for attack. And that moment had to include freeing Velika. Unbidden, Lan's hand went to his lips and ran along them, remembering the feel of the woman's soft kiss, the tears burning his flesh. His breathing came harder, and his hand trembled slightly in anticipation. As he ran over various scenarios in his head, his spirits rose to dizzying heights.

Krek sensed this.

"I fail to understand the workings of that thing you humans call a brain. How one such as yourself

can be beaten senseless, robbed of valued treasure—
from my web trove, yet—and your paramour whisked
away, then laugh and sing afterward, is a total
mystery."

"You think you have problems understanding
us?" Lan laughed out loud. "If I live to be a hundred, I'll never understand you."

"I am a hundred, and then some," mused Krek.
"You are right. If you did live as long as I have,
you would not appreciate us spiders." This satisfied something in the arachnid's twisted mentality,
for he began loping along with the spring in his
gait that Lan remembered so well from the time
they had entered the Egrii Mountains.

Krek suddenly stopped and dug his claws deep
into the soft earth until he found bedrock. He
"listened" for a moment, then announced, "Soldiers come this way."

"How many?"

"Enough" was all Krek said. He sank to the
ground alongside the road, appearing to be nothing more than a small dark hillock. Lan found a
tiny culvert and draped the silk cape over his shoulders, then camouflaged himself with a few strate-
gically placed branches and leaves. They waited
less than five minutes before a pair of horsemen
galloping hard came into view.

One sported the grey of a soldier under the banner of Waldron, while the other dressed in gaudy,
flowing layers of silk, the garb of a member of the
merchant class. Lan didn't care about the quality
of the man's clothing, as his interest lay in arming
himself. Both men sported swords and daggers.
And protruding from one's swordbelt was the butt
of a wheel lock pistol identical to those carried on
Lan's home world. He watched the men carefully,
frowning. The one carrying the pistol wasn't of
Lan's world. Lan waved his hand to signal Krek
that he planned to attack as the pair galloped by.

Lan had no chance to mount his attack. Krek's bulk blasted from concealment and bowled over the soldier's horse. The frightened animal struggled to its feet and raced off, minus its rider. The merchant's horse reared and vainly pawed the air to fend off the giant spider. Krek pounced, and two savage slashes of his mandibles left the horse bleeding on the ground, more dead than alive.

Lan hastened to the fallen soldier and discovered Krek had already done his work for him. A broken neck ensured that this man would never again lift a sword. Lan dragged out the knife sheathed at the soldier's belt and turned to face the merchant. It became readily apparent the man had no desire to fight.

On his knees, he begged, "Master, call off your demon! I am sinless! Don't steal my worthless, pitiable soul! I am too good for such a vile fate. I—"

"Silence!" roared Lan. The man blanched, then fell, touching his forehead repeatedly to the ground at Lan's unshod feet. He wanted to laugh but decided avenging angels didn't make sport of their victims in that manner.

"Strip. I want your clothes."

"Please, master! They forced me into the service of King Waldron. I was only a poor merchant on the bleak world, struggling for a living. King Waldron came and seduced me away with tales of riches, tales of people eating regularly. I was weak. He convinced me I should do his bidding and come to this world. Believe me that I didn't want all those gold coins they demanded I take for—"

"Silence, I said," he snapped again. "And get those clothes off. I might decide that is recompense enough for your sins." Lan didn't have to hear all the merchant's garbled confession to know the man was greedy and had probably done worse in his day than steal clothing needed to cover nakedness. If anything, this man probably had sold the clothes and jewels already taken from Lan by the grey-clads. He had the air of the illicit about him.

Somehow, Krek's looming bulk added speed to the merchant's fingers as he disrobed.

"How do I look, Krek?" asked Lan, pirouetting to display the gaudy, flowing clothing stolen from the merchant. The thin material billowed out from his lean body and lent an air of massiveness to him that wasn't his. In spite of the fine clothing, he kept the silk cape spun for him by Krek. Never had he found a garment so light and warm. The heavy sword swinging at his side comforted him, too. The body of the fallen soldier was neatly covered in the culvert after he had stripped it of the weapons he wanted. The wheel lock pistol felt hard and firm and substantial in his fist—and it gave a poignant reminder of his lost home. The sheathed knife completed his armament. While he could hardly fight off an entire army, he felt plucky enough to handle anything up to a company.

The spider crouched down and came close to looking him in the eye. His only comment was "The coarse weave of the fabric offends my craftsman's sensibilities."

Lan laughed. That was the best he could expect from the spider. If Krek hadn't commented in a sarcastic fashion, it would have bordered on a miracle.

"Very well, Krek, your opinion's duly noted. Now let's set off and find some that will be less objectionable to you—and less gaudy for me."

Krek let out a screech that made Lan jump. He had anticipated some bit of sarcasm, but not outright fear. He spun to face another arachnid fully half his height taller than Krek. Lan didn't have to be told that this was "the lovely Klawn." He read it in Krek's horrified response. Instinct guided him.

His blade flashed wickedly in the sunlight as he drew and slashed at the female spider's legs.

Agilely, she leaped and avoided his sword. She simply ignored him in her single-minded drive to get to Krek, now cowering beside the road and blubbering incoherently. Lan wished the spider would at least attempt to defend himself, but knew this might be impossible under the circumstances. He didn't blame his spider friend for not wishing to attack his mate; such behavior was frowned upon in most human cultures, Lan had found, and the consequences in the spider's culture appeared even more dire.

"Klawn, you are too good for me," whimpered Krek. He might have been a beaten child, so high and thin and tremulous sounded his voice. Lan didn't hesitate in reinitiating his attack. The sword resheathed, he dived forward and tackled the back two legs, giving impetus to Klawn's attack. The spider overcompensated and tumbled down in a furry pile of legs and snapping mandibles.

Lan writhed around to avoid the ominous crashing of those serrated death scythes above his head. He knew better than to release his hold on the hind legs. Allowing Klawn mobility meant death. He pulled upward on the legs held tightly in the cirlce of his brawny arms as he rolled to one side and snared still another leg. With three of the giant spider's legs under his control, he found it relatively easy to capture a fourth. Klawn kicked and fought but failed to reach and devour Krek, as her mating ritual demanded.

"Get me some rope, dammit!" flared Lan, struggling to maintain his grip. "I'm going to tie her up!"

"Oh, Klawn, my precious darling, please believe I was not in my right mind. I do not know what possessed me to rush from your fond embrace. I—"

"Krek! *Get me a rope!*"

This shook Krek from his fright long enough to

see what his human friend attempted. With ponderous movement, he plucked a lariat from the pile of discarded possessions taken from the merchant and his soldier guard. As if the rope might burn him, Krek gingerly tossed it to Lan. The human continued cursing under his breath, inventing new tortures and destinations as well as finding increasingly improbable conjugal possibilities, while he looped the rope around Klawn's four back legs. Then he went to work grabbing and securing the front legs. It took him the better part of fifteen minutes, but he finally hogtied Krek's bride in such a way that she couldn't easily get those razor-edged mandibles back to snip through the rope—or him.

"Let's race the wind, Krek, before she gets loose."

"Yes, let us make haste," the spider agreed. "And thank you, Lan Martak, for not injuring her." He vented a gusty sigh as he added, "Is she not the most lovely creature in all the world? Such fine legs, such lovely fur adorning them."

"She's certainly got enough legs," Lan said, remembering the chitinous claws tipping each one.

"That she has," said Krek with a sigh, longingly peering backward at the still-struggling Klawn.

Lan spurred the stolen horse to a full gallop and let Krek try to match the pace as well he could. He had little time for the lovesick spider or the oversized Klawn. All that mattered to him centered on recapturing Velika—and proving to her that he wasn't the wastrel and fool she had seen in the village and after.

His hand brushed over his lips. The sting of her tears remained.

"I don't believe it," he said, awestruck. The huge castle battlements reared up two hundred yards before ripping the sky apart with crenelations of obsidian. He dug his heels into his horse's flanks until he braced himself enough to reach out and touch the wall. Slagged glass slid under his fingers. Using the point of his dagger, he thrust directly against the translucent material. Blue sparks danced away, leaving the stone with only a tiny cicatrice.

"A house adequate for a king," observed Krek, crouching down while Lan continued his explorations at the base of the wall.

"Adequate isn't the word. This place could withstand a generation-long attack and still remain unscathed. But there has to be a way in. No matter how well contrived a structure, there is always some unforeseen way in."

"Human philosophy?" asked Krek. "I can conceive of structures with but one means of ingress. Why, in the Egrii Mountains, I once spun this fabulously intricate web-trap capable of holding a snow bear. It held so well I failed repeatedly to get the carcass out. The bear finally rotted away in the silken prison."

"How interesting," Lan said dryly. "What's that have to do with getting inside the castle and rescuing Velika?"

"Nothing," answered the spider.

Irritated, Lan guided the horse around the tower of glass until he found an observation point where he could spy on the people coming and going from the castle. The huge drawbridge lowered to cross a chasm fully fifteen yards wide. The cunning series of switchbacks immediately after crossing the bridge cancelled any plan he might have of charging the gate while it was down and storming the castle before the grey-clad soldiers responded. By the time he'd clear the second inner wall, even their dead could have been summoned to pick him off with their firearms, all of which looked as if they'd been imported from his home world. And none of the soldiers appeared lackluster in performing his duty. They paced their posts with an intentness that made Lan wonder at the punishment for falling asleep on patrol. But there had to be some way of sneaking in, if only he could find it. No amount of wishful thinking discounted the brilliantly colored hot-air balloon tethered just outside the drawbridge, either. An army could be seen, as well as a lone individual, from its dangling basket. Lan cursed the military mind that had invented the aerial spy.

Krek lumbered up beside him and studied the terrain. Finally the giant spider declared, "You might steal the balloon and float into the castle."

Lan's hope surged anew. Single-handedly attack the balloon and kick open its burners to lift over the walls of the castle? This appeared the only path open to him, dangerous as it was. All other surreptitious or overt routes had been guarded against with the thoughtful cunning of a paranoid mind.

"Do you really think I can sneak under the balloon, crawl up the anchor line, kill the guards, and then float upward and over the wall?" he asked.

"No," was all the answer he got.

He turned bitter.

"Then why did you even mention it?"

"I simply wanted to present yet another method of gaining entry."

"Another method?" Lan cursed the spider's nonlinear, nonlogical mind.

"Yes. I can spin a silk strand long enough and strong enough to easily scale the walls."

Lan put his head in his cupped hands. He didn't know whether to cry from relief or frustration.

CHAPTER EIGHT

The glittering strand of web material shot upward faster than Lan could follow. The bulb at the very tip touched the glassy wall some fifty yards over their heads, but the spider didn't seem concerned about the possibility of its coming loose. Blithely, as if he took an afternoon stroll in the warm sun, Krek walked up the wall until he reached the spot where the web stuck. Lan strained to see what he did then, but failed. Another loop of web rocketed upward from the spider's spinneret. Krek followed this strand as he'd done the first. The process repeated until Krek's now distance-diminished form perched high atop the obsidian battlements of Waldron Ravensroost's supposedly well-guarded, impervious castle.

"What now?" Lan called up.

Seeing the boulder hurtling down from above, he dived too late and found himself crushed under a ponderous, enveloping weight. Struggling only entangled him more in the sticky material. When he realized this, he relaxed and allowed Krek to reel him in like a fish on a line. All the way up, he cursed under his breath. Krek should have told him what to expect; the spider undoubtedly assumed this to be lodged already in Lan's memory and yet another indication of arachnid superiority over frail humanity.

"Get this gunk off me," raged Lan after his feet felt hard stone battlement under them. "It's getting into my nostrils and suffocating me." He kept his arm over his nose to protect against such an unhealthy occurrence.

"One moment, foolish human."

Lan cringed as a shower of astringent fluid bathed his entire body, but he shook his head once and the sticky strands began to melt away. In less than a minute, he stood free of the web material, most of his silk clothing also eaten through by the acid.

"My skin! What'll this do to me?"

"Nothing," Krek said, unconcerned. "It eats only my web and, apparently, those inferior garments. I told you they were of mediocre construction. Now perhaps you will believe me in the future."

Lan pictured the spider sitting down, crossing his legs and folding his arms in a smug manner. The spider, of course, did no such thing. He simply stood watching Lan, waiting for the next move. Lan brushed his curly hair back from his eyes and pulled a tattered strand of clothing from his arm. He shook all over like a dog thrown into a lake and material flew like water droplets. Only the broad leather belt remained unscathed from Krek's dissolving acid.

"I've got to find more clothing."

"Of better quality this time, I hope," added Krek.

"Yes, of course." Lan stalked off down the walkway on the ramparts, taking care when he entered a guard post. It was deserted and showed little sign of having been recently occupied. A quick search failed to reveal anything of more than passing interest.

"What now, Krek? Are there soldiers patrolling the walls?"

Krek's claws noisily scraped against the smooth obsidian of the walkway, and the faraway look came into his chocolate eyes. His body undulated to an unheard tempo as the coppery strands of fur on his legs bristled.

"A lone guard approaches from the east."

Lan killed the guard with a quick thrust to the back. As the dead body slumped to the floor of the guard room, Krek observed, "Will it not be hard explaining the dagger rent and bloodstains on the back?"

"The only way any of Waldron's men can see me from that direction will be if I run. I plan to attack." Lan rapidly stripped the fallen soldier of the grey uniform, wondering if the red stripes of the sleeves were indicative of rank. He had failed in his attempts to figure out how greys marked their officers. The commander of the forces back on the bog world had slightly less red piping than the man now dead at Lan's feet, yet this man obviously marched patrol around the walls of the castle, not the work of a commanding officer.

Smoothing down the too-small uniform's wrinkles, Lan asked, "Does this pass inspection?"

Krek didn't answer, but his motions reminded Lan of a man smelling a long dead fish. How the spider had come to be such an expert on human tailoring and style was something Lan would have to extract from him at some future time.

Striding out as boldly as possible in the tight trousers, Lan surveyed the inner keep of the castle. It, too, was cast in heroic proportions like the castle's battlements. Companies of grey-clad soldiers drilled on the bare grounds surrounding the central spire, too many men for Lan to avoid if he simply walked across to the keep. Not knowing if he carried rank in the three red stripes on his left sleeve also deterred him from attempting such a foolhardy excursion. Since everything inside the castle walls seemed geared perfectly to a military operation, Lan feared passwords might also be required at some point. While the keep loomed less than a hundred yards from the wall, it might as well have been on the other side of the world.

"Impressive design work," said Krek. "I am particularly taken with the intricate patterns etched into the black glass of the central building. Most architects feel the only decoration needed is a gargoyle here and there. Ingenuity as well as taste are always at a premium."

"So who made you an art critic?" snapped Lan, worried about being seen standing and peering so intently at the keep.

Krek paid him no attention.

"Pillars of some contrasting color, perhaps bone-white marble, would be most effective in front of that massive black door leading into the keep. All those guards simply litter the picture. A few more of those cunning arches would hide the soldiers posted to . . ."

"Be quiet, unless you can give me a quick and easy way into that pile of glass." Even as he mouthed the words, realization burst on him. The distance was greater than that across which Krek had shot the sticky strand of web material in climbing the outer wall, but the target was horizontally placed, not vertically.

"Naturally, I can," Krek smugly answered the unasked question. "A trifle of web shooting." A silver strand arched upward to follow a parabolic path to the roof of the distant keep. "Grab a leg, friend Lan Martak, and I will demonstrate how a Webmaster of the Egrii Mountains conquers space."

Lan barely had time to fold arms and legs around one of Krek's furry limbs before he felt himself precipitously yanked out into thin air. Once, he glanced down and saw the marching troops. His stomach flipped over as he felt poised in midair with nothing below, and he almost lost what little he had eaten for breakfast, but the flight ended abruptly, saving his meal and his sanity. Never had solid flooring pleased him more than this treacherously slick glass under his boots.

"See? It was the work of a moment," said Krek,

satisfied with the task. A quick dab of his acid
erased all vestiges of his web. Lan's only agitated
thought was that Krek had missed his calling. As a
cat burglar, he'd have been unmatched. Then he
settled his mind to cope with the fighting he knew
to be ahead of him.

"Let's find Velika and get free of this place."

"Do not forget the glorious jewels, friend Lan
Martak. Once they belonged to me; it is a personal
affront that they robbed you of *my* web treasure."

"I won't forget. Now let's find our way off this
roof and into the audience chamber of our unwilling host." It took twenty minutes to find the door
and another fifteen to pry it open. Never had Lan
seen such a well-locked door onto a roof. It was as
if they expected invasion from the skies. He didn't
know enough of this world to put credence to it,
but the balloons hardly seemed adequate for the
task, and there existed scant evidence of ensorcell-
ment to promote flying. In fact, Lan had seen little
magic used on this world. Even his minor fire-
starting spell constituted a major enchantment.

One renegade warlock could tie this world around
his spell-ring finger.

"Down?" Krek asked tremulously. The flare of
torches lighted the stairway and frightened the
spider.

Lan placed a reassuring hand on the spider's
nearest leg and stroked it as he would a kitten.

"I won't let any sparks set you on fire. Trust me.
I trusted you in that aerial leap across the gap." He
repressed a shudder thinking about it.

"But that was safe!" protested Krek. "*This* is
dangerous."

Lan managed to guide the reluctant spider safely
down the spiralling stairs without once endanger-
ing a tinder-dry bit of fur. The rest of their brief
journey proved uneventful, and for that Lan muttered heartfelt thanks to several gods and a dozen

demigods. The staircase ended in a balcony over-looking the great hall. Balanced precariously on four upright sword points stood a throne of blinding white. Seated on it with awesome majesty had to be Waldron of Ravensroost.

He didn't merely observe the throng gathered at his feet; he exuded a regality that Lan felt. A haughty look and fine garments added to the effect, but the pair of ravens perched on the man's shoulders pulled the scene from base affectation and pushed it into one that Lan dreaded. Waldron was no common soldier on a wild spree; he *commanded*. His presence dominated the room.

Lan circled the railing and jockeyed for a better position. The postures of the two men kneeling in front of the lambent throne indicated that they were senior officers. Straining to hear confirmed Lan's suspicion.

"Well done, General Wixxel, very well done," congratulated the ruler. "If this world's subjugation is almost complete, mass transfer of my subjects will begin immediately."

"A few outposts remain defiant, liege, but our forces apply growing pressure on them. They must fall soon. And when they do, we can move on to still another world."

"All in time, General, all in good time. I have just returned from our home world, and last season's crop failure has extended into this season, too. If we hadn't completed the conquest of this world according to the Great Plan, many more would starve this winter. Aid is being sent even now until they emigrate."

"My world also supplies them, liege," said the other man. "While total subjugation of my world is many months away, foodstuffs are plentiful."

Lan froze at the voice. He strained to see the man speaking more clearly. His worst suspicions were verified when Waldron answered.

"You have done well, Kyn-alLyk-Surepta. Of our new generals, you have accomplished the most."

"Under your leadership, all is possible," said Lyk Surepta.

Lan felt himself blanching. His hand trembled as he reached for his dagger. It was an impossible dagger toss, but he had to try. As he pulled back to send the blade cartwheeling, a furry limb restrained him.

"Is life so worthless that you throw it away like this?" asked Krek.

Lan relaxed slightly, the dagger no longer considered.

"He killed Zarella."

"Zarella? Oh, yes, your paramour on your home world. But I thought you wanted to retrieve your paramour on this world? Which is it to be, Lan Martak?"

Lan knew Krek was right. Zarella was dead and worlds away. But vengeance would be his! Kyn-alLyk-Surepta had sold out their home world to the murderous Waldron, and killing him would eliminate both a danger and a traitor. He turned his attention back to Waldron.

". . . and take the bitches captured on the road. I understand they are comely enough even for nobles such as yourselves."

The general smiled wickedly and bowed deeply. "Thank you, liege."

"My heartfelt gratitude," echoed Surepta.

"When you tire of them, allow your men to play with them. All my officers can use some . . . recreation."

All three laughed boisterously. Lan had to fight to hold his anger in check. He knew with certainty that those "bitches" were Velika and Inyx. He silently motioned to Krek as the officers backed from Waldron's throne, then turned and strutted off.

*   *   *

"We mustn't lose them, Krek! If we do, we'll never find Velika." Lan grew more panicky as he tried to keep the general and Lyk Surepta in sight. The going was made even more difficult by the need to avoid the sporadically placed guards. Explaining Krek's presence to a guard would be too difficult.

"I fail to understand what you see in that female. She appeared rather ordinary to me."

Lan remembered the way the blond woman's grey-green eyes had implored him to protect her, the way her slender fingers crushed his arm so passionately, her fragrance, her beauty, the burning touch of her tears. For a moment, he felt as if his head spun wildly through a cosmos far removed. When he recovered from the brief vertigo, fire burned within. He must rescue Velika. He had promised to defend her against all danger, and he had failed. To regain his own besmirched honor, and the woman with whom he had fallen in love at first sight, Lan Martak felt morally obligated to fulfill his self-appointed duty. He must rescue her. And, of course, Inyx. She came under the same stringent code he avowed concerning Velika.

"Human stuff, Krek. I can't explain it to you right now. Call it a matter of honor and let it go at that."

"You continue to astound me with your bizarre honors and dishonors. One day, when I am feeling less put upon, I shall sit down and contemplate all this. Truly, walking the Road is instructive. But the knowledge I gain seems so worthless to me. I ofttimes wonder if—"

"Krek, be quiet. Unless you can help me keep Surepta in sight."

"Oh, is that all you desire? It is quite simple. The pair you seek went down this corridor." Krek flexed his claws and inserted them into crevices in the interior walls. His eyes got a faroff look as he concentrated on "feeling" the location of Surepta and the general. After a few seconds, he bobbed his head rapidly and said, "It is as I thought."

"What?"

"I am right. They still go in that direction."

Lan bit back the retort forming on his lips. Arguing with the spider while in the center of the enemy camp was both futile and dangerous. Later, when they were all safe and far away from King Waldron and his hordes of grey-clad soldiers, then he could set this miserable furry spider straight on proper conduct behind enemy lines. Lan made his way carefully along the hall, not wishing to alert any guards in the crossing corridors. Once, he had to use his dagger, then find a room in which to hide the dead body. He hated wanton killing like this, but the slightest alert from a patrol meant his death, Krek's—and Velika's. He dared not take such a frivolous chance with *her* life. Better a dead body than a tied-up soldier who might escape his bonds and condemn all their souls to the Lower Places.

"Lan Martak!" hissed Krek urgently. "Halt a moment. Let me . . . consider."

Lan looked over his shoulder in puzzlement at the spider. The spider's entire body shrunk as he watched. The huge arachnid crumpled to the floor like a scrap of waste paper. For a long, throbbing heartbeat, Lan said nothing. Krek might be ill. He knew so little of the spider's needs; only his too-apparent fears surfaced. Had the spider encountered a vagrant current in the halls carrying some substance poisonous to his kind? Lan imagined a castle such as this protected against insects of all types. Perhaps a ward spell to this end had unbalanced Krek's metabolism.

He shuddered at the prospect. The only such insect-killing spells he knew acted directly to speed catabolism. The delicate balance of life was upset in such a way that the offending bug died rapidly, its bodily systems failing to offset the increased rate of dying.

Lan closed his eyes and muttered a simple detector spell, attempting to find what magical wards were at work. A dull throbbing attacked his temples, making his head feel as if it were a rotted melon ready to burst. He recognized no familiar spell. Pursuing the source of the aching in his head produced no useful information. Power of great magnitude flowed through the castle now, but to what end Lan failed to discern.

"Lan Martak, do you feel it, too?" came Krek's voice, strong as ever.

"What is it?"

"Another path from this world has opened. Waldron Ravensroost has discovered the secret of opening gateways other than through the cenotaphs. He can come and go from this world at his own discretion. It is as I thought. An artificial Road!"

Lan considered this. Whatever the strange power that Krek possessed, he must have it in some small measure, too. While he couldn't detect the fainter emanations from the "natural" Cenotaph Road, he did receive strong impressions from Waldron's manufactured one. A threshold factor might be at work. But, as interesting as this was, and answering many questions Lan had, he wasn't free to pursue it further. Velika must be his primary concern.

"The Road Waldron opens lies in that direction." Krek used a hairy leg to indicate the corridor perpendicular to the one they traversed. He stood and started down it on shaky legs. Lan ran and pulled the spider to a halt.

"Velika! We've got to rescue her first. Then we can explore this. Please, Krek. You can feel out where Surepta went. Tell me!"

"Hmmm? Oh, him. I seem to have lost the vibrations distinctive of his walk: Ahead lies a large number of soldiers. Perhaps one of them can be persuaded to answer your questions."

Lan Martak had never felt more torn in his life. The possession of the secret of interworld travel at will was a prize far exceeding a few jewels, even ones of the size, water, and clarity that he had so foolishly allowed to be stolen. But no prize, even the key to the Road, matched the treasure of Velika. He decided the best course to pursue was a rescue of the woman, then flight along Waldron's Road to another world. That saved them the trouble of fighting their way from the interior of the enemy stronghold into a world already conquered by King Waldron's grey-clad soldiers.

"Let's continue, Krek, and you warn me of guards." Lan wiped the sweat from his forehead that formed in spite of the clammy dampness of the hallway. He settled his mind and dried his wet palms on the sides of the uniform tunic. His sword mustn't slip when he met Surepta again.

"Ahead, ten paces past the junction of the corridors," came Krek's monotone voice. The spider jerked his head to the left, indicating the direction of the posted guard. Lan took a deep breath, held it for an instant, then exhaled quickly. Tense, but more relaxed than before, he walked into the intersection, performed an admirable left face and marched up to the sentry.

The man was half a head shorter than Lan. This helped him cow the guard with a snapped command from superior height.

"Where is Kyn-alLyk-Surepta? I have an important message."

"Down this corridor and in the commons room with the two wenches. They get all the . . . what? You're not a courier. Who are you?"

Lan's fist punctuated the sentry's question. As the man doubled over, a sharp knee to the chin put him out. Before he collapsed fully, Lan's strong hands gripped under the man's arms and pulled him to a nearby room.

"Krek? Is the room empty?"

The spider's claws tapped lightly against the door panels.

"Yes, it seems so. No one answers my knock."

Lan sighed at the spider's tactics but pushed into the deserted room. He dumped his prisoner on the floor and debated slitting the vulnerable throat. The idea didn't appeal to him. Instead, he bound the man, using strips of material torn from the man's uniform.

Pinching the unconscious guard's earlobe until a tiny half-moon of blood appeared forced the man's senses to return in a rush. The man shook his head, trying to avoid the fingernail gouging into his tender ear.

"St-stop it! Hurts!"

Lan slapped him, the echo of the blow ringing loudly in the empty room. The pain helped to further focus the soldier's attention. When he saw Krek looming, almost three yards of furry menace, he turned as white as flour.

His words tumbled out, "I . . . I am a true believer. Why send me to the Lower Places, O Great Minnpolus? I pray every seventy-third day as you decree!"

"Silence," commanded Lan, slapping the sentry again. "You aren't dead. Not yet. But you will be if you don't answer my questions. Where is Kyn-alLyk-Surepta?"

"I t-told the truth. In the commons room, not half a hundred paces down the corridor. On the right. A huge door. Red leather with brass studs. A . . . a hydra knob to open the door. It . . . O Great One, why me?"

Krek moved closer and towered over the bound man. With a choked, incoherent cry, the man fainted. Krek bounced up and down on his rubbery legs and finally said, "You humans give up your senses so easily. Or did you frighten him too much?"

Lan didn't bother correcting the spider's mistaken opinions by telling him that the guard no doubt considered him to be a demon from the lowest levels of Hell. That would only cement the spider's conviction that humans were frail and silly.

"We've got what we need from him. I doubt if he'll come to soon. And if he does, the fear of eternal damnation will be upon him. But to make sure ..." Lan tightly bound the man's mouth with another strip of cloth from his tunic. "There. Now let's find Velika."

"Yes, let us do that very thing. Perhaps then you will stop making all those silly noises about her."

The rollicking laughter from inside the commons room told Lan that he was too late. He pushed through the door and peered in at the scene, something out of a demented artist's mind. Huge flames leaped toward the shadowed ceiling, fed by canisters of bottled gas at each corner of the room. The movements of the men were stroboscopic, jerky, unmistakable.

Velika lay on the central table, her skirts mostly ripped off. From the look on Kyn-alLyk-Surepta's face and his obvious physical condition, Lan knew he'd arrived too late. The woman struggled weakly to fend off his amorous kisses, but the dishonor had been done.

Again Surepta had shamed Lan Martak.

A noise resembling two cats mating came to Lan's ears. In the corner of the huge room stood Inyx, a wooden stick in her hand. She swung repeatedly at the general's head every time he advanced on her. Although her clothing was ripped, Lan didn't doubt for an instant that her honor remained intact. She jabbed viciously at the soldier's head, then followed it with a looping kick to his groin. He grunted, taking the brunt of the kick on crossed forearms.

"Damn, but you're a feisty one," he muttered. "Surepta has already had his pleasure. Why not surrender yourself to me gracefully? You will like it, I promise!"

"The promise of a slime-pig. Kill me or let me go. I accept nothing else!" Inyx kicked out again, this time sweeping the man's foot from under him. He fell in a pile of thrashing arms and legs. A hard blow from the chair leg she brandished put him out of the fight temporarily. But instead of running, Inyx turned to Velika, still passively accepting Lyk Surepta's overtures.

"Scum!" Inyx flared. The wooden rod whished through the air and landed on Surepta's unprotected kidneys. He howled in anguish and turned to face his attacker.

"So he failed with you, eh? A woman such as you needs to be tamed by a real man." Surepta stood and moved lithely to one side, avoiding a second blow from her club. "You'll be more exciting than this passive lump of flesh." Surepta paused, a look of confusion crossing his sharp features. He looked down at Velika and the tears streaming down her cheeks. His hand worked against his tunic as if he wiped away grime. Only a damp spot from the woman's tears appeared on the lush fabric. "Still, she had her moments," he said in a choked voice. Then his normal arrogance flared back. "She might have been dead for all the pleasure I got from her!"

Lan and Krek slipped into the room, bolting the door behind them. Lan wanted no outside intervention.

"Behind you!" screeched Krek, his long legs springing straight. The huge arachnid launched through the air like a furry skyrocket. He landed between Inyx and the groggy general.

"Take care of him, Krek. Lyk Surepta is mine!" shouted Lan. But he found himself bowled over by a sudden rush. The attack cost him both his sword and pistol. Rather than attempt to recover either fallen weapon, Lan locked his arms around Surepta's body. Whatever else the man might have been, he was no weakling. Lan felt the flow and play of powerful muscles. He experienced a curious déjà vu feeling, remembering the night in the Dancing Serpent so long ago when he and Surepta had fought over Zarella.

Now they fought over Velika.

Lan gritted his teeth and tightened his bear-hug. Doubting he could win with this tactic, but fearful of letting go and allowing Surepta to pick up his own sheathed sword, Lan continued to squeeze with all his might. An adept twist sent him flying across the room.

He landed and rolled to his feet. As he faced Surepta, he saw death advancing on him. The gleaming length of blade between them was both sharp and well used. From the step-glide, step-glide motion, Lan knew Kyn-alLyk-Surepta meant to end this quickly.

"So, Dar-elLan-Martak," snarled Surepta, "we meet again. The sheriff thought you had escaped through the Road, but I never expected to find you here. It's my pleasure to kill you now as I should have done before!"

Surepta's first thrust was intended to be the last. Lan's counterattack only partially succeeded as he avoided the blade and drove his fist toward an unprotected throat.

The sharp, searing pain told him his right side had acquired another scar. But the meaty thunk of his fist drove Surepta to the ground. Lan felt a murderous rage seizing him. Surepta had killed his lover, poisoned the old sheriff against him, driven him from his home world, raped and killed his half-sister, and now he had raped Velika. Lyk Surepta deserved no mercy.

He got none from Lan Martak.

Powerful fingers clamped around the straining throat. Slowly, inexorably, life fled from Kyn-alLyk-Surepta's body until only a corpse remained behind.

Lan Martak stood and shook in nervous reaction, looking down at the dead body of his adversary. He realized then that the Resident of the Pit had been correct. Surepta had been brought to justice, but Lan's revenge tasted bitter and dry. There should have been more.

Lan turned in time to see Inyx hit the general over the head with the chair leg while Krek taunted the man. As the soldier fell forward, Krek's mandibles snapped once. They hardly slowed as they passed entirely through the body. Lan put his hand to his mouth at the gory sight, holding back his gag reflex.

"Well done, spider," Inyx congratulated her bloodstained ally. "A blow worthy of any warrior."

"You fared well alone, friend Inyx," answered Krek. "A pity you are not a spider."

"If I were, I'd shave my legs," came back Inyx, stroking over the rough bristles on Krek's front leg. "Still, I prefer this form, thank you."

"Humans are like that," Krek agreed. "Irrational about their frail forms. I must admit, though, there is something to be said about possessing appendages capable of firmly gripping a club." He attempted to pick up Inyx's fallen chair leg and failed, his chitinous claws not curving properly to hold the small-diameter stick. "I might have more luck with a sword."

The spider hoisted a fallen sword, holding it through the guard. With a quick flinging motion, Krek sent the blade arrowing through space to sink half its length into the wooden door. The giant bobbed up and down, silently congratulating himself on the feat.

Lan turned his attentions from the mutual admiration society forming and went to Velika. She still sprawled gracelessly on the table where she'd been raped, hardly moving during the fight. At the sight of Lan bending over her, she threw strong arms around his neck and pulled his lips to hers. Her tear-dampened cheeks brushed his; electric tingles passed through his body, exploded in his brain, ignited passions he'd never before known.

After a satisfactory kiss, she sighed and said breathlessly, "I knew you would come to save me."

"I was a bit late. Seems the best I did was avenge your lost honor." Lan looked at Surepta and felt the cold rage billowing inside him again. But a broken neck and stilled heart ensured Surepta would never again harass him.

"What honor?" asked Inyx contemptuously. "She spread wantonly for that beast, no doubt thinking to save her precious hide. Honor? She knows nothing of the word."

"Another few seconds and you'd have ended up the same as her," snapped Lan. "If we hadn't come along . . ."

"*I* would have died defending myself. I never will give my life but rather will sell it dearly. And with my life goes my honor."

"Humans," shrilled Krek, "please perform your silly ritual of mutual insults at some later time. I feel a company of men marching toward this room. Whether they come to avenge the deaths of their leaders or to partake of the peculiar mating ritual decreed by their king, I cannot say. It seems to me that nothing in this horrid chamber can turn for the good. Those awful leaping flames! I cringe at the thought of them singeing my fur." As the spider rambled on, he shrank down to rock size, all the while detailing how terrible a fate it was being allied with humans.

"The gods protect us," muttered Lan. "All right. We can escape this castle and flee to another world through an artificial gateway constructed by Waldron."

"He need not use a cenotaph?" asked Inyx, her green eyes glowing at the thought. "That secret must be mine! I can then travel to the ends of the universe. I can even return to Klendalu, a conquering explorer of the premier rank."

"All that's come to my mind, too, Inyx," said Lan. "But of more immediate importance is getting out of here unscathed."

"My lord!" cried Velika. "You bleed from a hideous wound." She hid her eyes in cupped hands and turned away from him. Inyx walked over and pulled away the matted grey cloth with a jerk that made Lan cringe, but her fingers probing the wound were curiously gentle.

"You'll live, more's the pity. Such a stupid person would be better off dead, yet I fear you'll soon fulfill that minor prophecy. I pray you won't take us with you as you die." All the while she muttered and cursed Lan's stupidity, she was binding his wound. When she finished tending him, she'd applied a tightly bound bandage. He experienced a twinge of stiffness, but little pain. Inyx had proven herself useful at doctoring wounds.

"Let's make haste for the new Road," said Lan. "Come, Velika, the blood's all gone." Her relieved look filled him with warmth that made up for the lack of blood. Her safety was all that mattered to him.

"Leave her, Lan Martak," advised Krek. "She is hardly worth the effort of squiring along with us. Speed and a modicum of ruthlessness are needed to win free from all these cavorting flames." The spider cringed as he looked into the corner containing one of the gas torches. "Such horrid people, having those spider-burning flames open like that. And do try to avoid the awful wetness that continually leaks from her eyes. It seems so . . . unhealthy."

"I agree with Krek," seconded Inyx. "Leave her. She faints at the sight of blood. If we walk the Road, even one of Waldron's manufacture, blood and death will be our constant companions."

"No. She comes along. And consider the treasure I'm abandoning. I'm willing to remain a pauper for Velika." His reward was a small frown.

The looks Inyx and Krek exchanged were even less respectful.

CHAPTER NINE

"Are you so greedy that you'd risk our lives in this way?" demanded Inyx. "Never have I heard of such stupidity."

"Dammit," exclaimed Lan. "I'm not going to argue with you. That cask of jewels belonged to me by right, and it was stolen. I'm going to get it back."

"It strikes me, friend Lan Martak, that this sudden desire for wealth instead of life did not take possession of your brain until it was placed there by her." Krek bounced up and down on springy legs and balefully looked at Velika. The blond temptress said nothing, but the way she clutched even harder at Lan's upper arm supplied all the impetus for his reply.

"We search out the jewels. If you and Inyx wish to try and win through to the Road opened by Waldron, do it!"

"You know we can't do such a thing, you fool. You saw the guards around that chamber," said Inyx angrily. "This entire place is a maze of twisting corridors. If we don't all work together to escape this accursed castle, we shall all die within its walls. Treasure hunting will buy us unmarked graves. Is that what you want?"

"We can get the gems back and escape," Lan doggedly told her. "I haven't come this far to turn back. Look at it my way. You've already been liberated from Waldron's clutches. That's fine for you, but I want all that's due me. Waldron's men stole the jewels, and I demand the right to fight and regain them."

"Isn't killing Kyn-alLyk-Surepta enough?" the spider asked. "Your mind is fogged by her presence. She bewitches you in some fashion a poor weakling spider such as myself cannot discern. Oh, how I wish I were back in the blessed Egrii Mountains, swinging idly on my noble web, feeling the wind sensuously singing through the fur on my legs. And Klawn, lovely Klawn!"

"May your 'lovely Klawn' burn, damn you," snarled Lan. "And I'm sick of you moaning all the time. Velika hasn't ensorcelled me. I come from a world where magic is commonplace and can defend myself against all but the most arcane."

Inyx snorted. "There's none quite so blind as a lovesick jackass. And I wonder about that. She holds a strange power over you that seems more than simple idiotic infatuation. But," she said, holding up her hands in acquiescence, "we cannot escape if we are divided. I shall help you in this idiocy, though it means our death. I will go out fighting, not snivelling." She cast a venomous glare in Velika's direction.

"I, too, shall add whatever pitiful efforts I can to the quest," said Krek, slumped to the floor in a giant, furry mass. "How I can aid you against that abominable firemonger, I am at a loss to say, but the attempt is the important thing. But a Webmaster deserves a better fate than being roasted."

"I agree," Inyx said, sullen and withdrawn.

"Then if you both agree, let's be off. Which way did you say the vaults were, Velika?"

"Might have known she'd seek out the riches first," muttered Inyx. Lan ignored her. He thought she was only jealous of Velika's glossy hair and womanly figure.

"This way, my lord."

"My lord," echoed Inyx sarcastically, then fell silent. She hefted a dagger taken from the dead general's belt, then tested Surepta's blade with a few quick lunges. Lan had to admit secretly that she looked as competent a swordsman as he'd ever seen. The test would come later, though, when she faced trained soldiers. Anyone can appear expert waving a blade around in thin air.

"Lead on, Velika, and we'll follow." Lan cast a silencing glance at his two companions to stifle any retort. For his own, he couldn't have been happier following Velika. The blond woman's every move showed liquid grace, almost snakelike in its bonelessness, and the tatters of her gown revealed intriguing patches of gloriously bare skin. Lan began idly daydreaming, and only Inyx's strong hand on his shoulder pulled him out of his reverie.

"Guards. Ahead. Use Velika to decoy them or we'll never get past."

"Go ahead, Velika. Don't be afraid. We'll protect you. Just distract them long enough for us to attack."

The frightened look on her face called for action on Lan's part. He placed his forefinger under her chin and raised her lips to his own in a soft kiss.

"There, a token of my esteem for your bravery." Her smile was reward enough for any man.

"The female makes an adequate decoy," observed Krek. "I do not understand it, but you humans have such a complex set of behavioral traits. Could you explain this to me, friend Inyx?"

"I won't lower myself. Besides, I'm not sure I understand, either. Ah, now. *Now!*"

With a surge of speed, Inyx burst onto the guards, with quick flashes of her sword to the left, right, then a long lunge directly ahead. Three guardsmen died before the first hit the ground. Lan followed suit, slaying two more. The five cooling bodies presented mute evidence of their teamwork.

"Well done, Velika," said Inyx. "We at last find your usefulness lies in deception."

A cold laugh echoed down the length of the corridor.

"It seems you are the deceived one, lady of the sword. Take them alive or take them dead, it matters little to our liege."

Krek backed up and sank to his knees, sobbing loudly.

"Trapped like an insect in my own web. A common bug and no more. Oh, have my brains turned to mush? Why should I be forced to show my stupidity to the world?"

The soldiers advanced in a line, more of them than Lan could count. He motioned to Inyx to cover his left flank and called to Krek, "Guard the back way. It might be our only way out."

Velika gasped when Krek mournfully said, "Trapped, I said, friend Lan Martak, and trapped I meant. A phalanx of brutes approaches from behind. I am powerless to hold back so many well-armed humans."

"Do not surrender to these scum-eaters," cried Inyx. "Sell your life for a hundred of theirs. Krek, do it! You are powerful! We need your strength, not your weakness."

"Oh, very well, but it is simply useless. No power on this world can turn the tide of such malevolence."

"I agree with the spider," said Velika hurriedly. "Please, Lan darling, surrender and throw ourselves on their mercy. They won't slay us if we surrender." Tears rolled down the woman's cheeks like waves against an ocean strand. Lan's fingers dampened with the tears. His entire body stiffened as if monumental conflict took place within.

"They'd cut their own grandmothers' throats if it amused them. Are you so eager to be raped by an entire army, girl? I for one will fight. Are you with us, Krek?"

"I suppose it is my woeful lot, Inyx. Yes, I will fight at your back for as long as strength flows through my now-rubbery limbs."

"Lan?"

His mind raced. Kyn-alLyk-Surepta. Waldron. Zarella's death. The grey-clad soldiers on the bog world. But then there was Velika. She wished him to surrender. His hand burned as if he'd thrust it into a fire. Lan fought off the waves of emotion wracking him and making him giddy, confusing his senses. There could be only one path to follow. His decision was made.

"We fight," Lan said, his voice choked. The conflict within died down and his resolve firmed. He did the proper thing. "I'm not going to allow Velika to fall into their hands again. Fight, Krek, fight as you did on the bog world."

Lan lunged *en quarte* and skewered the soldier in front of him. He pulled back, his blade dripping gore, and the body fell heavily, forming the foundation of a barricade in the hallway. Inyx added another before the wave of soldiers broke on them full force. Lan's mind went blank. All he knew was lunge, parry, riposte. He accumulated minor cuts and one of a dangerous potential on his leg. But the snick-snick of his blade against those of the grey-clad soldiers demanded his full attention. Like Inyx, he'd go down fighting.

After all, his own greed had caused them to fall into this trap. His own greed—spurred on by Velika.

Velika!

Lan cast a swift glance over his shoulder and saw her cowering against the wall, crying openly. As he turned his attentions back to the fight, he witnessed Inyx in action and thought his eyes deceived him. She weaved a curtain of steely death in front of them, every third cut drawing blood, or so it seemed. The death count for her more than doubled Lan's. He fought harder to match her; she shouldn't have to bear the brunt of fighting because of him.

Behind her, Lan heard the clacking of Krek's awesome mandibles. Once, a shower of blood rained down on him, forcing him to disengage and take a second to wipe sticky gore from his eyes. Krek had overenthusiastically severed a soldier's head from his torso.

Lan Martak knew that no three had ever fought more valiantly against the soldiers, but with that same certainty came the ugly knowledge that they were tiring rapidly. Soon, the grey tide would wash over their dead bodies and leave Velika to their crude amusements. This gave added strength to Lan's arm, more cunning to his blade, faster movements to his feet. But still the soldiers fought on, one immediately taking the place of a fallen comrade.

Krek screeched, "She comes! How did she find me? Oh, woebegotten spider, your end is near!"

"What're you talking about, Krek?" gasped Lan, parrying a strong thrust barely in time to keep his arm and wrist connected. "Who's coming?"

"Klawn has discovered where I am, and she comes to devour me! Why should she desire to consume a wasted spider such as myself? I am lost, lost, I say!"

The roar of the guards echoed throughout the castle. As an earthquake sunders the ground, so did Klawn split the ranks of the grey-clad soldiers in her headlong rush to finalize her nuptial arrangements with Krek. The huge female spider leaped along the ranks of the struggling, now-frightened soldiers, using her mandibles more as a slashing knife than as snipping scissors. A full two dozen fell before her savage, mindless attack.

Lan panted and yelled, "Stop the big spider before it's too late!"

Whether it was the air of command in his voice, the confusion, or the red blood altering the remnants of the soldier's uniform to give him the desired rank, he didn't know, but the soldiers closed on Klawn, blades singing their death songs to little avail. The spider proved too powerful for even their combined might.

"Here, Lan, Krek, here's our escape," cried Inyx, shouldering open a heavy door a short distance down the hallway. "Though we don't find treasure, at least we keep our lives."

Lan pulled Velika through the door an instant before Inyx slammed and bolted it against outside intrusion. The scowl on her face told Lan that, to her way of thinking, she had failed by allowing Velika entry. But Inyx said nothing as she wiped the worst of the blood and gore from her tunic.

"Ah, my beauty, they have escaped. Amazing. I hadn't thought the barbarians of this world showed so much determination. But are they really of this world? Or another? Can you tell?" Waldron held his gloved hand up level with the balcony railing so the huge raven perched on his wrist could peer down into the immense courtyard. A raucous caw was all the answer the conqueror received.

"Yes, I believe you are right. The spider is of this world. The flaxen-haired woman, possibly, also, but the dark-haired woman and the man who wields the sword so well cannot be."

Waldron leaned against the railing as he studied their movements so far below him in the convoluted maze of corridors he had ordered constructed. He peered into the darkness and sighted Klawn struggling against the door that Inyx had so securely latched. He reached down and scribbled a note on a piece of vellum, then tied it to the raven's leg. With a casting motion, he sent the bird fluttering into the air. The black bird fell a few yards, then powerfully stroked against the humid air, cawed and soared like a shadowy bullet for the other side of the castle. Klawn would soon be neutralized by closing siege doors on each side of her, but the others presented a unique problem for Waldron.

A unique problem and a unique amusement.

Holding his wrist out and emitting a screech similar to that of the bird just flown, Waldron captured another airborne raven, wincing slightly as the bird's metal-sheathed claws cut into his padded gauntlet.

"My beauty has been hunting again, eh? Would you like to become a herder of sheep? Or perhaps I should say people who can become sheeplike? You would? Excellent, my winged ally. Seek out those below and force them along the Chaos Path."

Waldron chuckled as he watched Lan, Inyx, Krek, and Velika dodge the plummeting death messenger. The raven's talons slashed more savagely than any falcon's. Soon, little knowing where they were being herded, the foursome fought and struck out against the raven, but inexorably they moved into the diabolical maze toward their deaths.

"Accursed black fiend!" screamed Velika. "Stay out of my hair!" The raven took a special delight in only plucking the strands of her golden hair away from her scalp. The others were decorated with red striations left by the raven's steel talons.

"A door, Lan, quickly," called Inyx, holding the heavy wooden portal open for them. Velika raced for the safety offered by the door, and Lan followed in a rearguard position, still swinging his sword futilely at the darting raven. Only Krek hesitated on entering.

"Hurry, Krek, or we'll be ripped to bloody shreds by that filthy creature."

"Friend Lan Martak, I feel an ominous presence lurking within. Are you sure we can cope with it better than the winged death? I am so weak from the fight and the encounter with lovely Klawn that I would be of little use to you."

"We'll get by. Now, dammit, get in here!" Lan took one last stab at the raven as Krek lumbered into the darkness and Inyx swung the door shut. A resounding click told them all the door was self-locking. And, in the dark, none could find the freeing latch.

"What do we do now?" sobbed Velika. "It's so dark."

Lan circled his arms around her and felt hot tears and breath against his skin. The curious effect of acid burning seized him once again, but he barely noticed. No matter what they'd been through, it was worth it for the moment. Velika needed him; that was something no one else could claim. Zarella had laughed at him, being too intent on her own pleasures to dare care for one such as he.

"Don't worry, Velika. We'll get through this."

"A fire! Let's light a fire!" the woman cried out. Lan's fingers hardened around her wrist to keep her from running blindly into the darkness. He pulled her closer to keep Krek from disemboweling her at the very idea of a fire so close.

"We don't have fuel for a fire, Krek," he said hastily to reassure the spider. "We'll find our way out of here without one."

"Out of here?" the spider asked, his voice curiously mild. "I rather like this place now that I have come to study it. There is a peculiar play between worlds, almost an eddy current, that amuses me. And Waldron's gateway is ahead. I feel as if I can reach out to it, in spite of the thickness of the surging color."

"Color?" asked Inyx. "What color? All I see is blackness."

"Perhaps I tolerate this blackness, as you call it, better than a human. To me, this is a fine night, all the discarded objects glowing with an inner light."

"Objects?" demanded Lan. "Such as?"

"This." A clicking noise sounded. From the echoes, Lan guessed the area around them to be huge, walls and ceiling so distant he couldn't touch them. Yet, curiously, he felt as confined as if the walls crushed him. His magic-sensing ability had left him like one blinded, and the only senses he had to work with were those of hearing and smell. And Krek's hearing was far more acute than his.

A beam of light stabbed out abruptly, penetrating the veiling curtain of black. Krek valiantly struggled with a small lantern, his claws and mandibles doing a poor job of controlling the device. Inyx gingerly reached up and took it from the spider.

"This is sufficent light to guide us. But where do we go?" She cast the light in a circle, and Lan felt sudden chills. No sign of the door through which they'd come was visible. Indeed, they might have been standing in the center of a deserted field. The lantern beam, strong and thick, played around, only to be gobbled by immense distance.

When Inyx shone the light onto what Lan thought to be the floor, he experienced a surge of vertigo. No floor existed under him. He hung suspended high above a galaxy of stars, gently spinning through eternity, and he was falling into the flaming core. He shrieked and grabbed out, clutching wildly at Velika, but she squirmed away from him and left him to soar and dive and plummet on his own.

A hairy leg pulled him close. Hardened hands gripped his. A resounding, stinging slap made his head ring like a summons bell. His attention was forcibly pulled away from the limitlessness under him and back to his companions. Heart beating fiercely, sweat running in broad rivers down his body, he turned wild-eyed to Inyx and Krek.

The woman's jet-black hair floated in wild disarray as if she had been running frenzied fingers through it or a typhoon had ripped apart the gentle braids holding it intact. Krek's up-and-down motion reminded Lan so much of a furry rubber ball that he had to laugh. He laughed harder and harder, soon succumbing to hysteria. Another slap from Inyx's punishing hand calmed him.

"I . . . I don't know what happened," he confessed. "The sight of *nothing* under me did something to my head."

"Do not worry, friend Lan Martak," said Krek. "Many hatchlings experience such fears. Even we spiders are not immune to attacks of vertigo."

"Yes," hastily added Inyx, "it takes much exposure before you get used to the sensation. I experienced it many times on many worlds along the Cenotaph Road."

"Then we're on Waldron's Road?" he asked weakly. He wished his magic-sense weren't so confused.

"I fear not, for the energies surrounding us are of a different nature. Rather, it seems to me that we are on a path leading to the Road. And what lies along this path, I am terrified to even guess."

"Thanks, both of you." Lan wiped sweat off his forehead and allowed the smell of fear to vanish from his nostrils before attempting to stand. Shaking, he got to his feet, only to find the floor underneath solid and opaque. The illusion had been good, too good for his liking, and he wondered if more of the same had to be endured before they reached Waldron's artificial cenotaph.

"Velika!" he called out, suddenly worried for her safety. "Where are you?"

"Here, Lan darling," she said, sidling up to him, her arm snaking around his waist. "I was so frightened when you went stumbling away like that."

"If you'd held on to him, he wouldn't have experienced the full effect of vertigo," accused Inyx. "Afraid you'd tumble after him?"

"I was afraid," she said. "I don't want to die."

"That's all right, Velika," said Lan, holding her close and feeling the heart beat strongly in her breast. "This is strange and frightening—to all of us."

Krek whined a little, and Inyx simply turned her back on Lan. He wondered what it was they both held against Velika, then forgot the little tiff as Inyx said, "This direction appears a likely one." She pointed into the darkness, no discernible reason for it. Lan started to protest, then bit back his argument. He'd follow her for the moment. One direction was as good as another in his present condition.

"Do we have to go with her, Lan? I don't like her," Velika said softly. "I think she hates me."

"You're imagining things. Inyx has different customs than those you're used to, but she doesn't bear you any malice. And yes, it's best we stay together. For a while."

"As long as I'm with you, Lan, I know everything will be fine."

Lan puffed with pride at the confidence she showed in him. Taking her hand, he walked off after Krek and Inyx, making certain to keep his eyes fixed straight ahead. He wanted no more vertiginous tumbles into infinity. They were too undignified.

The four trod silently on the substance of the floor for some time without seeming to make progress. Lan lost all track of direction in this nonspace, but trusted Krek's senses to be sharper than his. But he began to worry when a pungent odor assailed his nostrils. He took a deep breath and almost gagged on it. Sickly sweet, it reminded him of something long dead and now rotting.

"Inyx, hold a minute." The woman turned and cast the beam of light over him. Lan squinted and moved to one side to avoid being blinded. "Do you smell anything unusual?"

"No, nothing. Do you, Krek?"

"You humans are simply inventing this spurious smell-sense you boast about endlessly. I cannot imagine what it would be. If I cannot see or feel it, if I fail to hear it or 'vibe' it, surely it does not exist."

The spider seemed satisfied that nothing alien and evil approached. Even Inyx with her survival-trained senses failed to detect the vile odor. For a moment, Lan wondered if he were imagining this. Then he knew he wasn't. The lizard-thing slithered up, gobbets of rotting flesh falling from its ponderous bulk. As it surged from the veil of darkness into the tiny circle of light cast by their lantern, Lan pulled his blade from its sheath and drove mercilessly into a blind, atrophied eye, hoping to penetrate all the way into the creature's brain.

A geyser of pink ichor blasted down the length of his blade and onto his hand as he twisted the sword and lunged again. The sticky, warm blood fountaining from the wound spattered upward into Lan's face, momentarily blinding him. But still he slashed and lunged, flailing wildly, his gorge rising along with his panic.

The monstrous creature rolled over and twitched feebly. Lan stood, staring at it as a numbness claimed his soul. It had come so close to killing them all, and only he had the nerve to fight it. Even Inyx had denied its existence.

"Are you all right, Lan?" came Inyx's concerned voice. "What's wrong?"

"That thing," he said with loathing tingeing his words. "It's dead now, no thanks to all of you."

"What thing?" asked Krek mildly. "I am feeling poorly and cannot fend off any sustained assault. Oh, why did I ever leave my web, even for this transient thrill of exploring between worlds? Stupid, I am stupid beyond belief!"

Lan's jaw dropped in amazement as he went to wipe the gore from his blade. The carbon steel blade gleamed in the lantern light, as clean as the day it came from the forge. And nowhere did he find the carcass of the blind lizard-thing. Not a trace existed on the floor or on his tunic. Even the malodorous taint to the air had mysteriously purified. Whereas the others had shared the vertigo at the beginning of their trek through the velvet black wasteland, none of them had even seen this creature.

"You're not going mad, are you?" demanded Velika, shrinking from him. "Did you see something or not?"

"Don't badger him, Velika. I want to hear him out. It might cast some light on the nature of our surroundings." Inyx sat the lantern down and stood, hand on sword, waiting for an explanation. He gave it to her as succinctly as possible.

As he finished, Krek wailed, "Woe! A lizard grown too large for Krek to eat! The world shifts on its axis around me. I am powerless to do a thing. Pull me free of my noble web and I am nothing. Klawn, lovely spinner of delicate webs, why did I ever think to leave you and our bliss?"

"Hallucinations," said Inyx forcefully. "That is the answer. And for some reason, you are the most susceptible to them. Or perhaps Waldron has singled you out for this unique attack."

Lan shuddered, thinking of bearing constant assault by these all-too-substantial wraiths. While he had been fighting, it had been *real*. Nothing had seemed more real to him in his life, and this datum set his mind racing for the answer.

"Can these images be dredged from the pits of our own minds? Could Waldron be tapping our inner fears?" he asked.

"Doubtful. Otherwise, we would have seen Krek dancing amid a fire, and I would be drowning in an ocean without shores. I detest water in bodies larger than those conveniently stepped across," confided Inyx.

"You, too?" said Krek, almost cheerful now that he had found a companion to share another of his private fears. "Water makes the fur of my legs twitch dreadfully. Nothing in the world do I hate more—save fire."

"And I do not care for the feeling of insecurity," chimed in Velika. Lan pressed close to reassure her with his nearness.

"These creatures and happenings might leak through from other worlds," said Inyx. "Perhaps, since we are all creatures of different origins, our senses are subtly tuned to one world line but not another. Lan might be sensitive to creatures from certain worlds and we from others."

"Aieee!" screeched Krek, his mandibles slashing at thin air. The giant spider hopped backward and slashed again with his man-killing pincers. Lan freed his sword from its sheath but feared to attack something he couldn't see. Foretelling where Krek might dodge or leap proved impossible as he bounced and ducked his invisible foe.

"Finally, my weakness proved an asset," said Krek. He shook himself and fluffed his fur, then sank down to rock size beside them. "A vicious swarm of gnats the size of your fist. Dangerous to one in my pitiable condition, but tasty when taken singly."

"We'd better hurry. If these things are finding us with greater regularity, we might be attracting them simply by our presence in this nothing-world," said Lan. "Inyx, you seemed to know where we're headed. Start out. I have no idea at all where the Road lies from here." Even closing his eyes and attempting to regain the throbbing headache he now associated with the presence of the interworld gates, Lan couldn't find the proper direction in the darkness. The gate seemed to be everywhere and nowhere.

"Do you know where it is, Krek?" she asked. "I was simply following your lead."

"I did, but my powers wane rapidly in this

nonworld. But if memory serves, and at any moment I might fade into senility from all the shocks to my system, this is where our destinies lie."

He rose and trotted in the direction he'd pointed. For long hours they trooped beside him, Inyx's head swivelling from side to side like a mechanical toy and Lan holding Velika's hand in a death-grip, sure that any moment might be their last. Lan was the first to notice a gradual lightening. Soon, the others commented on it. When the level of light reached that of false dawn, they turned off the lantern.

"It looks like a junkyard," said Velika. Scattered around them were bits and pieces of machinery long rusted, huge beetle-shaped metal shells with wheels large enough to use as battle shields, and myriad smaller metallic implements. Lan stooped to examine some. Their feel assured him of their reality.

"It might be a razor blade," he said. "But who has ever seen one so small and difficult to hold?" Casting it aside, he picked up a smooth yellow cylinder. On impulse, he pressed his forefinger against the sharpened end. A long blue streak appeared on his skin. "A scriber! Imagine. And those things over there are paper fasteners such as clerks use."

"Someone's discard pile. But why here, between worlds?"

"Ever lose anything?" Velika asked. "Maybe this is where it goes."

The other three scoffed at the idea, but Lan wondered if she might not have an inkling of some cosmic truth. His intellectualizing was cut off abruptly by the eerie sensation of being watched. He carefully turned and surveyed the littered nonworld. Rising silently from the rusty remains of metal came a skeletal being, ligaments of wire and bones of steel and eyes of glaring red glass. It would have been an amusing parody of a human had it not carried a long length of chain in each pseudohand. Rippling motions like a muleskinner's sent the chains outward in perfect sine waves.

"I don't know what it is—or if you can even see it—but it looks nasty." Lan heard Velika's horrified gasp and knew she saw it, too. Inyx drew her sword and crowded close to his side. Krek bobbed up and down on the other.

"Separate a bit, and keep a lookout behind us, Krek," commanded Lan. "I don't want this thing's friends to sneak up on us." His mouth filled with cotton as he watched the graceful motions of the metallic being as it neared. The chains sang death songs now, snapping as if they were made from leather.

"How do we kill such a construction?" asked Inyx. "In all my travels, never have I seen its like."

"We take it from two sides at the same time. Maybe lopping its head off will do something. The way those eyes flash on and off makes me think it might have a brain of some sort, even if we can't see anything in its head but a small black box."

Then the time for talking passed. The skeletal being lashed out with the left chain. Lan danced aside and slashed viciously at a steel wrist with his blade. Sparks danced as contact was made, but the sword refused to penetrate and slithered down the creature's arm, leaving only a shining nick as evidence of the blow. Lan's entire arm had been numbed by the force of the stroke. He barely recovered in time to avoid the chain swinging in a short arc for his legs.

Inyx used a massive two-handed overhead blow to embed her sword in the right-arm socket of the robotic thing. Placing her foot against the skeletal leg, she twisted. Her blade snapped clean and left the attacking scrap pile with only impaired dexterity in its right arm.

164 ROBERT E. VARDEMAN

"What are we going to do? Krek? Can you . . ."
Lan ventured a hasty glimpse over his shoulder.
Krek silently defended them from one of the huge
metal bug shells rolling on four soft wheels. It
pulled back and shot forward, trying to crush Krek
under its weight. At least, that seemed its only
form of attack. Lan wished the same could be said
for his opponent.

A whistling arc of chain swept his feet from
under him. The pain lancing into his body almost
robbed him of consciousness, but Lan continued
to fight. He lunged awkwardly for the creature's
face. As his blade slid into where the mouth might
have been on a living being, an electric shock
jolted the blade from his hand. At the same instant, the creature jerked violently backward.

Inyx saw the reaction and pounced, her dagger
out and aimed for one of the glass eyes. A tinkling
noise sounded as the knife broke a crystyalline
eyeball. The robotic thing went berserk, thrashing
around, using the chains as much against itself as
to attack Inyx. Lan painfully pulled himself erect,
drew his dagger, and took careful aim. The blade
tumbled twice in midair and impacted firmly in
the creature's other glass eye. As if poleaxed, it
sank to the ground.

Lan stumbled, then steadied himself. Inyx rubbed
her arm where a wicked welt colored as the result
of too-close contact with the chain. She tossed Lan
his dagger, then pulled her own free from the
shattered socket.

Lan considered giving her his sword to replace
her shattered one, then knew with innate certainty
that the proud woman would refuse it. Their eyes
met and locked for an instant, and a silent communication flowed between them, the reassuring
message of one ally to another. He sheathed his
sword as she averted her eyes.

"I'm glad this is over," she said. Then, eyes widening, she turned and yelled: "Krek!"

Lan had forgotten about their furry friend. He twisted and looked at the spider in time to see it catch the front of the attacking metal bug and flip it over. Twin snips from huge mandibles cut cables underneath to ensure immobility.

Lan glanced back at the fallen metal skeleton as if afraid it might spring back to life, then went to Krek and lightly asked, "Do you spiders keep a trophy of your kill? If so, I'd like to present you with a wheel." He hefted one of the beetle-thing's soft wheels and tossed it to the spider.

Krek caught it easily between his mandibles. He squeezed the rubbery ring, then cast it aside.

"No good. Too chewy."

Lan laughed, and Velika came up beside him and joined in. For a brief instant, anger surged in him. Why should she enjoy the camaraderie they shared along with the danger? She had hidden and had not helped in the common defense. Then he forgot his irritation. Her kiss was wet and passionate against his lips, promising much more when the situation was right.

"My hero!" she whispered hotly in his ear. Embarrassed by Krek's and Inyx's glares, he pushed her away and said, "Later. We've got to find the Road. Then . . ."

"Yes, then!" she smiled, looking at him with adoration shining brighter than the lantern in the darkness.

"I feel its pull. It is close," Krek said. "Yes, even in my debilitated condition, I sense its nearness. It is as if it opens and closes like a door."

Lan felt the throbbing headache pummel his head. It had come as if a switch had been thrown. Even he sensed the immense power released nearby.

They turned and walked toward the nexus of power.

CHAPTER TEN

Lan Martak ran forward to take the glowing crystal globe in his hands. A definite radiation exuded from the pulsating sphere that pulled him closer the way a magnet attracts iron filings. His eyes caught vagrant moonbeams dancing in the depths of the globe and followed them inward, down into infinity. Nothing mattered quite as much as actually possessing this wonderous door to other worlds.

Without straining, he felt power rippling through his being. He saw new worlds, he saw different futures, he witnessed the slow parade of a million histories. He held the power of the Resident of the Pit. He knew now what eternity meant. Worlds were his for the taking. He blinked and universes changed before him. The smallest particles, the largest worlds, all were his.

"Stop, friend Lan Martak," came Krek's quivering voice. "I do not know the nature of this device, but it *is* Waldron's answer to the Road. Woe is me. I should have paid more attention to my mentor when she instructed me on such things as the Road, but no, lazy and foolish, I simply allowed such knowledge to slip through my feeble brain." The spider vented a human-sounding sigh that lightly touched Lan's face and brought him back to his senses.

The orb, pinkly warm and appearing soft rather than glassy-hard, still drew him closer, but now he successfully resisted the pull. Studying it more carefully, he witnessed a cavalcade of worlds flashing through the ball, each a separate reality beckoning to him, offering him things no other world could. The temptation to walk the Road soared inside him again.

"That's all we sought?" came Velika's petulant voice. "I've seen treasures far exceeding that. Why, Lan's jeweled casket taken from him by those awful grey soldiers was worth more than this."

"Judge not by appearance," snapped Inyx. "I'd trade an empire for this. How a knave such as Waldron came by such a fine piece of magic, I'll never know."

"It's of no use to us! Who'd buy it? And who wants to leave this world to go stumbling among others? This world is enough for any sane person." Velika gripped Lan's arm even harder, but he barely listened to her pleas.

Magic, yes, and he felt the flux all around him now. His magic-sensing ability had returned in full force, so much so that his head ached horribly and his eyes felt as if they'd been placed in burning vises. Powerful spells were used in complex ways to generate this globe of transition. He knew that the Cenotaph Road demanded the personal energies of a person of great heroism and death-honored but unfulfilled by actual burial. Whatever the spells cast over an empty grave, they tied down that person's essential bravery and soul-force to an eternity of maintaining a gateway between worlds. Some led one way, like the first he'd taken into the bog world. Others were so potent they opened both ways. Still others were rumored to span several worlds, so great was the power and honor of the unburied dead.

But this globe . . .

Lan saw at least a score of worlds passing in panoramic review. He wanted to learn all he could of this masterwork of sorcery, attune himself to it, and then follow the Road to each and every world shown. Velika might protest at first, but Lan knew they'd explore together where none from this world had trodden before. He felt a tightness in his throat as he thought of the blond woman, and again he experienced the twisting inside he couldn't explain. She did things to him, that woman. The tension had made him giddy, nothing more, he told himself.

Or was it only tension?

"This is what I needed years ago," said Inyx in a hushed, almost reverent tone. "To walk randomly among the worlds is folly when one can choose with this."

"Yes," agreed Krek, "my own journey would have been immensely easier using such a device. My precious energies need not have been squandered fleeing shadows caused by fire and damp. Surely a world exists in that vista where neither flame nor water exists. What a find it would be! Sheer paradise for these creaking joints."

"I am glad you approve of my toy," came a cold voice from above. They looked at one another, then elevated their gaze to where Waldron Ravensroost leaned indolently against the balcony railing, one elbow resting on a rude wooden box. "Your triumphs in my little maze astonished me, to be sure. I was particularly amused by your confrontation with the metallic skeleton, a remnant from one of the most mechanized worlds inside that."

His finger pointed to the depths of the pinkly pulsating crystalline globe. A shimmer like heat across desert sands came and then a gradual focusing until one specific world snapped into clarity. Millions of darting mechanical devices purred and whined and screeched back and forth, raising such a din that Lan placed both hands over his ears for protection.

"Ah, you do not like that world, eh? Let us try another. From my study of the Kinetic Sphere, I suspect you are native to this world." With no discernible motion on Waldron's part, the globe obeyed his spoken command. A jumble of colors, a silent, thick wind stirring the viscous mass, then Lan's world came into view with heart-wrenching pellucidity. One of the demon-powered cars chuffed along, frozen mist on the bottom of the boiler while steam plumes arched high overhead from the dual stacks. And sitting ramrod-straight in the carriage was the old sheriff, looking apprehensive being so close to the symbol of progress on his world.

Straining, Lan imagined he heard the old man's rough voice.

"No," said Waldron, "you cannot speak to him, nor he to you. One day I shall learn to control that feature of the Kinetic Sphere. Until I do, all that is open to me is searching out the locations where I and my men enter a new world. That, by the way, is a likely world for our Great Migration. Pleasant, the people are relatively unwarlike, and the abundances of food already flow to feed my people."

"Who manufactured this . . . Kinetic Sphere . . . for you?" demanded Lan. "This thing is beyond your power."

"I sense meaning to your use of the word 'power' that escapes me. But I shall be frank with you. A mage named Medolinev or Shastry, or possibly even L'ao Shu or Claybore, is responsible. He who constructed it is loath to give voice to his proper name for fear I would gain power over him." Waldron laughed harshly, changed elbows on the wooden box resting on the balcony railing, and added, "As if that matters to him now. But he refused to share this fine gift with my people, so . . ." A careless gesture of Waldron's hand across his throat indicated what had happened to the niggardly magician. "You continue to amaze me, though, in that you sensed my inability to construct such a device. How did you know? A guess?"

"Hardly. I've been around magic-users all my life and, while I'm unable to cast more than elementary spells, I can feel *power* around me. You are lacking."

"Lacking in that form of power, perhaps, but not in others. I tire of this conversation, so allow me to congratulate you on pleasing me for so many hours during your journey through the maze. People walking between worlds as you did seldom survive, although the actual distance you traversed is less than ten yards."

"We'll continue to survive, eater of small children!" raged Inyx, her hand pulling at her dagger.

"Alas, I cannot oblige you that minor request. You have two choices open to you. My captivity until I decide how you might be of best use to me or random passage along the Road."

"The Road!" cried Inyx.

"Yes, if my weak legs will carry me forward," agreed Krek.

"Come, Velika, let's go through the gateway while it's open," said Lan, pulling at the woman's hand. But she refused to move. Yanking harder as Inyx and Krek advanced on the Kinetic Sphere and the curtain of radiant energy now surrounding it, Lan found himself off balance and stumbling. He slipped and bowled over Krek. The giant spider's wildly thrashing limbs sent Inyx tumbling. Velika stood over the pile of bodies and shook her head.

"Better a dungeon than being lost in that welter of crazy, dangerous worlds!" she cried out, tears flowing copiously down her cheeks. Lan started to go to her, but some inner force held him back, an inexplicable one akin to his intuitions about magic use. Those tears . . .

Inyx surged to her feet, but the globe had lost its lustre and the energy curtain had closed. No more coalescing colors in the ball; it remained inert, dead, shut to them. And the ring of crossbowmen assured her that fighting now was tantamount to suicide. Turning on Lan, she screamed, "That bitch has signed our death warrants! I consign you both to the Lower Places for this!"

Lan Martak had no answer, for he felt much the same about Velika's reluctance to walk the Road. It had just cost them all their freedom—and their lives.

"Hmmm, such a motley group you are," said Waldron, looking down at the four in chains. As Krek rattled his bindings ominously, several of the guards insinuated themselves between the giant spider and their liege lord. Waldron shifted the wooden box he carried so that it safely rested under his arm, then made a vague gesture in the air with his free hand as he said, "It's all right, men. My armorer assures me even this ponderous creature will be unable to break through the special steel chains on all of his legs."

"Begging your gracious pardon, Saviour, but the armorer also assured us that the other spider could not escape the chamber in which he placed it. It took less than an hour for the beast to break entirely free and escape."

Waldron's face tightened.

"Why wasn't I informed of that immediately? Damn that man! You, Commander Ells, remove the armorer and find a suitable replacement. And report back to me afterward."

The indicated soldier, dressed in the grey of Waldron's army, bowed to his liege and backed out, bobbing his head in agreement. The other stirred nervously, glanced at Krek, and obviously doubted the strength of the chains on all eight furry legs.

The soldier jumped when Krek clacked his mandibles together and said, "Lovely Klawn has escaped! How wonderous!"

Waldron straightened his courtly robes and held out his gloved hand. A caw and a flutter of wings, then a large raven perched impudently on his wrist. He stroked the greasy feathers and talked quietly to the large bird.

"You wouldn't allow such a tasty, oversized morsel to do me harm, would you?" The answering caw sounded more like laughter from a demented fiend than the normal screech of a bird.

"My human guards are fallible, but my winged ones aren't. They protect me with their very lives— and have done so. But this audience draws overlong. I see that it isn't possible to imprison the likes of you," he said, peering at Krek past the black bird flapping for balance on his wrist, "so that eliminates several possibilities."

"You said you'd let us walk the Road you opened in the chamber. It was a mistake that we didn't. Allow us another chance," said Lan, fearing all was lost. The answer sealed their fate.

"No." Harsh, flat, final. "The decision has been made. A moment's leniency weakened me. For a time I thought your bravery should be rewarded. Or perhaps that I could use you. Since you killed Kyn-alLyk-Surepta, I require a native of your world to act as liaison in my continued dealings there."

"Betray my world to you?" raged Lan.

"Yes, that's the reaction I predicted. Hence, death for all four of you." Waldron moved the raven to a padded shoulder perch and shifted the wood box again.

"Lord, no!" pleaded Velika, throwing herself at the man's feet. She reached out and touched the soles of his boots imploringly. "Anything but that, master. Anything!"

"Anything?" he echoed, then laughed. "You offer

yourself in exchange for these others?" Waldron waved aside Lan's protest before it even came to his lips.

"No, master, I offer myself wholeheartedly and ask for nothing in return." Tears ran in ever-increasing rivers down her cheeks. Waldron brushed one away, then stiffened slightly, his face turning into a mask with unreadable emotions. He shook slightly as he again touched the tear-stained cheek, then straightened.

"Direct, to the heart of the matter, yes," he mused, rubbing his chin with one hand while bouncing the flapping raven with the other. "Very well, blond seductress. I am sure that Kyn-alLyk-Surepta enjoyed many pleasures with you before he died."

"And I can show you ever so many more, master, if you'll allow it." Velika's eyes shone with fear as she mouthed the words. Lan wanted to silence her, prevent her from degrading herself further, but the guards and the chains effectively stopped him.

"Chamberlain," Waldron called out. "A point of protocol. Since Diamerra died of the cold last winter, I have been without wife. Should I happen to take this woman, who is not of our world, must it be as legal wife?"

An old man dressed in flowing grey robes shuffled up and turned tired eyes to Waldron.

"Saviour, this need not be so. This world and two others under your aegis allow concubines."

"Concubines," said Waldron, rolling the word over his tongue as if it were new to him. "Yes, that might be the answer to this vexing dilemma. On this world I will take a concubine." To Velika, he asked, more gently, "What is your name, flaxen-haired one?"

"Velika L'spurota, master."

"The proper form of address is 'Saviour,'" said

the dour chamberlain. "He has delivered all our
people from great sadness and, for this service to
our bleak world, will live forever on our hearth and
in our heart." It sounded like a litany the man had
learned and was now tired of repeating.

"Saviour! Yes, you are my saviour!" babbled
Velika. "Anything you desire of me will be yours."

"I am pleased," said Waldron dryly, "especially
since I can take it whether you desire it or not.
Never mind that. The other three. Take them to
the north tower and execute them at first light.
That much I will grant since I have no quarrel
with any of them."

"No quarrel and you would still murder us?"
bellowed Lan. "What manner of beast are you?"

"Silence, fool," hissed the chamberlain. "He could
have you executed now while it is still dark and
allow the demons to devour your souls. The Saviour
does you great favor by allowing the sunlight to
drive off the demons before removing your spiteful
heads."

The last thing Lan Martak heard as they dragged
him from the audience chamber was Velika's soft
purring, "Anything at all for my wondrous saviour!"

He wondered what evil magic Waldron had used
on the woman he loved to turn her so much against
her will.

"You deceive yourself if you really think that,
Lan," declared Inyx, trying to keep her voice gentle, and failing. The harshness crept in and made
her words sting more than she intended.

"You're wrong, I tell you, wrong! Velika did it to
save us. There's no other reason she'd go to
Waldron's bed so swiftly. She is plotting our escape even now. How could she do it if she were
thrown in here with us?"

"She might be a simple whore," observed Krek.

The spider bobbed out of the way as Lan took a vicious swing at him. "Are you upset over this possibility, friend Lan Martak? I merely stated what seems a fact. You humans have the oddest sensibilities to offend. The very concept of whoredom amuses me, and I have oft thought on it during the long nights I spent alone along the Road. While I personally cannot conceive of Klawn being a whore, it would please me to find one like her who could give me the same amount of sheer bliss and then not demand to devour me afterward. Yes, that would be quite nice."

Lan rattled his chains savagely as he paced the confines of the narrow tower cell. The three slits in the stone walls looked out over the castle, but, under the cloak of darkness, there was little of interest to see. Lan still pressed his face close and peered down in the vain hope of seeing Velika sneaking across the courtyard, keys to their chains dangling from her slender fingers.

"She will come. She has to. I know she will," Lan repeated to himself.

"While he's mooning over a traitorous bitch, let's figure out our own escape, Krek," said Inyx, seating herself next to one of the spider's furred legs. She rested against the post-thick leg and rubbed her back until her muscle strain eased. "These offensive chains are the key to our escape, as I see it. We can do nothing as long as we wear the shackles of a tyrant."

"Oh?" Krek said mildly. "Is that all we have to do to escape this drafty, damp place?"

"Well, not all, but . . . aieee!" Inyx looked stupidly at her severed chains. Krek's mandibles had made one swift snap and left only shining metal where one link had been. She lifted the bracelet on her left wrist so that Krek could snap the metal without injuring her. In a double flash of chitinous material, her wrists were free. She sprang to her feet and whooped loudly.

"Friend Krek, you are a marvel!" she crowed. "That is the slickest cut of hardened steel I have ever witnessed. You should rent yourself as a blacksmith's assistant. For a modicum of work, you could earn a young fortune!"

Lan turned dull eyes to them and said, "He could've done that a long time ago. He's versatile," then went back to his lonely vigil at the window.

"Let him cut your chains, Lan; then we'll figure how to get out of here!"

"I tell you Velika has a plan to free us. If we just wait, she'll free us and we can all four be gone from this pest-ridden castle and that bird-loving Waldron."

"Unless my eyes deceive me, friend Lan Martak, it lacks but a few minutes of dawn. Waldron seems nothing if not totally efficient in his slaughter. Linger much longer and we all die. And I am too insignificant a spider to come to such a fate. Please, Lan Martak, save me. Inyx? Lan?"

The tone made Lan turn and see a huge, salty tear forming at the corner of a limpid eye. He sighed in defeat and dejectedly held out his wrists.

"Snip 'em off, and hurry. You're right about the time. I just don't know what delayed Velika."

"She's probably having too much fun in Waldron's bed," Inyx muttered under her breath. The words were drowned out by the metallic snicks as Krek severed the last of Lan's shackles. Louder, so both Lan and Krek heard, she said, "Do we overpower the guards when they come for us? These lengths of chain hardly seem adequate weapons, although the metallic skeleton used them dextrously enough back in Waldron's maze. Or do we attempt to escape in some other way?"

Lan pointed to the window through which he'd kept his futile watch for Velika.

"Down the wall to the courtyard. It's still empty. We might be able to win free through the main gate from there."

"Down that wall? You're insane. It's too sheer. Why, the surface is slick glass. Not even fully outfitted for mountain scaling could I get down that way!"

"We don't have to scale it, just get down it. Krek? Honor us with a bit of web spinning." Lan watched as the spider emitted a coughing noise and began generating yard after yard of strong silken cable. In a few minutes, the pile on the floor reached up to Inyx's knees.

"Is this sturdy enough?" she asked dubiously.

"My dear lady!" said Krek, puffing himself up and banging the ceiling of the small chamber. "I am Webmaster of the Egrii Mountains, and this is the finest silk you shall ever see. Humph!"

"Sorry," apologized Inyx. "This does seem strong. Shall I go first?"

"Go on," said Lan, realizing this was Inyx's way of gaining forgiveness from the spider. "Krek will come down last."

He helped Inyx into the narrow window slit, his hands almost encircling her trim waist. For the first time he marvelled at her litheness, her strength, even her muliebrity. Then she dropped over the edge and adeptly swung lower and lower on the silken cable. When she touched the ground, Lan followed. Her hands were most welcome to guide him into the dense shadows at the base of the tower. Krek came hurtling down, descending the sheer wall ten times faster than either of them had dared.

Legs spread widely around his thick body, Krek sighed. "One day, I shall have the opportunity to rest. Just me, swinging to and fro in a simple yet elegant web, the soft, warm wind caressing me, making me feel less old, less tired, more like my original youthful self."

"Sure, Krek, sure you will, but let's talk about it later. After we're out of here." Lan glanced around nervously, wanting to see Velika's trim form, fearing to find a guard patrol instead.

"One moment," Krek said. He whistled and spat out a long streamer of gooey material that clung to the silk cable. In a few seconds, the silken strands were totally eaten away and all trace of their escape route erased. "Now, do we tread wearily on the Road once again? I sense that Waldron has reopened the route."

Lan pressed a hand to his head, knowing that Krek was right. The dull, throbbing ache between his ears seemed a sure indication of the artificial Road's coming back into existence. Still he balked at travelling it again.

"We've got to rescue Velika. It won't take long. She'll be in Waldron's private chambers. We . . ."

"We'll be shorter by a head if we stay," hissed Inyx. "Look and tell me how to fend off so many— and us without weapons?"

The troops marching in perfect syncopation stopped in front of the locked door leading up into the prison tower. The commander fumbled out a key, then ordered his men inside. The door locked again to thwart any escape of his supposed prisoners, the officer led his men up the spiralling staircase.

"Seconds, friend Lan Martak, before they discover our apparent dematerialization," said Krek. "I would like to stay and see you through your pointless excursion to rescue the lumpy human female, but my weakness and quivering fear overwhelm me. Please forgive me."

"And I am with him, Lan," declared Inyx firmly. "I refuse to watch Waldron's talons close around us still another time, and all for that worthless whore of yours."

"She's no whore!" blurted Lan. Then he calmed. He took a deep breath and slowly released it. He had to admit they had a point. Waldron was not stupid; he would not allow them to escape still another time if he caught them now. While Lan didn't agree with Krek and Inyx about Velika's merits or lack of them, he saw it was unfair and dangerous to insist they stand beside him while he attempted a rescue.

"The Road opens again," Krek told them. "A huge flow of power surges between worlds. It makes the fur on my legs bristle, so great is the force."

Lan nodded, his head pulsing strongly and making it difficult for him to think clearly. Why did the gate open now, just when he needed the clarity of his senses to rescue Velika? He hardly noticed Inyx pulling him along through the deserted courtyard until they were outside a blackened door, the product of some raging fire long forgotten save by the tortured grain of wood.

"Inside is the Kinetic Sphere," said Krek. "My abilities to find other Roads are blurred by its stark power."

"I'll be leaving you here, Krek. Good Luck, old spider." Lan stroked fondly over the fur of the leg nearest him, then turned to Inyx. "And I'm sorry to be leaving you, too. I can't help but feel things might have been different in a less strained circumstance." Lan bathed in the radiance of her smile and realized for the first time how lovely Inyx truly was. Shakily, he held out his hand and was surprised to find her pull him close for a proper kiss.

"I shall miss your bullheaded ways, you stupid fool," she said softly, but without sting of sarcasm. Lan wanted to say just the right words, but none came.

"Lan Martak, we are trapped!" came Krek's warning. Lan shot a glance over his shoulder in time to see the commander of Waldron's guard run from the prison tower, scan the courtyard, and spy them. A shout caused a drowsy sentry to ring the warning bell and rapidly fill the castle grounds with sleep-dazed, half-armed men. When the grey-clad soldiers came fully awake, the trio would find themselves prisoners once again—unless the gateway produced by the Kinetic Sphere still quivered open between worlds.

"That's the door. Hurry!" Lan cried, pushing the others in front of him. It proved difficult herding Krek, but necessity lent strength to his efforts. Slamming the door behind, he searched frantically for a locking bolt. There was none.

"The Road is still open," said Inyx. "Quickly, Lan, let's all tread that path again."

"Get going," he ordered. "I'll hold them as long as I can. And don't stand around arguing."

"He is lamentably correct, friend Inyx. Go and forge ahead for us. We shall come shortly."

Inyx nodded, then ran for the shimmering curtain drawn between them and the ball. It seemed a perfect stereographic projection, each point on the surface of the sphere corresponding to a point on the planar sheet of dancing, scintillant energy. Inyx plunged through, vanishing from the sight of the two remaining behind.

"Go on, Krek, before Waldron shuts the damned thing down and strands you here, too."

"I go. Hold tightly," he said cryptically. Krek trotted to the edge of the gateway, then shot out a sticky strand of the web stuff that curled around Lan's middle. He continued holding the door shut against the increasing efforts of the soldiers outside. Lan then felt himself jerked into the air and sliding along the smooth floor toward the interworld portal. Krek bounded through, and Lan followed, a human balloon on a string.

The entire world turned black, then shattered around him. He thought his head had exploded, then worried that it hadn't and he'd gone insane. The pain finally drove away consciousness, and soothing dark velvet wrapped soft arms around him in silent greeting.

CHAPTER ELEVEN

A herd of multilegged beasts cavorted joyfully on his head. Lan Martak put his arms over his head to protect himself from their manic depradations, but this did no good. If anything, it increased the roar and pain inside his skull. Opening his eyes didn't prove as traumatic for him as he'd feared from the interior throbbings. The dismal greyness surrounding him was almost soothing. Then came the grating harshness of human voices.

"He'll be fine in a while. Took a nasty blow to the head as you dragged him through."

"I suspect my feeble efforts are not so much to blame as the closing of the gateway just fractions of a second after he came through to this side."

"That might be true. Even I felt the vortex of energy seething around the path, and in the past I've never been particularly sensitive to such things."

Lan rolled over and peered at the two. Inyx sat, her feet neatly tucked under her, facing Krek. Beyond was a world lacking contrasts. The sky stretched a leaden grey as if rains were imminent, the grass shone with an odd mottled greyish-green, the trees sported redolent, brittle swordlike leaves hardly differing in hue from the grass, and the very air hung with scummy grey particulate matter, the residue from too many coal and wood fires. The only thing colorful in the entire world was the red pain searing through his head like a heated battle ax.

"I assume we made it," he said slowly, the words thick and muddled. "Unless this is our reward for a lifetime of sin and evildoing. It looks too much like the bog world for it to be anything else."

"A reward it might be, but we still live," pointed out Inyx. "Waldron failed to cut off the Road soon enough to prevent our passage. I cannot be sure, but I think a heavy wagon passed along just before us, one laden with all types of foodstuffs."

"The mention of food reminds me how feeble I have become. It seems years since a good meal of grubs and bugs rested lightly in my digestive tract. Let us find sustenance, then discuss more worldly matters," urged Krek.

"I think the spider has a good idea. Can you move yet, Lan?"

"Whether I can or not, we'd better make tracks away from here. If Waldron sends a patrol after us through the gateway, they are sure to find us if we simply lie around." He peered around, wondering why Waldron had chosen this particular area for establishing a roadway through his Kinetic Sphere into Krek's web world. There seemed little to recommend the location other than the brownish ribbon of dirt road slithering off toward the gently hillocked horizon. A heavy grey-green pall swirled in eddies no matter which direction Lan peered.

They staggered along for some time until Krek accumulated enough small insects to form a brief repast. Inyx ordered Lan to rest while she hunted food for them. The throbbing in his head had cleared, but he was grateful for her offer. He even slept, only to awaken with the smell of roast rabbit in his nostrils.

"This seems an unappetizing world, save for the rabbit," he said. "Never have I seen such featureless terrain, lacking in color, texture, and character. Even the bog world I met Krek on held some little variation."

"And the air is thick with ugly odors, too," Inyx

added. "Friend Krek is luckier than we on that score."

"Lucky, you call it? When such small bugs are all I can find to eat? Why, I shall surely starve to death in a fortnight without proper food. I am already weakened to the point of starvation, and the distance from my web further saps my strength. Oh, how do I find myself in these impossible situations?"

"You cast your lot with us," said Lan dryly. "But what world is this? Can it truly be Waldron's home? I thought a conqueror's world offered something more than this spent countryside."

He attacked the burnt rabbit with the ferocity of a man too long gone past his mealtime. The grease only added flavor; it seemed at odds with the blandness of the world. After he and Inyx had shared the meager portion of the brains for dessert, Lan leaned back against the smooth trunk of a tree and picked his teeth with a small bone taken from the rabbit's leg. In spite of the fact that Waldron probably had droves of grey-clad soldiers on their trail, he felt complacent and even content with his lot in life.

"No reason why not. In point of fact, friend Lan Martak, we might query those starvelings about it."

The roadway rumbled with the sound of a lop-sided dogcart with wear-flattened wheels being pulled by two people. Their heads held low, they saw nothing but the dirt in the road bed. Lan called out to them, then waved, saying under his breath, "Vanish for a short while, Krek. We don't want to scare them too badly."

The spider gusted a sigh. "Even my friends are ashamed of me. Pity that I am such a poor creature, unable to fight the good fight, to maintain myself in the manner to which I would like to become accustomed." Then, after he seemed no more than an inert rock in the grey countryside, he added, "Ask for any insects they might have on them."

Lan shuddered when the pair drew closer. The only bugs likely to come from these two would be body lice.

"Welcome, fellow travellers," Lan called out in what he hoped was a cheerful tone. The suspicion with which the two viewed him made him think a picture warrant for his arrest had preceded him. Yet the reactions of the two seemed more of inbred rampant paranoia than specific fear.

"Are you from the other side?" asked the woman, taking the initiative while her man stood watch over the pitiful belongings stacked helter-skelter on the dogcart.

"Yes, we both walked the Road," said Inyx, motioning Lan to silence. He propped himself against the tree, hoping to appear at ease and not a threat to these people. Without sword or dagger, his head still ringing like a ceremonial bell, either of these two emaciated grey-worlders might have bested him.

"You look well fed. I suspected that you did," the woman said. Lan tried to figure out if she were old or merely appeared old. It made little difference; life was obviously harsh on this world.

"We have been most recently in King Waldron's castle on the next world," Inyx said boldly, hoping this would add stature to their position with the couple.

"Aye, and that's a good thing. The Saviour needs to keep his finger on the world pulse. Are you to report back to him? You have the look of couriers, though you don't wear the uniform of the Service."

"We are supposed to go among the people and listen to their pleas. Could you tell us yours?"

"That I will," spoke up the man for the first time. "Hail the Saviour! Praise the great Waldron!

We are currently making way to the new settlement outside Ligginton. The wealth of other worlds flows into this one, at long last! Bless the day of our Saviour's birth!"

"And bless the day when we, too, can take part in the Great Migration and leave this miserable world for other, lusher ones," the old woman added.

"You were more poorly off before?" asked Inyx, surprised anyone's condition could be more miserable than these two now appeared.

"Aye, that we were. Seven sons and a daughter died of starvation, and my very own mother failed of the consumption, spitting out blackened lungs for a solid month before the demons took her. Breathing the foul air did it to her, it did."

"Foul air from what?" broke in Lan, curious.

"From the forges, man, from the steel mills, from the factories, from every damn thing burning peat. But with the new gas wells capped off and the food and finery from the conquered worlds acoming in, we have hope of surviving."

"So you feel Waldron is truly your Saviour?" asked Inyx.

"Aye, that he is," chimed in the man. "Bless him!"

"Shut up, Gorly," the old woman said tiredly. "Aye, Waldron of Ravensroost brings life to this exhausted world. Without him only misery would be our destiny. He was smart enough, he was, to grab that sorcerer that came awandering through from another world and make him spit up the secret of the other places."

"Sorcerer? You mean Shastry or Claybore?" asked Lan, vainly tying to remember the other names Waldron had so casually mentioned.

"Never heard his name, lad. But he plundered at will, taking even from poor folk like Gorly and me, until Waldron put an end to it. And discovering the Road, he calls it, opened up a source of food and clothing for us."

"Food and clothing not around here. Bless the Saviour. Long live Waldron!"

"Shut up Gorly," the old woman said.

They truly believed Waldron to be their Saviour. No trace of guile existed; both meant the praise they gave for Waldron. Lan prodded the woman by asking, "Do you know Waldron lives lavishly on the other world?"

"Aye, he comes back to speak with us now and again. He's promised that we will all one day have such finery. Why, he even gave Gorly here a golden ring. Show these couriers, Gorly." She nudged the man in the ribs with a scrawny elbow.

The man fumbled in his pocket until he produced the end of a leather thong. Pulling, he fished out a massive ring inset with a precious stone. He proudly allowed it to spin slowly just below eye level.

"Why don't you trade that for food? It's worth a young fortune."

"Trade it? You hear that, Gorly? Trade it, the young one says. You are long away from this world. There is naught to trade for. Our poor farm produced scarcely food for one, much less the pair of us—and we were the most successful in the old Thull Valley. Nay, the new settlement is enriched with alien fertilizers and food is abundant, wagons coming in every day from conquered worlds. And there is even rumor we will no longer burn peat to keep from freezing. Magic from the other worlds will warm us. They even trade the gases from the swamps for other-world goods not sent in proper tribute to our Saviour. Imagine! They use our swamp farts!"

"I see," said Inyx, slowly assimilating the wealth of information she'd received. "I am sure the Saviour will smile on you again. And may you have more children."

"Pah! I am no fool. If we get food enough to fill our bellies, why add to the problem with more mouths? Come, Gorly, let's be off. If we make Ligginton before sunset, we can feed this day."

The two hefted the sidepoles and began pulling their pathetic cart along the dusty road leading to their chimerical city filled with such unbelievable commodities as food and warm shelter.

When they were out of sight, Krek rose up and stretched cramped legs. He yawned once, clacking his mandibles together, and finally said, "It seems evil Waldron is a saint to his people. I must admit this is a most dismal world. Why, even the mere-spiders spin paltry webs, as if their hearts aren't in the endeavor."

"This is a tired, overused world," said Inyx. "But it is wrong to loot adjoining worlds along the Road for the betterment of this one." She looked around and shuddered. "But why can't they add some color other than grey? This is *so* depressing."

"I agree about that," muttered Lan. "Krek? Find us another cenotaph to get off this world and onto another, more hospitable one."

"You have given up your futile quest to regain the treasure lost and that Velika female?"

"No," Lan said slowly. "But I'll be in a better position to launch an attack against Waldron after I've had some substantial food and a nice bed to catch up on lost sleep. This world cannot furnish those, so I'll recuperate, then rescue Velika."

"As if she needed rescuing," snorted Inyx. "That's one bitch who can roll with the punches and come to her feet. Or rather, end up on her back. Never have I seen such selfishness or viciousness."

"In Velika?" asked Lan, startled. "Hardly. She's quite the opposite, in fact. She can hardly protect herself in the world Waldron's created. And you are a fine one to talk of bloodthirstiness. I've seen you swinging a sword and slaughtering soldiers left and right."

"At least my ruthlessness is open, not under the covers like Velika's."

"You misjudge her." Lan lapsed into silence, worried at the way both Krek and Inyx felt about Velika. While he had hardly been charmed by her disavowal of them in front of Waldron, he was positive that had been part of an abortive plan on Velika's part to rescue them all. Something had gone wrong; that was why she had failed to free them from the prison tower before their execution time. Lan felt his innards twisting about in confusion. A burning sensation, more from memory than physical reality, stung his lips, his fingertips. His head ached horribly and threatened to explode like a bomb with his internal emotional conflicts—and he didn't even know what the opposing sides were, much less what they fought over. He hadn't the objectivity to study it, nor the time. He had to decide this matter once and for all time.

Velika wasn't the vicious schemer Inyx pictured her as. Velika's failure to free them in time proved that. Otherwise she'd have succeeded easily in getting them out of their chains and Waldron's castle.

"Where's the cenotaph leading off this world, Krek?" repeated Inyx. "I tire of this dreary world—and the company we're keeping."

"Everyone tires of my company because I am such a pitiable creature. And I am sure you will heap further indignities on my head when I tell you that there is no cenotaph on this world that opens the Road. Only Waldron's artificial gateway impinges on my muzzy mind."

"That figures." Inyx sighed. "No one of sufficient bravery has ever existed on this world to create the confined energies needed to open the

Road. They're probably all too busy scuttling out a living from the thin soil to go adventuring."

"That means we've got to go back through Waldron's gate or we'll be marooned here. That's why Waldron hasn't sent his soldiers. He knows we're trapped on his home world." Lan reached for his sword and found only emptiness. Fighting back to the other world—and Velika—seemed more difficult with each passing second.

"Still another wagon of food and clothing," said Inyx, squinting slightly into the afternoon glare. The grey clouds had lifted a little but not enough to bolster their flagging spirits. The armed guards standing on either side of the shimmering curtain of pure energy effectively barred their return. They might kill one or two of the grey-clad soldiers, but to eliminate all five in such a way that an alarm wasn't raised appeared impossible. Waldron's skill as a general showed even in small details such as sentry duty.

Inyx had scouted the countryside while Lan had rested, finding the reason for the gateway's existence here. The town of Ligginton lay only a few miles down the road. Through the gate passed food to supply the city, such as it was. Inyx reported that the town consisted of little more than hovels pushed together to share common walls.

The idea that this polluted, overcrowded, dirty, ill-supplied city was superior to a farm had revolted her. Yet that seemed to be the case.

"I shall sacrifice myself," announced Krek. "I am too cowardly to kill myself. This will redeem me in your eyes for all my past cowardices. Oh, why am I such a disgrace to all spiderdom?" He wailed like wind curling through an aeolian harp. Lan felt the dejection, too, but didn't show it. He didn't want to further depress the spider.

"A possibility exists," said Inyx, after considering the situation for a few more minutes. "Can the guards see through the hindside of the path opened by Waldron?"

"We can see into the other world. I don't understand why they—of course! If all we can see from this side is the world to which the Road opens, then they can't see us sneaking up on them, using the gateway as a shield!" Lan felt more enthusiastic about their chances of returning than ever before. "Thay might not think to post men there, and if they did, we can remove them without the others seeing."

Walking up the hill using the Road as concealment proved easier than Lan had thought. He simply had to remember he could see the guards perfectly while they were unable to see him at all. Three guards fell before the other two noticed. And one jump from Krek, a lightning slash of mandibles, and the fight ended.

"A sword!" yelled Lan, holding it over his head and waving it in circles. "I feel dressed again." He stripped a pair of daggers off the bodies and said, "Through the Roadway before Waldron senses something amiss."

The passage back proved far easier than the prior one. A moment's vertigo and he stood in the black chamber containing the pinkly glowing Kinetic Sphere. Assaulting the limits of his vision wavered the actual projection of the gateway. He hefted his sword, then held aloft his left hand. A small chant produced flames licking from his fingers. A frightened yelp from Krek went unnoticed as he studied the now dimly lit chamber.

Lan had thought Krek's cry resulted from the sudden magical fire leaping from fingertip to fingertip. Now he saw real danger lurking just beyond sword's reach.

"Fardorus take me!" exclaimed Inyx, her blade dancing out in a complex maneuver to meet the attack of the ghostly creature. The substance of the wraith's body might have been in question, but the evil glint of the steel sword it brandished brooked no doubt about its death-dealing capabilities. Inyx parried, cut over, and parried again. A quick disengage carried her point through the misty body with no visible effect.

"Waldron raids the space between worlds for his soldiers now," she panted, maintaining a purely defensive fight. She slashed viciously across the insubstantial neck and almost lost her balance. The blade of the mist-creature sought out her flesh and left an ugly, deep cut that bled profusely.

He saw that simple sword play wouldn't destroy this being. Summoning his magical powers, Lan fed the full force of his being into the flame spell. Lances of fire blasted from his fingers and engulfed the vaporous spirit. It screamed wordlessly and popped! back into whatever world it had originated on.

Lan abandoned his flame-spell in favor of a healing chant directed at Inyx's wound. He closed to attack from the side when a shuffling noise alerted him of more immediate personal danger. He sidestepped the cyclopean giant confronting him, swung his blade, and employed a twist of the wrist to send the sword threatening Inyx's life cartwheeling through the air. He returned to his own defense in time to catch the point of the cyclops's pike on the edge of his own blade. As he dropped to his knee to combat the overwhelming power, he heard Inyx's blade whir and bite deeply into an unprotected side. The one-eyed giant bellowed and turned to face its new attacker. Lan's admiration for the monster's intelligence evaporated as he spitted it through the groin.

Both Lan and Inyx joined Krek in combatting a multiarmed beast. The creature lacked mobility, but it needed none. Apparently able to use nine swords effectively, it seemed able to fight to the last arm without moving. Lan changed his tactics and closed to sword and dagger distance. A quick bind carried two swords from his path, while his dagger pinned another. Inyx shot through the gap he'd formed and drove her blade into juicy, pulpy flesh. The nine-armed beast emitted a curious sigh and evaporated like fog in the morning sun, leaving only nine swords behind on the floor as mute reminder of its existence.

"We do well as a team, Lan," Inyx told him, clapping him heartily on the shoulder. He grunted wryly at the compliment, turning his attention to the wound-healing chant to close the gash on her arm. She glaced down at it as soon as she felt the magical fingers gently closing off tiny veins and arteries; then her eyes rose and locked with his for a moment. Again they recognized more than simple teamwork existing between them.

Uncomfortably, Inyx shifted about, no words coming to her lips. Lan finished his healing spell and felt the same strange need to speak and the inability to put his feelings to voice. Krek relieved both of their fumbling needs.

"We had best remove ourselves from this worldless place. We spiders usually love out-of-the-way interstices, but I fear my overwhelming weakness and outright cowardice will betray us all."

"Right, Krek. I . . ." and Lan felt the floor vanish from under him. As had happened before when they'd entered Waldron's dimensionless maze, he hung suspended light years above the slowly spinning galaxies as he began his plunge to infinity. But this time the vertigo didn't totally seize control of his senses and cause wild panic. Inyx's arm brushed his and gave a reference point to the real world.

Or was it the real world? Nothing seemed to belong to the reality with which he was accustomed. The very fighters sent against them by Waldron were phantasms, ghosts, creatures of dubious existence. Reality flowed like a clear stream in the springtime, sometimes overrunning its banks, while at other times drying up almost entirely. Could he be so sure he wasn't falling through space and time on an endless journey to death?

And if he fell long enough, mightn't he find that timeless place where the dead resided?

To find Zarella!

His heart raced at the thought of the lovely woman. The the heart's beating stilled to nothingness. She was only a wisp of memory to him now. Gone, long gone on a world also vanished from his reality. Tears welled in his eyes at the thought of never returning, yet he'd had his revenge on KynalLyk-Surepta. And it had been as ashes in his mouth.

The Resident of the Pit had been correct, all too correct. Surepta had found justice at his hand, but Lan felt no sense of revenge, of fulfillment at the other's death. And still he spun through the galaxies yawning under his feet, seeing the slow march of stars and worlds without number.

"I witnessed a duel of wizards on a world similar to this one," came Inyx's disembodied voice. "They turned the entire glade dark and sent us whirling through space at a furious rate. I closed my eyes and concentrated on what I knew had to be my proper surroundings."

Proper surroundings? Lan was uncertain what that was now. He belonged to the universe. He roved among the stars at will. He was lost in eternity.

But the woman's words kept repeating over and over in his mind. Lan screwed his eyes tightly shut and pictured the Kinetic Sphere pulsating with its almost obscene pseudolife, the ebon darkness of the surrounding room, the high-gloss floor, the fire-blackened door leading into the courtyard, other doors leading off into unknown directions. The dizziness passed, and he fought to maintain his mental picture against the new assaults on his senses. The interworld creatures couldn't harm him now; he had substance and they did not.

A sharp pain lanced through his leg. He stumbled and fell. He hazarded a quick look and saw a quarrel piercing his calf. Breaking off the squared head, he withdrew the shaft and tossed it away. Wherever it had come from, it wasn't from the nothingness of the wraith-dimension he fought his mental battles in.

"Why am I afflicted with this insane urge to leave my web?" moaned Krek. "I was happy. No spider could have been happier. I was content swinging across the Egrii Mountains. But no, fool that I am, I took to wandering. Oh, why, why!"

Inyx vanished from sight. Lan swallowed hard and fought down the pain rising in his leg like the ocean's surf. The illusions diminished in intensity, and Lan thought it might be due to the pain from his injury. Pain drove out all mirages of the mind. A scuffling noise drew his attention and the point of his sword. A muted cry, then a body fell lifeless to the floor.

"Thanks for your quick sword, Lan," the black-haired woman said. "I thought you were still whirling in your orbit around all space."

"To tell the truth, I was until that crossbowman pulled me back to the here and now." He grimaced and sat down on the floor to begin the healing chants.

Inyx crouched beside him, then looked up at Krek and said, "Guard us for a few minutes. His magics take too long to work." She ripped away his pants leg and used the material to expertly bind the wound. Although the quarrel had missed all important bones and tendons, the wound still burned as if infested by a hill of acid ants. "There," she said finally, "that'll take care of you for a short while. Later, when we have the time, you can chant away the cut with your spells."

"You're expert at this. It seems you spend as much time repairing me as you do fighting."

"I'm an old hand at both. Until my brothers were killed, I spent my spare time sewing them back together. And Reinhardt . . ." Her voice trailed off, and Lan saw the twinkling speck of an unshed tear forming in the corner of her eye.

"Reinhardt? One of your brothers?"

"My husband, now dead a full year and more." She stood and said sternly, "On your feet. We must still fight free of the castle."

She helped Lan to his feet, and he found he could walk—after a fashion. He wondered how much more fighting would be necessary for escape.

And to rescue Velika.

CHAPTER TWELVE

"I can't believe we were allowed out of the chamber so easily," worried Inyx. "That is unlike Waldron."

"Easy?" asked Lan. "What do you mean, easy? We fought for our very lives back there. We could have been killed at any instant." The dull pain in his calf told him exactly how near a brush with death he'd had. He didn't like Inyx even thinking it had been too easy to escape from Waldron's treachery.

Yet . . .

A thought niggled. He felt something amiss, though not the ease of their escape. At every turn, he had expected Velika to appear, breathless and flushed, newly escaped from Waldron's clutches. Some minor detail relating to the blond woman and Waldron bothered him. The expression on the man's face as his hand touched Velika's tears. Unconsciously, Lan rubbed his own fingers over his grimy, bloodstained tunic, then stopped guiltily, as if caught at some unclean act. The confidence Waldron had shown had been wiped out in an instant—turned to confusion—by the blond woman. Lan couldn't figure out what that meant. He'd reacted similarly to her when they'd first talked in the field, after he'd rescued her from a life of slavery in some merchant's pleasure den. When he had time, he would have to put this perplexing reaction to Velika to serious thought, but now his entire energies had to be directed toward staying alive.

The courtyard was denuded of all but the small weeds growing at the periphery; nothing stirred but tiny dust devils whirling mindlessly across the barren ground. The wind whistled ominously through the pile of stone and glass comprising the castle and its battlements, but not a human sound was to be heard.

"Have they deserted this fine castle?" asked Krek. "I might enjoy spinning my web from yon tower to this point and then over to the central keep. Not a large web, barely fifty miles of strands, but enough to satisfy me in my old age."

Lan hobbled forward, sword in hand, peering up at the towers, expecting the glint of sunlight off an unguarded crossbow or helm or sword tip. All humanity had been stripped from this now-desolate place. A chill crept up his spine and made his hand tremble. If Waldron had abandoned the castle in favor of another—or another world—Velika would be with the self-appointed Saviour. Lan might never find her in the myriad worlds of chance along the Cenotaph Road. A needle in the ocean was simple to find in comparison; a magnet attracted iron. But what magnet drew Velika if she were lost among the probabilities of all the worlds?

"The Kinetic Sphere is still in its chamber," he said suddenly. "Waldron wouldn't abandon it. He must still be here. But why the emptiness?"

"Perphas he feels the need to expand or loot to further fuel his own world with goods for their coming winter," opined Krek. "If I were not so tired, I would consider leaving right away and tending my own affairs. My web must be in gross disrepair by now. The hatchlings are not up to tending it now that I am absent and Klawn searches for me. Ah, Klawn," he moaned softly, "where are you?"

"Krek, please, not so loud. They said something about her escaping from their dungeons. You might inadvertently call her."

"Do I deserve more justice than she is likely to dispense? No! I shirked my duties, a cowardly thing to do. But this obscene desire to see more of the world seized me again and pulled me away at a crucial time." The spider shrank down in size until hardly more than a large rock. Lan didn't bother trying to cheer up the disconsolate spider. He had learned nothing worked well, but Inyx continued to cajole the creature.

"Krek, please, for me. We've got to get out of here. I feel a trap. Spin a strand for us over the wall so we won't have to go through the main portal. Please." She stroked the spider's hairy legs until he actually shivered with joy.

"No one needs me. You would be better off to look for another means of escape. Dependence on my feeble talents will lead only to ruin."

"Nonsense, Krek. You're one of us, part of the team. The three of us belong together. Together, we can defeat Waldron and his whole damned army!" Inyx waved her sword around with wild abandon until Lan cringed. And he didn't much care for the way the woman limited their number to only three. Velika made the fourth. Just because she was held captive didn't mean her heart wasn't with them and their efforts to defeat Waldron and walk the Road.

Yet the niggling thought made him wonder. Did her love for him extend that far? Lan didn't know. He was no longer certain of his own love for the blonde at times.

"Oh, very well. This one time only. I simply have not the strength to do more." The spider made a coughing noise preparatory to spewing out the sticky strand of web-stuff, but he paused as he took aim on one of the crenelations along the battlement. "I fear I dallied too long. Company of a winged variety approaches, and quickly."

Lan strained his eyes against the sky and finally

saw several hard black dots moving slowly. Predicting where the specks flew proved impossible because of the angle, but Lan felt a sinking feeling that these black birds were winging to stop them. No matter where Waldron had gone, his feathered bodyguards adequately protected the castle from all invaders.

"Inside the great hall," he urged, pointing toward the central keep. "If we can prevent them from entering, we stand a chance to kill them one by one."

Inyx snorted as if she didn't believe him. Lan didn't blame her for the skepticism; his own faith flagged dramatically upon finding the castle deserted after the fight required to win free from the chamber cradling the Kinetic Sphere. Better to meet Waldron face to face than to fight off the droves of those evil black ravens. The first hit and sent him stumbling before he had covered half the distance to the doorway. The next streaked down and left ugly, bloody tracks across his shoulders. A third almost clawed off his ear with a mighty swoop that caused the bird's pinions to creak and snap under the strain.

"Hurry, Lan," said Inyx, standing in the doorway, one hand sweeping an arc over her head to keep the darting ravens at bay. "I'm not going to come and pick you up!"

The words galled him. Pick him up! Power flooded into his injured leg, and he propelled himself in a flat drive through the door. He skittered along the polished floor and collided with a wall, his teeth snapping together hard enough to give him a bone-jarring wrench. The torn remnants of two ravens told him that Krek had already beaten him to the cleanup detail. Blood dripped from the mighty pincers and glued small black feathers to the hard, serrated surfaces.

"Did I do that smartly enough for you, highness?" he asked sarcastically. "I wouldn't want to delay you more than a few seconds in your noble quest to beat a cowardly retreat."

"Cowardly!" snarled Inyx. "Stupid is what you are to want the likes of Velika. Can't you see her for what she is? Pah! I want to return to the Road and leave an oaf like you behind."

"And I will go with you, for a short while, if you will allow it, Inyx," said Krek. "I tire of all this petty bickering over the lumpy female."

Lan felt sheepish as he propped himself against the stone wall. Krek was right. He was being churlish.

"No more arguing?" he said, holding out his hand. Inyx hesitated, then took it firmly in her own.

"None."

"Then how shall we ever decide how to get past all those filthy ravens? You humans do nothing without arguing."

Lan only sighed.

"We are not alone" was Krek's appraisal. "I hear the ravens beating themselves senseless against the door, and there is another sound deep in the halls, a slight noise hardly worthy of mention. But I note it solely in the event you missed it." Krek spread his long legs, claws biting into the stony walls.

Lan exchanged glances with Inyx, then drew his sword again. Perhaps this was an enemy who'd die by the sword, unlike the flapping cloud of gnatlike birds outside. Lan silently railed against the ravens, then tottered and weakly put his hand out to maintain balance. The building swung in a large arc, making him so dizzy he fought down the giddiness it brought.

"Are you all right?"

"No," he said weakly, dropping to his knee. Putting one hand on his forehead as a support while resting an elbow on a knee helped quell the revolt inside his brain for the span of a heartbeat. Then he sank completely to the floor.

"Krek, have you ever seen anything like this wound before?" Inyx's voice sounded muffled, distant, as if she spoke from the bottom of a well. Even her face refused to come into focus.

"A spider learns to brew many poisons, since it is our stock in trade. I suggest bleeding him to relieve the poison from the raven's talons. And perhaps tourniquets here and here and here."

"You idiot," raged Inyx. "Putting a tourniquet around his neck will kill him instantly."

"Oh."

"But the rest of your suggestions are sound. Help me." Inyx drew the point of her dagger along each wound inflicted by the birds. When they flowed profusely, she dabbed away the excess blood and bandaged the new wounds. "I hope that will help," she said, worry tingeing her words. "The poison seems to have gotten a foothold already. Look at him twitch about."

"He has always appeared twitchy to me," observed Krek. "But then, most humans do. You say a poison affecting his nerves was used? This is the basis for my own personal brand of killing poison. It paralyzes the body without inhibiting thought, although in his case there was precious little brain to begin with. Why, I remember once when we . . ."

"What are you getting at, Krek?"

"Oh, nothing, save that I might be able to concoct an antidote for the poison if I obtained a small sample."

Inyx speared one of the dead ravens with the tip of her sword and held it out for Krek's inspection.

"Is this satisfactory?"

"Not quite." He took the raven and devoured it in front of the woman's horrified eyes. "Ugh, such a vile, stringy texture that meat has. I fail to see what you humans enjoy about it. Bugs are much more satisfying." He sneezed, sending a cascade of feathers spiralling about his mouth. Then he sank to the ground and pulled Lan nearer. "The poison is simplistic for one of my acumen. Allow me." Krek's mandibles punctured veins on the inside of each of Lan's wrists. Tiny drops of yellowish fluid beaded at the hinge of his pincers to run down a duct to the very tip where the viscous ichor entered Lan's blood stream.

In a few seconds, Lan went into convulsions. Krek's powerful legs held him, and the spider commented, "Humans lack a certain tolerance to this, it appears. But fear not for his safety."

True to his word, Krek soon released Lan, who looked up and smiled weakly.

"He is cured, of course," Krek pronounced with insufferable superiority. But neither Lan nor Inyx noticed. The man managed to get his feet under him again, and when the world stopped precessing, he felt as good as he had before the poison coursed through his veins.

"I owe you one, Krek," he said, solemnly squeezing a convenient leg.

"One what?"

"Never mind. I'll let you know when the time comes. Did you notice any activity further inside the keep? Waldron?" He didn't have to add "Velika."

"Several are inside. Perhaps as many as a platoon."

"A holding force?"

"More likely a bodyguard. For Waldron," said Lan grimly. "And if he's still here, I'll wager Velika is, too. I don't feel too great, but this might be our only chance to free her." He started off on shaky legs, his hands trembling and his vision still slightly blurred.

"A moment, Lan," demanded Inyx. "We—Krek and I—have no interest in that blond bitch, but we will aid you in return for your promise of the Kinetic Sphere. To be able to walk the Road without searching out the scattered cenotaphs, and not having to bow to their haphazard destinations, would be a boon of incalculable value."

"If we possess the glowing sphere," added Krek, "I would be unable to find the natural cenotaphs, anyway. The power is far too great for me to penetrate the occluding veil it casts, but it would not matter if we sought out worlds we desired to explore. I remember one I spent some little time on years and years ago. Grubs as thick as your wrists! Never a worry about food. And . . ."

"I get the idea," said Lan, his mind racing. As much as he would have loved to keep the Kinetic Sphere for himself, he had to admit it would be better used by Inyx. And if he and Velika settled down on this world after Waldron was properly routed, why did he need to walk the Road at will? "I accept your offer, and in return, not only will I give you the Kinetic Sphere, but all the treasure you can carry."

"Fair. Shake." Their hands gripped once, then slipped down each other's forearm to signify a permanent pact. Both started when a furry leg was added to theirs.

"Your sword—your nearness!—is a gift I can scarce repay, Inyx," he said, his voice choking slightly. "And Krek, without you I'd be dead many times over." He hurriedly wiped a tear from the corner of his eye and saw Inyx surreptitiously do the same. It would be difficult without her and Krek.

But for Velika!

What would he *really* do for the woman? Lan struggled with the inner turmoil again, the internal war that confused and bothered him. He loved her. He did! Yet . . .

"Let's get this over with while you're still able to

stand upright," said Inyx gruffly. She swung off down the hall, with Krek and Lan following a few steps behind. Lan didn't know if it was the possibility of sudden death or his eyes slowly opening to the world around him, but never had he seen Inyx so trim, so athletic, so beautiful. Her loveliness didn't match Velika's, but there is beauty and beauty. While Velika was the sheltered rose, the hothouse-nurtured beauty, Inyx impressed him as more of the wildflower growing in spite of adversity and appearing all the more desirable for it.

Then all such poetic nonsense flew from his mind as the hallway filled with grey-clad soldiers. He lunged well past Inyx, using his superior reach, and pinked the officer's arm as he drew forth his blade. The enemy sword clattered to the floor when Inyx spitted him through the hollow of the throat. The other four men were as easily removed by quick snips of Krek's fast-moving mandibles.

"Inside the audience chamber," came the spider's appraisal. "Only a handful of humans there."

"Watch for the damned ravens," cautioned Lan as he kicked open the door. None of the winged messengers of death attacked, but he found himself fighting swordsmen far better than he. His wounds slowly took their toll of his strength. He had to rely on stealth rather than strength if he were to live much longer. Using every trick he could remember, Lan killed one man. Then he used a quick cut over to slay a second. The third demanded more attention and skill. And Lan found his stamina fading like a flower petal before winter's onset. The man executed a bind that sent Lan's blade sailing through the air. Before the death stroke landed, a dagger blossomed in the soldier's side.

Inyx had accurately cast her knife, saving Lan still another time. He didn't have time to thank her, except by joining against the three men she held at swordpoint. Her skill was great, but their lunges were longer, their attacks appearing to snake from impossible distances.

"Here goes nothing!" she cried, then heaved herself into the trio. She slashed the legs from under one, and the other two stumbled under her weight. Lan had no time for a chivalrous fight. Seated on a throne to the right of Waldron, who calmly watched the slaughter, was Velika.

Lan pledged the first death for her. And the next.

Inyx spun and gave the final death stroke to the remaining soldier vainly trying to get his slashed leg under him to continue the fight.

Sword dripping gore, Lan walked to stand before the throne.

"I have come for her," he said simply.

Waldron's eyebrows rose a trifle and he laughed. "You came for *her*? That's rich. I thought you lusted after the secret of the Kinetic Sphere. Or possibly just a few trinkets to amuse you on wintry evenings. But her?" His laughter annoyed Lan; then he took a firmer hold on his emotions. Waldron was expert at manipulating public sentiment; he knew the precise method to needle Lan, make him act without thinking, and thus kill him the more easily.

"Fight or die where you sit, scum!"

"Very well, put that way, I can hardly deny you the right of dying. I had really hoped to avoid this unpleasantness. Would a few carts of gold and jewels buy you off?"

"You try to bribe me? Why do you stay here? If I were you, I'd've been long gone. Or at least ensconced in a safe place with troops to protect me."

"Protection from my own people is the last thing I need. My vassals are content, having more to eat than ever in the history of our world. Why do you think I offer you worthless jewels? You cannot eat pretty silicates. My people need only food—and that I give them, along with hope for a better future. As for my troops, they are scavenging the countryside for food even now to offset the bitter winter wearing down half my world. If you had not forced your way through the artificial gateway, I, too, would be out importuning this world's peasants for charity. But alas, no, I must stay to deal with you."

"Charity! You steal and then force them to call it charity?"

Waldron's expression flowed from a dark scowl to bemusement. "I don't know what you mean. Yes, I subdue those who oppose me, but I never kill wantonly or steal food from the mouths of those who sorely need it. I am the Saviour of my world and the conqueror of this. Treacherous behavior would cause the people to demand my head—and get it!"

"I demand your head for the vile things you've done to my world."

Lan Martak remembered lovely Zarella and his half-sister Suzarra and how Kyn-alLyk-Surepta, in the name of Waldron Ravensroost, had slain them. The old sheriff was living out his days watching the grey-clad soldiers slowly extort power from him. And that was a world with only the barest of toeholds. What of the others?

And Lan could never forgive Waldron for what he had done to Velika.

He had lost Zarella to Waldron's men. He would not lose Velika to Waldron.

"I demand your head!" raged Lan, his blade slashing in the air, scattering red droplets of blood before him.

"Really, you are the one who should apologize," said Waldron, his voice level. "You kill my best generals, come raging through like a berserk pard, and now you demand the-gods-alone-know-what."

As he spoke, Waldron reached beside him and lifted a small wooden case. One side hinged upward. Waldron lifted the door to expose a desiccated skull inside.

"Good-bye," said Waldron, smiling wickedly. He thumped the back of the box.

Lan watched in frozen awe as the skull impossibly opened empty eyes. In the hollows, dull red coals began to smoulder, then burn, and finally take on a fire that dazzled him, that set his magic-sensing ability screaming. He instinctively rolled to one side to escape the incandescent path of that gaze.

The table behind him vanished with a dull *whoof!* Lan Martak kept rolling as Waldron followed him around the room. The twin beams from the skull's eyesockets removed object after object from the throne room. It became immediately apparent to Lan that simply hiding behind some massive piece of furniture wouldn't save his hide.

In mute fascination, he watched, helpless, as Waldron swung the box around and lifted it to bring the dual beams of ruby destruction in line with the floor in front of him. The floor simply vanished. As Waldron raised the box to point directly at Lan, Inyx moved. Her dagger cartwheeled through the air and thudded into the meaty portion of Waldron's upper left arm.

The box containing the skull fell to the floor, the lid snapping shut as it hit. The double beams of death winked out of existence.

Cold rage clouded Waldron's face as he clumsily pulled his sword from its sheath. Blood ran in a steady torrent down his left arm, then slowed, and finally coagulated.

"If the sorcerer's skull isn't enough to dispatch you, then by all the gods, my sword will prove more than adequate. Die, dog meat, die!"

Waldron's lunge missed Lan by a wide margin.

The would-be Saviour of the grey, dismal world silently sidestepped Lan's steely reply and settled into an en-garde position, obviously composing himself after the initial wild rush. All the years of training stood Lan Martak in good stead. He did not wildly attack.

Faint magical emanations came from Waldron's sword. His blade carried a spell locked to its metal. Magic seemed a rare commodity outside of Lan's world, but none had used it as well as Waldron. The Kinetic Sphere, the deadly skull in the box, now this unknown sword and its mysterious qualities.

"I see you realize the nature of the blade you face." Waldron executed a stylish lunge that took Lan by surprise. He parried thin air and felt the razored edge slice his arm. Yet his parry had been directed in line at the precise point needed for riposte. Again and again he missed his parry by a hair's-breadth.

"Surrender and I will allow you and those two passage along the Road. Refuse and I'll cut your manhood off!"

"The word of one such as you is worthless," flared Lan. He settled down to an increasingly defensive fight as he tried to understand the nature of the weapon he faced. Slowly, as new and deeper wounds opened on his torso and arms, he came to the conclusion that the blade emitted a distortion field around itself, causing him to subtly misjudge the true position of the sword. A few parries confirmed this, but his magical training was insufficient to allow him to conjure a counterspell, even if he hadn't been actively fighting for his life.

He glanced around to see how Inyx and Krek fared. They were locked in battle in the far corner of the room, fending off a half-dozen grey-clad soldiers. The battle between him and Waldron was a solitary one; he knew he could expect no help from Velika, who sat on the throne, her eyes wide and a lily-soft hand clutched at her throat.

Lan kept hoping that the wound in Waldron's left arm would impede him. It didn't. The flow of blood had stopped totally now. It hurt, of that Lan Martak had no doubt, but Waldron was a skilled swordsman and no doubt pushed such minor annoyances from his mind until afterward.

But the very use of a spell sword meant that Waldron depended more heavily on trick than skill. Gambling on his own skill, Lan closed his eyes and "felt" the steel blades as they slashed at one another. Depending on feel rather than sight allowed him to react by instinct, using a quick disengage, a beat, and a powerful follow-through.

Lan's blade pressed firmly into Waldron's throat. Waldron attempted to bring his dagger into play, but the wounded left arm hindered him. Lan's leg snaked out around Waldron's, and a quick kick landed the man on his back. The spell sword fell from his grip. Lan kept his point at Waldron's throat as he picked up the other's magical blade.

"It pleases me to kill you with your own sword." He pulled back for the stroke, only to have Velika hang on his arm and prevent him from a clean kill.

"Stop, Lan, don't do this! He's a great man. He isn't the tyrant you believe him to be."

"He's tried to kill me at every turn. And look how he's ensorcelled you. For that alone I'll kill him!"

"I love him, I truly do!" Velika cast a tearful glance down at Waldron, then pulled with greater urgency on Lan's sword arm. "I beg you to spare him." Tears flowed freely. Lan pulled away from her, the sight of those tears making him uneasy. Velika was obviously torn between them, the freebooter and the warlord, and had made her choice, no matter how painful it had been for her. Or Lan.

Lan's sword rose. He felt the acid tingle of her tears as they dropped onto his hand. He actually cringed away, his resolve to kill Waldron gone.

"Spare him," came Inyx's advice. "He does seem to have the best for his own people at heart, even if his methods are extreme."

Inyx came and stood beside Lan, her sword dripping the blood of the fallen grey-clad soldiers.

"Even after he enslaved you, you beg for his life?" Lan asked, astonished.

"Would you have done so differently in his place?"

"Of course!"

"Remember the grinding poverty on his home world. And there are no cenotaphs off. He needed the Kinetic Sphere."

"I, too, vote to spare his life. Without his knowledge of the operation of the Kinetic Sphere," said Krek, " we might never ascertain the proper ways of activating it." Krek's advice was sound.

"Your life," said Lan Martak, "is still in my hands. Tell us how to use the Kinetic Sphere, or I *will* kill you."

"No," said Waldron adamantly. "That is the sole possession of any value on my bleak world. There is no other way off that grey, spinning ball of sludge. I hold a heritage that must be preserved, even if it means my death."

"Then die!"

"Lan, please! I'll tell you how to operate it." Velika's frenzied tone convinced Lan that the woman knew and wasn't merely using this as a ploy to add a few extra seconds to Waldron's life. "I'll show you all you need to know!"

"Velika, you can't!"

"Waldron, I must. If it means your life, I will do anything!"

Lan laughed harshly. "Your spell binding her to you is fading, Waldron. Velika returns to her old self. She'd do anything to help me—and prevent me from further bloodying my hands."

Inyx snorted disdainfully, and Krek said, "I will bind him, friend Lan Martak." A gurgling noise followed by a hiss, and sticky strand after strand of silken web stuff cocooned Waldron. The more he struggled, the more he entangled himself.

"You can't take the Sphere. You can't!" he yelled, furious at Velika. "I love you, but if I were free, I'd gladly strangle you to prevent this theft. My world needs it! Millions will starve without it!"

"Come along," said Lan, nudging Velika toward the corridor leading to the chamber holding the Kinetic Sphere. "The sooner we're gone, the better I'll like it." As Lan sheathed the ensorcelled weapon at his side, he heard a thin, reedy voice cry out.

"Take me, too! Take me along with you! I can show you wonders undreamed of in your feeble fantasies."

"Lan," said Inyx softly, her hand on his arm. "The box spoke!"

"Leave it!" snapped Waldron. "It means your death to touch it."

"You'd love to see me dead," said Lan. "The box means something more."

"I created the Kinetic Sphere. He imprisoned me in here. Take me with you!"

Lan hefted the box containing the sorcerer's skull. Gingerly, he opened the lid, making sure the empty eyesockets were pointed at a distant section of the room. The twin ruby beacons did not shine forth. Instead, the jaw hinge of the skull twitched slightly.

But the words Lan heard were as plain as if spoken by flesh and blood lips.

"I am Claybore. He stole my Kinetic Sphere. I conjured it; he saw and coveted it as I passed through his dismal world. He stole my creation!"

Lan glanced quickly at Waldron, still struggling in his silk coffin. He believed Waldron capable of any deed, including one as perfidious as this. The fallen Saviour-king would have killed off entire worlds to feed his own. The death of a single sorcerer meant nothing to him.

"Claybore, eh? I've heard the name. But you're not from Waldron's world?"

"No! I am from . . . a great distance away, even when reckoned by the Sphere. Take me with you and I shall explain the workings of it."

"He lies. His treachery forced me to—"

"Silence!" shouted Lan. He didn't doubt Waldron was capable of any treachery, but the sight of the virtually fleshless skull unnerved him. He remembered the beams of destruction leaping from those hollowed eyesockets and wondered at the truth.

"We'll take you along, Claybore," said Lan, snapping the lid closed on the box. "And we'll talk later."

He heard the words of thanks, although he knew that the throat of the long-dead sorcerer was separated from the skull by an infinity of worlds.

"Tell us about the Kinetic Sphere, Velika," he demanded. "Quickly. The grey-clad soldiers hammer at the doors again." Already, outside the doors barred by Inyx and Krek, more of the grey-clad soldiers hammered to gain entry.

"This way," she said, her voice strained and her eyes downcast. "It is another way into the chamber holding the Sphere. It's Waldron's private passage." They raced along a corridor opening into the throne room and soon entered the chamber containing the Kinetic Sphere. It lay like a pink, pulsating pearl in a bed of black velvet. World after world spun by in a never-ending parade inside the crystalline depths, and Lan had to force his attentions back to Velika and this world. It would be difficult abandoning the Road, but for Velika he'd make the sacrifice.

Yet so much lurked just an arm's length away. . . .

"Y-you need only allow the worlds to pass in review. When you see one you want, simply say," and she chanted a complex rhyme, mnemonics for the key words needed to freeze the gateway on the desired world. Lan had her repeat the rhyme several times until he was sure he had learned it, then asked of Krek and Inyx, "Sufficient?"

"I can remember," said Inyx simply.

"A child's verse in its simplicity," Krek assured him. "Why, we spiders carry our entire heritage in vastly more complex word patterns, not being able to write, you see. I can recite—"

"Thanks, Krek, later." Then Lan remembered that there wouldn't be a later time with the spider. And they'd been through so much together. But he'd not signed any document stating life would be full of simple decisions. Velika, as soon as Waldron's hold on her diminished, would prove a far more loving companion than the egotistical, weakness-proclaiming spider.

"How is the shimmering curtain of the Road itself summoned?" asked Inyx, eyeing the world chosen in the globe.

"I do not know," said Velika.

"It is merely another chant," came the strong, baritone resonance of Claybore's voice. "This one."

"And the cancellation?" asked Inyx.

The rhyme Claybore chanted burned in Lan's mind, and he saw in it a palindrome. The symmetry of the spell fascinated him, gave him clues to the innermost workings of the universe itself. To have the knowledge to construct such a device drew him. And it was all Claybore's. And Claybore's head rested in the box under Lan's arm.

"Carry the Sphere with you through the curtain simply by reciting the spell on the far side. It . . . it slips through," said the decapitated sorcerer.

"Lan," cried Velika, clutching again at his arm.

"He—it—has shown you all you need to know. Now give me my freedom as you promised."

"What?" he said, stunned by the request. "I said I'd spare Waldron's life. Don't you want to stay with me?"

"Why? To stumble along in the darkness of that cursed Road of yours, to allow the fleas to enjoy gourmet dining on my flesh, to be cold and hungry and miserable? I never loved you, Lan, not the way I love Waldron. He's kind and—"

"And powerful and rich," interjected Inyx. "It seems the minx worships power more than freedom."

"Yes, yes, that's true," raged Velika. "I *love* the power being Waldron's consort gives me. Why shouldn't I? A lifetime of deprivation is at an end. He rules seven worlds and will rule a dozen more! Take the Kinetic Sphere and leave us!"

Krek began to point out the logical inconsistency in Velika's statement, but Inyx cut him short.

"Lan. You heard her wish. Will you join Krek and me now?"

"She's under a spell. Come, Velika, come with us and away from the evil spell that steals your mind and emotion."

"I will see your liver drying in the sun, animal-lover!" came the snarled threat from Waldron. The strands of silk web-stuff still clung to his arms and sides, but he had done a rough, thorough job of cutting his bindings with a tiny knife.

Lan started to draw his blade, but Velika hung on his arm and prevented him from carrying out his bloody desire. He turned to her and, eyes blazing angrily, spat out, "You're under no spell, are you? You willingly desire to be with Waldron." It sounded like an insult the way he said it, but Velika took the meaning differently.

"You finally understand, you bumpkin fool! Waldron's a thousand times the man you claim to be." The triumph in her eyes as she went to Waldron infuriated Lan Martak. Something inside him burst, and he attacked in the worst way he could.

Words flowed from his lips, and the Kinetic Sphere glowed brightly, solidifying the gateway onto Waldron's grey, dismally appointed world. Lan's fist smashed hard into Waldron's face, the nose breaking under the impact. He then threw the man back into his own world, a blaze of light throughout the curtain signalling Waldron's precipitous return.

"I'll follow and kill you for this, scum!" screamed Waldron from the other side of the energy curtain, blood spurting over his entire face from the damaged nose. "My entire life has been for the betterment of my world, and you've taken away the only chance for our survival."

"Waldron!" cried Velika, who stumbled forward, following the path just taken by the lord of the grey world.

Lan watched, numbed to the core of his being. Velika had actually followed Waldron back to the impoverished world, even knowing what Lan would do next. His lips moved in the patterns necessary to close the gateway. It crackled and collapsed in a fountain of wild color.

"Pick us another world, one far from the greyness," said Inyx, shivering at the fate of Waldron and Velika.

"Allow me to perform the ritual," spoke up Claybore from the security of his box.

The worlds spun by in a crazy kaleidoscope until Lan felt dizzy. But he managed to watch and listen carefully. Before the glittering sheet of pure energy formed, dotted with its dancing motes of rainbow hues, the scene in the Sphere had shifted more slowly, one world at a time parading by until one was chosen like a single specific card being plucked from a deck. Claybore had selected a world, and not at random.

"She actually followed him. I can't believe she did it," a distracted Lan said sadly.

"She did it," said Inyx. "Now hurry before those grey-clad soldiers break through the door and find us. We can't fight them across all eternity, but without Waldron, their empire will soon collapse in petty squabbles."

"Velika chose him over me. Why?"

"Come, Lan," insisted Inyx. "We have the universe in the palm of our hand!"

"But she didn't willingly follow him," spoke up Krek. "Friend Inyx, you pu—" Krek howled in pain as Inyx ground the point of her knife into his leg. Krek subsided, muttering to himself. "Strange mating rituals, these humans have. And they express amazement at the civilized behavior of us arachnids."

The world shattered around all of them as the Road opened onto a new world, and again they followed it.

CHAPTER THIRTEEN

"My legs ache so," complained Krek. "Must we carry that useless box with us?"

"I'd walk if I had legs. Lend me a pair of yours," snapped Claybore from the inside of his wooden box. "Or perhaps I can conjure enough to take them from you."

"Enough of that," cut in Lan. "We're in this together. No squabbling." For a moment he feared that the sorcerer could do exactly as he threatened. He remained in awe of the talking skull, and mingled with that awe came a touch of fear. Claybore's power had been severely limited when his skull had been imprisoned in the wooden box by Waldron, but Lan couldn't erase from his mind the memory of the twin beams of ruby destruction.

"Wherever *this* is," added Krek.

Lan sighed and sank to the ground under a convenient tree. He rested his tired back and felt the weight of the world descend on him. He'd lost Velika. She had chosen Waldron over him. And all he had to show for the emotional pain was a crystal globe capable of moving between worlds—and the head of the sorcerer who had originally conjured it into existence.

Sorry fare in exchange for one he'd loved so.

Inyx came up and laid a surprisingly gentle hand on his shoulder and said, "Be glad for her. She is with the one she truly loves."

Lan didn't hear Krek mumble, "Yes, herself."

"You might be right," Lan said, "but that doesn't make the ache any less real."

She squeezed his shoulder in a way that was more than comradely, then told him, "We have all we need from Waldron. We have the Kinetic Sphere. We can walk the Road and find treasures undreamed of, even in our wildest imaginings."

He nodded, not trusting himself to speak. He might have lost Velika, but the Siren's call of unknown worlds still tugged mightily at his sleeve, urging him onward.

"Which of those worlds do we choose?"

"Any—all!" cried Inyx. "What does it matter? Aren't we free to venture where we please?"

"Yes," cut in Claybore. "Take this world for example. A lovely world simply waiting for your presence. Explore it! Experience it!"

Lan Martak remembered how Claybore had spun the worlds by in the Kinetic Sphere, then slowed and appeared to seek out this particular one. But he pushed the thought from his mind. Too many other things rushed in to confuse him. Velika. Inyx. The Kinetic Sphere. Krek. The jumble was too great to worry what it was about this particular world that Claybore specifically sought.

"This does appear to be a kindly world for one as old and infirm as myself," said Krek. The trilling words came with a modicum of animation now. The spider rejoiced in his own way of being free of his home world and his overamorous bride, Klawn-rik'wiktorn-kyt.

And Lan rejoiced, too, for him, for himself. What the old sheriff said to him so long ago about Zarella came back. He belonged in the country, not locked in the city. This countryside stretching off as far as the eye could see was for him. He didn't believe Zarella—Velika—would ever have appreciated the sylvan beauty, the simplicity, the intricacy, the life-giving feelings he now felt.

"I'll explore ahead. Any direction pleasure you

more than that one?" asked Inyx, pointing into the setting sun.

"That's fine," said Lan. He glanced into the box containing the sorcerer's skull and saw an eerie caricature of a smile form on the exposed teeth. He started to ask Inyx to scout elsewhere, then thought better of it. Better to see where Claybore wanted to go than to blunder unsuspectingly on it.

A sorcerer's surprises were often fatal.

As Inyx walked off, almost strutting, Krek came to Lan and said, "A brief discussion with you, friend Lan Martak. I am still woefully ignorant of human customs."

"What is it, old spider?"

"Why do you moon over Velika? That human female appeared far less desirable than Inyx."

"So what do you know of human tastes?" Lan shifted uneasily, not liking the way the conversation turned. He didn't know if he was up to exposing the emotional wounds yet or not.

"Nothing, and that is why I request information. Maybe I am stupid as well as ignorant, but I must try to sift these things out in my enfeebled brain. Velika was headstrong, greedy, and ambitious and obviously cared for no one but herself. Where lay the power, so did she. You were only momentarily in such a position, whereas Waldron commanded vast legions."

"You don't know a thing about love."

Krek thought for a minute, then jerked his head around in a tight circle. "I fear you are right. We spiders are civilized."

"But Klawn tried to eat you!"

"Of course, what is more civilized than that? It is I who am the barbarian. I am, of course, disgraced, but in my current state of debility, I cannot worry over such things. Rather, I worry over you."

"Thanks, but it isn't necessary."

"Could Velika fight as nobly as Inyx? Could she

provide you better companionship? I see an active, noble human female in Inyx."

"You and she get along well together. You never cared for Velika."

"True, but this does nothing to detract from Inyx's charms."

"I don't want to talk about it, Krek. Besides, the wound in my leg is beginning to ache again. In fact, I ache all over. My body has been slashed and stabbed and bruised and beaten too much. Let's camp here for the night."

"I feared you would say that because of the stream of running water being so close." The spider shivered and moved from Lan's side.

"Your wounds are minor," piped up Claybore. "A simple spell will heal them. Allow me."

"*No!*"

But Lan didn't voice his objections quickly enough. He felt the familiar lethargy of a potent healing spell stalking his senses. His own brand of magic was puny in comparison; he feared Claybore's power even as he felt the positive effects of the spell beginning to heal deep inside. In a few minutes, all the pain had been washed from his body and the gaping wounds were closing visibly, leaving only tiny hairline scars by the time Inyx returned from her scouting.

"You're healed!" she exclaimed, examining the once-wicked wound on his leg. "Claybore?"

"Your humble, obedient servant," spoke up the skull. "I am pleased to be of assistance to those who rescued me from that tyrant."

"How did Waldron ever get you . . . I mean, how. . . ?" Inyx was momentarily flustered.

"How did he come to decapitate me and place me in this wooden prison?" the sorcerer finished for her. "I hardly expected a primitive from a world such as Waldron's dismal mudball to strike so cunningly. He was a genius in his way. He instantly recognized the Kinetic Sphere for what it was. Even as I bent to acknowledge his sovereignty over his world, he drew and struck a dastardly blow that severed head from torso."

Inyx shivered. Lan had to admit this was less than toothsome commentary.

"But the box?" asked Krek, seemingly unaffected by the gruesomeness of the description. "How did your head come to remain in it while your body was elsewhere?"

"Waldron attempted to bury my body to create the strains in the universal fabric necessary for a permanent gate. He failed. But a sorcerer as powerful as I hangs tenaciously to life. My head lived on—if this can be called living."

"What of the beams of destruction?" asked Lan, realizing Claybore held back more than he revealed.

"They tr—" The sorcerer cut off in midword. "They are manifestations of my power, the only power I retain."

"Living imprisoned thus in a box," mused Inyx. "A horrible fate."

"It is better than wandering the cosmos as a totally disembodied spirit," answered Claybore. "I live, after a fashion. I am content."

Again Lan sensed the untruth. Uneasily, he shifted around and asked Inyx, "What did you find?"

She smiled and breathlessly told him, "A caravan! People, Lan, people! And from the richness of their dress, this is a most prosperous world."

"Good. I just wish we were as prosperous. Looting Waldron's vaults would have improved our position enormously."

"We have the Kinetic Sphere," she said, patting the crystalline globe. "This is worth more than a ton of jewels. And we have one another." She looked up and locked gazes with Lan. No true telepathy existed between them, but a definite communication without words developed. He reached out and took her hand in his.

"How far are these other humans?" asked Krek. "While I do not seek out humans, I feel that . . ." The spider talked on, unaware of Lan and Inyx rising and moving away from him and Claybore. When they were far enough distant, Lan pulled Inyx close, her lips first brushing his, then crushing down hard.

"Sure enough, there is the carvan you saw yesterday, Inyx," said Lan, his arm flush with the woman's. She turned and smiled at him. He returned a grin; then they swung off together down the hill.

"Friend Lan Martak, carefully study the scene ahead, and you will notice the reason the merchants are not moving along their highway."

"What? I don't see anything."

"They are under attack," came Claybore's cold words.

"Yes," clacked Krek, his mandibles snapping together. "And I see my first good meal in more weeks than I can remember." The spider lumbered down the hill in full charge. Lan pulled at Inyx's arm, urging her to more speed. He felt an obligation to fight alongside the spider.

"Fear not," said Claybore. "The spider is capable of defeating them."

"We'll help him, nonetheless," panted Lan, increasing his speed. Comrades fought together.

The guards from the caravan battled valiantly against the dog-sized grasshopper creatures, but the droves of insects washed over them like an ocean's tide covering a beach. Lan and Inyx swung swords and killed several of the grasshopper-things with each stroke, but sheer numbers would soon tire them out. Judging by the partially devoured corpses on the ground, the insects had a taste for human flesh.

But it was Krek who proved the most effective. He gobbled and gorged and fought with the ferocity of a hundred men. And somehow, this communicated to the grasshopper-things. Perhaps the spider was a potent natural enemy on this world, or they might have been intelligent enough to realize their potential meal dined off them. However it was, the grasshoppers began retreating with oversized froglike hind legs propelling them in immense jumps.

Krek finished his meal and looked up, belly full and now content in other ways. The way Lan's arm circled Inyx's shoulders, and her arm his waist, convinced the giant spider that all was as it should be. Even the mocking smile on Claybore's bony mouth didn't bother him.

Krek settled down and watched Lan and Inyx go to the merchant leading the caravan and begin the endless dickering over the value of their services. But Krek did wish the merchants would be more careful with their torches. One tiny spark and his furry legs would be ablaze. Humans could be so vexing at times.